Penguin Books
What's Happening to My Body?

Lynda Madaras teaches sex education in a school in Pasadena, California. She has written a number of books in the field of popular health and child care including *Child's Play*, *The Alphabet Connection*, *Womancare: A Gynecological Guide to Your Body*, *Lynda Madaras' Growing-up Guide for Girls*, *Lynda Madaras Talks to Teens about AIDS* and *What's Happening to My Body?: A Growing-up Guide for Parents and Sons*. Her growing-up guides were placed on the American Library Association's Best Books for Young Adults list.

Area Madaras is Lynda Madaras's daughter and assisted her mother in the preparation of this book.

Lynda Madaras

with Area Madaras

What's Happening to My Body?

A Growing-up Guide for Parents and Daughters

Penguin Books

PENGUIN BOOKS

Published by the Penguin Group
Penguin Books Ltd, 27 Wrights Lane, London W8 5TZ, England
Penguin Books USA Inc., 375 Hudson Street, New York, New York 10014, USA
Penguin Books Australia Ltd, Ringwood, Victoria, Australia
Penguin Books Canada Ltd, 10 Alcorn Avenue, Toronto, Ontario, Canada M4V 3B2
Penguin Books (NZ) Ltd, 182–190 Wairau Road, Auckland 10, New Zealand

Penguin Books Ltd, Registered Offices: Harmondsworth, Middlesex, England

First published in the USA, under the title *The 'What's Happening to My Body?'
Books for Girls*, by Newmarket Press, New York 1983
This revised edition published in Penguin Books 1989
10 9 8 7 6 5

Copyright © Lynda Madaras with Area Madaras, 1983, 1989
Illustrations by Will Giles
All rights reserved

Printed in England by Clays Ltd, St Ives plc
Filmset in Linotron Meridien

Except in the United States of America, this book is sold subject
to the condition that it shall not, by way of trade or otherwise, be lent,
re-sold, hired out, or otherwise circulated without the publisher's
prior consent in any form of binding or cover other than that in
which it is published and without a similar condition including this
condition being imposed on the subsequent purchaser

My half of this book is dedicated to my present school, SMASH (Santa Monica Alternative School House), especially to Linda Gesualdi, my maths teacher, Diana Garcia, my English teacher, and most of all, to my science teacher and advisor, Brian Lamagna (who I still insist is wrong, I won't take up writing as a profession). And this book is also dedicated to all the fathers of the world, since I don't believe they receive enough credit for the birth and upbringing of their children.

A.M.

For the students and staff at Sequoyah School, Pasadena, California
L.M.

Contents

Acknowledgements

The authors would like to thank Ms Toni Belfield and the Family Planning Association for their generous assistance in the preparation of this edition of the book. We are especially grateful for their help in preparing the material on sexually transmitted diseases and contraception.

Introduction For Parents

Why I Wrote This Book

It was one of those perfectly languid summer days when the heat is so rich and thick you can taste the scent of summer wild flowers in the air. My 8-year-old daughter and I were slowly making our way downstream through the woods by our house. It was one of those magic moments that sometimes happen between mothers and daughters. All the years of nappy changing, complicated child-care arrangements, hectic juggling of career and motherhood, nagging about bedrooms that need cleaning and pets that need feeding, all the inevitable resentments, conflicts and quarrels seemed to fade away, leaving just the two of us, close and connected.

We stopped to sun ourselves on a rock, and my daughter shyly told me she had some new hairs growing on her body.

'Down there,' she pointed.

I was filled with pride as I watched her scrambling among the rocks, a young colt, long-limbed and elegant and very beautiful. I marvelled at her assurance and ease. Her transition into womanhood would be so much more graceful than my own halting, jerky and sometimes painful progress through puberty.

I was also proud of our relationship, proud that she felt comfortable enough to confide in me. Never in my wildest imaginings would I have thought of telling my mother that I'd discovered pubic hairs growing on my body. It was simply not something we could have discussed. I was glad that it was going to be different between my daughter and me.

We didn't talk much more about her discovery that day. Weeks and months passed without further mention of the topic, but our relationship remained close and easy.

'Enjoy it while you can,' my friends with older daughters would tell me, 'because once they hit puberty, it's all over. That's when they really get difficult. There's just no talking to them.' I listened in smug silence. I knew the stereotype: the sullen, sulky adolescent daughter and the nagging harpy of a mother who can't communicate with each other; but it was going to be different for us.

My daughter must have been 9 or 10 when it first started – her introduction to the nasty world of playground politics and the cruel games young girls play with each other. She'd arrive home from school in tears; her former best friend was now someone else's closest ally; she'd been excluded from a forthcoming party at which friends were invited to stay the night, or was the victim of some other calculated schoolgirl snub. She'd cry her eyes out. I didn't know what to say.

'Well, if they're going to be like that, find someone else to play with,' I'd say.

The tears flowed on. It became a weekly, then a twice-weekly event. It went on for months and months. And then I finally began to realize that no sooner had she dried her tears than I would hear her on the telephone, maliciously gossiping about some other little girl, a former friend, and cementing a new friendship by plotting to exclude this other girl. I was indignant, and I began to point out the inconsistency in her behaviour.

'You don't understand,' she'd yell, stomping off to her bedroom and slamming the door.

She was right, I didn't understand. From time to time, I'd talk to the other mothers. It was the same with all of us. Why were our daughters acting like this? None of us had any answers.

'Well, girls will be girls,' sighed one mother philosophically. 'They all do it and we did the same when we were their age.'

I reached back over the years, trying to remember. Were we really that horrible? Then I remembered the Powder Puffs, a club my girl friends and I belonged to. Unlike the Girl Scouts and the other adult-sanctioned after-school clubs, the Powder Puffs had no formal meetings, no ostensible purpose, which is not to say that the club didn't have a purpose. It did. The membership cards, which were wondrously official looking since one girl's father had run them off in his print shop, and which we carried around in the cloudy cellophane inserts of our identical vinyl 'leather' wallets, certified us as members of the all-important Group. As if that weren't identification enough, we moved around in an inseparable herd, ate lunch together in our special territory of the playground, sat together giggling like a gaggle of geese in school assemblies, wrote each other's names on the canvas of our scuffed tennis shoes, combed our hair the same way, dressed alike and generally made life miserable for the girls who were not members of our group.

Today, some twenty years later, I can only vaguely recall the names and faces of the other members of the Powder Puffs. I do, however, remember one girl so vividly that I can almost count the freckles on her face. Her name was Pam and she was most emphatically not a member of the group, although she desperately wanted to be – so desperately, in fact, that she took to writing notes that she'd leave in my desk:

Dear Lynda,
Please, Please, Please let me join the Powder Puffs. If you say I'm OK, the rest of the girls will too. Please!!! Please!!!! Please!!!!! Please, please, please!

Pam

The notes embarrassed me horribly and, of course, the mere act of writing them doomed Pam for ever to the status of outsider. I have conveniently forgotten how Pam fared after that. I know she never got to be a Powder Puff, and I imagine we made her life even more miserable with sniggering and snubs, behind-the-back whisperings and the usual sorts of adolescent tactics. (I wonder if it would have been any comfort to Pam to have known that a year later, when my family moved to another area, I got my come-uppance. In the vulnerable position of 'the new girl', I was the perfect target and boarded the school bus each day, pretending to be oblivious to the sniggers and whispers that followed me up the aisle while I hunted for a seat.)

At any rate, what's really frightening is that I wasn't any more cruel than most adolescent girls. I talk to other women about their relationships with other girls during those years and hear the same sorts of stories. The milk of human kindness does not flow freely in the veins of pubescent girls.

We all remember how it was, and it was much the same for all of us. We had our best friend, from whom we were inseparable, with whom we shared our deepest secrets and to whom we swore everlasting friendship. And then there was the larger gang, the other little girls at school. Everyone had a role: leader, follower, victim. Although the role assignments shifted from time to time, the roles themselves remained constant.

The games we played with each other were standardized as well and not very pretty. Exclusion was the basic format.

One girl, for the crime of being the smartest, the prettiest, the ugliest, the dumbest, the most sexually developed or whatever, was designated the victim. She was cast out, ostracized by the group.

But what was even more important, what was in fact the central theme of my life in those years was a more personalized version of the exclusion game: betrayal by the best friend. In this case the formerly inseparable friend was now unavailable for after-school activities, Saturday afternoon movies and so on. Her time was taken up with the new best friend. We were abandoned, crushed and heartbroken; we cried our eyes out.

Little boys don't spend their energies in such melodramatic psychodramas. There's the gang or, more likely, the team, even the best friend and, undoubtedly, lots of exclusion, especially for the unathletic, quiet and gentler boys, but there is not the same intensity in their interpersonal relationships nor the petty and vicious aspects that characterize the relationships between girls of this age.

Maybe, I thought, the mother who sighed that business about 'girls being girls' was right. We all did it and now it was happening all over again. Our daughters were playing the same games by the same rules. Maybe it was inevitable. Maybe it was just the nature of the beast. I didn't like this idea, but there it was.

To add to the things I didn't like, there was a growing tension between my daughter and me. She was terribly moody and it seemed as if she was always angry with me. And I was often angry with her. Of course, we'd always quarrelled, but now the quarrels were almost constant. The volume of our communications reached a new decibel level. There was an ever-present strain between us.

All of this bothered me a great deal, but what was even more disturbing was the change in her attitude about her body. In contrast to the shy wonder that greeted her first pubic hairs, there was now a complete horror at the idea of developing breasts and having her first period. Like most 'modern' mothers, I wanted my daughter's transition from childhood to womanhood to be a comfortable, even joyous, time. I had intended to provide her with all the necessary information in a frank, straightforward manner. This, or so went my reasoning, would eliminate any problems.

But, here was my daughter telling me she didn't want to grow breasts or have her first period. I asked why, but didn't get much further than 'because I don't want to'. I countered with an it's-great-to-grow-up pep talk that rang hollow even to my own ears.

Clearly something was amiss. I thought I'd made all the necessary information available in the most thoroughly modern manner, but the anticipated results, a healthy and positive attitude toward her body, had not materialized.

I thought long and hard about all of this, and finally I began to realize that I hadn't given my daughter all the information I thought I had. Although she was amazingly well informed about the most minute details of ovum and sperm, pregnancy and birth, the physical details of inter-course and even the emotional content of love-making, she knew nothing, or next to nothing, about menstruation and the changes that would take place in her body over the next few years. She'd seen me in the bathroom changing a tampon and I'd tossed off a quick explanation of menstrual periods, but I'd never really sat down and discussed the topic with her. I'd read her any number of marvellous children's books that explain conception, birth and sexu-ality, but I'd never read her one about menstruation. Obviously, it was time to do that.

So, full of purpose, I trotted off to the library and dis-covered that there was no such book. There were one or two books for young girls that briefly mentioned the topic, but they were hopelessly out of date, and the tone was all wrong. Some of them even made menstruation sound like a disease.

If I wanted to teach my daughter about menstruation and the other changes that would happen in her body, I was obviously going to have to rely on my own resources. Coincidentally, I had just finished negotiating a contract to write a book on women's health care. I would have to do considerable research on menstruation for the book anyhow. (For once in my life, my career as a writer and the job of being a mother wouldn't be totally at loggerheads.)

The more deeply I researched the topic, the less surprised I was that there was no book for young girls on menstruation. Throughout history, in culture after culture, menstruation has been a taboo subject. The taboo has taken many forms: one must not eat the food cooked by a menstruating woman; touch objects she has touched; look into her eyes; have sex with her. We no longer believe that the glance of a menstruating woman will wither a field of crops, that her touch will poison the water in the well, that having sex with her will make a man's penis fall off, but the menstrual taboo is, none the less, alive and well.

Even today, in an era when the most bizarre of incestual and sado-masochistic sexual practices are the subject of cover stories in national news magazines, cocktail chitchat and television specials, the natural bodily process of menstruation remains an unmentionable subject. Indeed, as Paula Weidigger points out in her excellent book *Menstruation and Menopause*, when the subject of menstruation finally did come up on a segment of the controversial TV programme *All in the Family*, the network received more letters protesting public mention of 'such a thing' than had been received as a result of the airing of any other episode of the popular series (and this from a programme that had dealt with such topics as premarital sex, racial prejudice, impotency and homosexuality).

Of course, we are no longer banished to menstrual huts each month, as were our ancestral mothers in more primitive societies. But as Nancy Friday argues in *My Mother, My Self*, our release from monthly exile does not necessarily represent a more enlightened view of menstruation. Rather, Friday says, thanks to centuries of conditioning, we have so completely internalized the menstrual taboo that it's simply not necessary to bother any longer with menstrual huts. Our modern tribe doesn't need to go to such lengths to remove any disturbing sight or mention of menstruation from its collective consciousness. We do it ourselves, through our ladylike avoidance of any public discussion of the topic and our meticulous toilet-paper mummification of our bloodied pads and tampons.

Indeed, we are so embarrassed by menstruation that we cannot even call it by its rightful name, relying instead on largely negative terms such as 'the curse'. One male writer of a review of a book about menstruation, who Friday quotes, put it in a particularly telling perspective.

If men menstruated they would probably find a way to brag about it. Most likely they would regard it as a spontaneous ejaculation, an excess of vital spirits. Their cup runneth over. Their sexuality supererogates. They would see themselves as 'spending' blood in a plentitude of conspicuous waste. Blood, after all, is generally considered a good. 'Blood' sports used to be the true test of manhood. And at the conclusion of a boy's first hunt he used to be 'blooded'. All that is turned around when it is the woman who bleeds. Bleeding is interpreted as a sign of infirmity, inferiority, uncleanliness and irrationality.*

It is certainly true that we don't often hear women boasting about their periods. No 'cup runneth over' for us, no solemn and magic puberty rites. Hardly anywhere in the

*Nancy Friday, *My Mother, My Self*, New York, Delacorte, 1977, pp. 147–8.

anthropologies and histories of the kaleidoscope of cultures this planet has spawned are there societies where women take their daughters out at night at full moon to celebrate the ripening of the seeds of being we carry in our blood-lined bellies. There have rarely been joyous puberty rites for women. Instead, the years of puberty leading up to menarche, the first menstruation, are characterized by separation and conflict between mothers and daughters, and the whole topic is surrounded by a resounding silence.

So total is our silence that we ourselves are sometimes not aware of it.

'Oh, yes,' the mother says, 'I told my daughter all about it.'

'My mother never told me anything,' the daughter says.

Even if we are conscious of this silence and decide that it is time that this deplorable situation was dealt with, the taboos and our cultural embarrassment about menstruation may still take their toll. Wanting our daughters to have a positive view of their natural bodily functions, particularly if we have suffered in this area, we summon up our courage and carefully rehearse the proper lines. Intent upon improving the script our mothers wrote for us, we boldly announce to our daughters: 'Menstruation Is a Wonderful Part of Being a Woman, a Unique Ability of Which You Should Be Proud.'

At the same time none of us would think of hiding our toothbrushes under the basin or in the back corners of the bathroom cupboard, yet it is rare to find a box of sanitary towels prominently displayed next to the deodorants, toothpastes and hair sprays that line the bathroom shelves of most homes. Thus we constantly contradict our brave words and send our daughters double messages. We say it's fine and wonderful, but our unconscious actions indicate just the opposite. And, as we all know, actions speak louder than words.

The sad truth is that most of us have very little in the way of positive images to offer our daughters. Indeed, most of us are remarkably ignorant of even the basic facts about our bodies and our menstrual cycle.

'I'd hate to tell you how old I was before I learned that the Tampax I'd been inserting for years didn't enter the same passage through which I urinated,' writes Nancy Friday.*

'My experience has been that 75 per cent of the women in this country (and that's a modest estimate) couldn't give an explanation of menstrual periods to a sixth grader [12-year-old]. They don't know how it happens, have little or no idea what does go on in their bodies,' reports one health professional in Friday's book.†

As a result of the research I was doing, I was learning quite a bit about the physiological processes of menstruation. I could at least give a coherent explanation to a 12-year-old, but I was also learning that I had a whole host of negative attitudes about menstruation in the back of my mind, attitudes that I had not even been conscious of before. These attitudes were changing, but who knew what else might still be lurking in the dark corridors of my subconscious? If I talked to my daughter about menstruation, I could say the right words, but would my body language, my tone of voice (and all those other unconscious ways of communicating) betray my intended message?

I worried about all of this for far too long, until the obvious solution came to me: I simply explained to my daughter that when I was growing up people thought of menstruation as something unclean and unmentionable. Now that I was older and more grown up, my attitudes were changing. But some of the feelings I had were old ones

*Ibid, p. 137.
†Ibid, p. 137.

that I had lived with for a long time, all my life in fact, and they were hard to shake off. Sometimes they still got in my way without my even knowing it. This, of course, made perfect sense to my daughter, and from this starting point, we began to learn about our bodies together.

We didn't sit down and have The Talk. My mother sat me down one day to have The Talk and I suppose she must have explained things in a comprehensive way, but all I remember was my mother being horribly nervous and saying a lot of things about babies and blood and that when It happened to me, I could go to the bottom drawer of her chest of drawers and get some towels. I wondered why she was keeping the towels in her chest of drawers instead of in the linen cupboard where she usually kept them, but it didn't seem like a good time to ask questions.

Having one purposeful, nervous discussion didn't seem as though it would fill the bill. Puberty is a complicated topic and it takes more than one talk. I decided just to bear the topic in mind and bring it up now and again. It turned out to be a pretty natural thing to do since I was doing so much research on the female body. In one of the medical texts I was plodding through, there was a section on puberty that discussed the five stages of pubic hair and breast development, complete with photos. I read the section to my daughter, translating from medicalese into English, so she would know when and how these changes would happen in her body.

I talked to her about what I was learning about the workings of the menstrual cycle. I showed her some magnificent pictures taken inside a woman's body at the very moment of ovulation as the delicate, fingerlike projections on the end of the Fallopian tubes were reaching out to grasp the ripe egg.

A friend's mother gave us a wonderful collection of booklets from a sanitary towel manufacturer that dated back over a period of thirty years. We read them together, laughing at the old-fashioned attitudes, attitudes I'd grown up with.

In the course of our reading, we learned that most girls begin to have a slight vaginal discharge a year or two prior to menstruation. I had told my daughter that when she started to menstruate, I would give her the opal ring that I always wore on my left hand, and that she, in turn, could pass it on to her daughter one day. But when she discovered the first signs of vaginal discharge, we were both so elated that I gave her the opal ring on the spot. (She'll get a matching one when she has her first menstrual period.)

A few hours later, as I sat working at my typewriter, I heard my daughter yelling to me from the bathroom, 'Hey, Mom, guess what I've got twenty-one of?'

We had a pregnant cat at the time and, for a few horrible moments, I was struck numb with the thought of twenty-one kittens. But it wasn't kittens, my daughter was back to counting pubic hairs.

The time that we'd spent learning about menstruation and puberty had paid off. My daughter had regained her sense of excitement about the changes that were taking place in her body. This healthy attitude towards her body alone made our discussions worthwhile, but there were also other changes. First of all, things between the two of us got much better. We were back to our old, easy footing. She didn't magically start cleaning her bedroom or anything like that. We still had our quarrels, but they subsided to a liveable level. And when we fought, at least we were fighting about the things we said we were fighting about. The underlying resentment and tension that had been erupting from beneath even our mildest disagreements, engulfing us in volcanic arguments, was gone.

But the most amazing change, perhaps because it was so unexpected, was that my daughter's role in the playground machinations had begun to change. In *My Mother, My Self*, Friday suggests the mother's failure to deal with her daughter's dawning sexuality – her silence about menstruation and the changes in the daughter's body – is perceived by the daughter as a rejection of the daughter's feminine and sexual self.

This silent rejection of these essential elements of self, coming as it does just at the time in the daughter's life when these very aspects of femininity and sexuality are manifesting themselves in the physical changes of her body, is nothing short of devastating. The daughter feels an overwhelming sense of rejection from the figure in her life with whom she most intensely identifies. One of the ways in which the daughter seeks to cope, to gain some control over her emotional life, is through the psychodramas of rejection that she continually re-enacts with her peers.

I don't know if all this is true, but when I read Friday's book, I was reminded of a psychology experiment I'd seen in college. Rats in this experiment would press a lever and give themselves a jolting electric shock rather than receive random, intermittent shocks at the erratic whim of the experimenter. Self-administered shocks, even if they are more frequent and more intense, are apparently preferable to the anxiety of awaiting the unexpected, over which there is no control. Perhaps for little girls this small element of control, these self-administered rejections, are also attempts at reducing anxiety.

Or perhaps these dramas of rejection are more along the lines of the pecking-order behaviour we see among chickens. The largest, boldest chicken pecks another smaller one away from the food dish, that chicken retaliates by pecking on another smaller and more vulnerable chicken, and so on down the line. We cannot deal with mother's rejection directly by confronting her. We are too small, too vulnerable, too defenceless; so, in a classic case of displaced aggression, we turn around and attack another little girl. Or perhaps just the opportunity to act out rejection, whether we play the role of leader, follower or victim, to make this devastating experience familiar, to carve out roles we at least know and are used to, provides some measure of relief.

Whatever the particular mechanism, I can't help but suspect that the cultural taboo about menstruation, a mother's ignorance of and reluctance to deal with the topic, and the phenomena of playground politics are inextricably tied up with one another.

One morning, some time after my daughter and I had begun to return to our old footing, I was driving her to school when she started to talk about the problems she was having with her friend. I held my breath. This topic had become so volatile that I hadn't even broached it in months. I didn't want to say the wrong thing.

'I don't know what to do, Mummy,' she told me. 'I want to be Susan's and Tanya's friend, but they're always whispering and talking about Kathy, and they do it loud enough so she can hear. And I'm with them, but I really like Kathy too.'

'Well, can't you be friends with everybody?' I said, biting my tongue almost as soon as I said it. This had been one of my stock replies whenever we had talked about the subject and it usually caused a storm, but this time she merely answered me, 'But if I don't turn on Kathy with them, Susan and Tanya won't be friends with me.'

'So what do you do when that happens; how do you handle it?' I asked, trying to say something neutral.

'Well, I just kind of stand there. I don't actually say bad things about Kathy, but I'm there with Susan and Tanya, so it's like I'm against Kathy too. And it makes me feel terrible, like I'm not a very good person,' she said, starting to cry. 'I don't know what to do.'

'Well, look,' I said, 'Susan and Tanya are both really nice girls. Why don't you just go up to them and say "Look, I have a problem and it's really making me feel lousy", and then just tell them what you told me – that you want to be their friend, but you don't dislike Kathy and it makes you feel lousy if you join in putting her down.'

My daughter gave me a look that told me what she thought of my suggestion.

'Not such a good idea, huh?' I offered.

'No, Mum,' she agreed, and I kissed her goodbye as the school bell rang. Maybe my advice wasn't much help. Maybe it wasn't even very good advice, but at least we'd talked about the subject with each other.

Two days later, when I picked her up from school, she told me, 'Well, I tried doing what you said to do.'

'How did it work?'

'It worked. Susan and Tanya said that it was OK, that they'd still be friends with me even if I didn't hate Kathy.'

Big of them, I thought to myself, but I didn't say anything. In truth, I was pleased; my daughter had begun to carve out a new role in the game for herself.

Perhaps Nancy Friday was right. Maybe my daughter perceived my attention to the changes taking place in her body as an acceptance of her sexual self, and this, in turn, lessened her need to participate in these playground psychodramas of rejection. I didn't, and still don't, know whether Friday's theories are real explanations, but my experiences with my own daughter certainly seemed to validate her ideas. Still, I wouldn't want to go so far as to promise you that spending time teaching your daughter about menstruation and the other physical changes of puberty will magically deliver her from the psychodramatics of puberty or will automatically erase the tensions that so often exist between parents and their adolescent daughters. But my experiences with my own daughter and, more recently, as the teacher of a class on puberty and sexuality for teenagers and pre-teenagers, have convinced me that kids of this age need and want information about what is happening to them at this point in their lives.

This information isn't always easy to come by. Too often we parents simply don't have the facts to give our children. Most of us have, at best, a sketchy knowledge of menstruation, and it is a rare parent who can describe the five stages of breast or pubic hair development. This book was written to provide those facts.

The book is aimed primarily at girls between the ages of 9 and 16, but may be appropriate for younger or older girls as well. The bulk of the book deals with the physiological changes of puberty. The first seven chapters are devoted to female puberty. Chapter 8 discusses male puberty, as girls are also curious about what happens to boys' bodies as they go through puberty.

Because the changes that take place in children's bodies during puberty are sexual changes, young people of this age are curious about the other aspects of sexuality as well. So, although this book is primarily about puberty, it also discusses related issues. For instance, Chapter 9 deals with reproduction, intercourse, contraception, sexually-transmitted diseases and other sexual health issues. Chapter 10 deals with romantic and sexual feelings and touches on issues like crushes, dating, kissing, petting and making decisions about how to handle your sexual and romantic feelings. These two chapters answer some of the most commonly asked questions, but they are not a comprehensive guide to these subjects and don't cover everything you will need to discuss with your daughter as she moves into adulthood. They are only a beginning, a starting point that, it is hoped, will trigger more questions and discussions about sexual values, morality and codes of conduct.

This book may reflect values that are not the same as

yours. This doesn't mean that you can't use it. You don't have to throw out the baby with the bathwater. Instead, you can use this book as an opportunity to explain your own point of view. For example, masturbation is discussed in Chapter 5. The discussion reflects my attitude – that masturbation is a perfectly acceptable, perfectly healthy thing to do. This attitude may conflict with your moral or religious views. If that's the case, you can read this section with your child, explaining how and why you feel the way you do.

Ideally, this book is something that you and your daughter will come back to time and time again as she progresses through puberty. You may want to introduce her to the book when she is 8 or 9, before these changes have started to happen, so she'll have some idea of what to expect. But do come back to it again when she is actually going through them. What she is able to absorb when she is 8 or 9 will be very different from what she is able to absorb a couple of years later.

You may worry, as many parents do, that giving children the kind of information in Chapters 9 and 10 will get them 'too interested' in sex and will encourage them to go out and experiment sexually. Parents are particularly apt to worry that giving children information on contraception encourages sexual promiscuity. But study after study has shown that children who have a strong background in sex education, particularly if that education has come from their parents, are *less* likely to be sexually active at a young age, *less* likely to be promiscuous, *less* likely to develop a sexually-transmitted disease, and *less* likely to become pregnant as teenagers than less well-educated girls.

On the other hand, you may find that your child isn't particularly interested in some of the material in these chapters. For instance, my 9- and 10-year-old pupils are usually not too interested in discussing sexual decision-making. A lot of these girls are still in the boys-oh-ugh!/boys-are-horrible stage. If your child isn't interested in some of the material in Chapters 9 and 10, she may choose to skip these sections now. Of course, it won't do any harm for her to read this material, even if it's not very relevant to her life at the moment. It never hurts to think about these issues ahead of time. But it's been my experience that many of the younger boys and girls in my classes aren't too concerned with issues like how to handle your romantic and sexual feelings on a date. Typically, they're more interested in body changes and things like childbirth or other aspects of reproduction. So if your child doesn't seem ready for some of this information, there's no need to push it. However, here again, we hope you'll keep the book around, so your daughter can come back to it in future years when this information may be more relevant to her life.

I hope that this book will help you and your daughter understand the changes that take place in a girl's body during puberty, and that by reading it together, the two of you will become that much closer and more at ease with each other.

Chapter 1

Puberty

This book is about a time in a girl's life when her body is changing from a child's body into a woman's body. This time of changing is called *puberty*.*

Our bodies change quite a bit as we go through puberty. We get taller. The general shape or contour of our bodies changes: our hips and thighs get fleshier, and we take on a more rounded, curvy shape. Our breasts begin to swell and to blossom out from our chests. Soft nests of hair begin to grow under our arms and in the area between our legs. Our skins begin to make new oils that change the very feel and smell of us. At the same time that these changes are happening on the outside, other changes are taking place inside our bodies.

These changes don't happen overnight. Puberty happens slowly and gradually, over a period of many months or years. These changes may start when a girl is as young as 8 or they may not begin until she is 16 or older. Regardless of when they start for you, you'll probably have a lot of questions about what is happening to your body. We hope that this book will answer at least some of these questions.

'We' are my daughter, Area, and I. The two of us worked together to make this book. We talked to doctors and research scientists and pored over medical textbooks. We

---

*puberty (PEW-bur-tee)   The word puberty is pronounced with the accent on the first part of the word, PEW. You say that part of the word with the most emphasis. Throughout this book, there are a number of words that you may not have heard before. Whenever we use one of these words for the first time, we include a pronunciation key like this at the bottom of the page.

also talked to mothers and daughters to find out what happened to them during puberty, how they felt about it and what kinds of questions they had. You'll hear their voices throughout this book. Some of the quotes in this book are from boys and girls in my class. During the school year I teach a class on puberty once a week at Sequoyah School in Pasadena, California. (My daughter used to go to Sequoyah, which is how I happen to be teaching there.) The pupils in these classes and the mothers and daughters we talked to had a lot of questions and a lot of things to say about puberty. So, in a sense, they too helped to write this book.

We usually start the first puberty class of the year by talking about how babies are made. This seems like a good place to begin since the changes that occur during puberty happen to get the body ready for a time in our lives when we may decide to have a baby.

A talk with a group of boys and girls about how babies are made usually turns into a pretty giggly affair because in order to talk about how babies are made, we have to talk about *sex*, and sex, as you may have noticed, is a *very loaded subject*. People often act embarrassed, secretive, giggly or some other strange way when the subject of sex comes up.

Even the word itself is confusing, because *sex* can mean many different things and is used in different ways. In the simplest meaning of the word, sex refers to the different kinds of bodies that men and women have. There are a number of differences between male and female bodies, but the most obvious is that a male has a *penis* and *scrotum* and a female has a *vulva* and *vagina*. These body parts, or organs, are called *sex organs*. People are either members of the male sex or the female sex, depending on which type of sex organs they have.

penis (PEE-niss)　　　　　*vulva* (VUL-va)
scrotum (SKRO-tum)　　　*vagina* (vah-JIE-nah)

The word 'sex' is also used in other ways. We may say that two people are 'having sex'. Having sex, or *sexual intercourse*, involves a man putting his penis into a woman's vagina. Or we may say that two people are 'being sexual with each other', which means that they are having sexual intercourse or that they are holding, touching or caressing each other's sex organs. We may also say that we are 'feeling sexual', which means that we are having feelings or thoughts about our sexual organs, about being sexual with another person or about having intercourse.

Our sexual organs are very private parts of our bodies. We usually keep them covered up and we don't talk about them in public very often. Having sex, being sexual with someone or having sexual feelings are also usually private matters that don't get talked about very often. So when we come into a class-room and start talking about penises and vaginas and having sex . . . well, things get pretty giggly. (You can imagine how my poor daughter felt, having her mother coming to school to talk about *those* things. Before I started teaching the class, I asked her if it was all right with her. She wasn't entirely happy with the idea. Finally she said all right, but no way was she going to be in the class! As it turned out, the classes were a big hit. Other pupils were coming up to her and saying how much they liked the class. So eventually she joined the class too, even though she'd heard most of this stuff at home.)

I decided that if we were going to get all silly and giggly in class when we talked about these things, we might as well get *really* silly and giggly. So we start the first class of the year by giving everyone photocopies of the two drawings in Illustration 1 and red and blue pencils that we use to colour the drawings.

intercourse (IN-ter-korse)

Sex organs

Illustration 1 shows the male and the female sex organs. These sex organs are also referred to as the *genitals* or the *genital organs*. Everyone has sex organs on both the inside and the outside of the body, and they change as you go through puberty. These pictures show how the sex organs on the outside of the body look in grown men and women.

We usually begin with the male sex organs. We explain that the sex organs on the outside of a man's body have two main parts and that the scientific names for these parts are the penis and the scrotum. By the time we've passed out the copies of the drawings and have started talking about the penis and the scrotum, the pupils are usually giggling like mad, nudging each other or falling off their chairs in embarrassment. We don't pay too much attention to how they're behaving; we just say, 'OK, the penis itself also has two parts: the *shaft* and the *glans*. Find the shaft of the penis on your drawing and colour it blue.' Some pupils keep giggling and some get very serious, but they all start colouring. Why don't you colour the shaft too (unless, of course, this book belongs to someone else or to a library. One of the people we admire most in the world is a wonderful lady named Lou Ann Sobieski. She's a librarian, and my daughter and I would be in very hot water if Lou Ann thought we were telling people to colour in library books.)

After they've coloured the shaft blue, we tell the class that there is a small slit in the glans, right at the very tip of the penis, called the *urinary opening*. This is the opening through which *urine* (pee) leaves the body. We ask the class to colour it red. Next, we colour in the glans itself. We usually recommend blue and red stripes, but colour it any way you want, just as long as it's coloured differently from the other parts so that it will stand out clearly.

genitals (JEN-a-tulls)   *urinary* (YUR-in-air-ee)
glans (GLANZ)   *urine* (YUR-in)

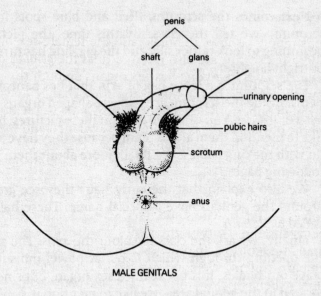

penis

shaft   glans

urinary opening

pubic hairs

scrotum

anus

MALE GENITALS

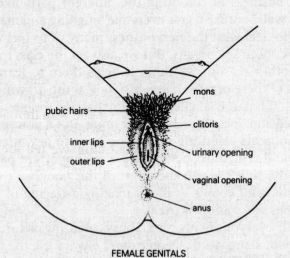

pubic hairs

inner lips

outer lips

mons

clitoris

urinary opening

vaginal opening

anus

FEMALE GENITALS

Illustration 1. The genitals.

Next comes the scrotum. 'Red and blue spots for the scrotum,' we tell the class. By this time, the picture is beginning to look rather silly and the giggling has turned to outright laughter.

The scrotum is a loose bag of skin that lies beneath the penis. Inside the scrotum are two egg-shaped organs called *testes* or *testicles*. You can't see them in these pictures, but we like to mention them at this point because they have a lot to do with making babies. We'll talk more about them in the following pages.

We also explain that the curly hairs they see growing around the genitals have a special name. These hairs are called *pubic hairs*.

Finally, we ask the class to colour the *anus*. The anus is the opening through which *faeces*, or bowel movements, leave our bodies. It is not really a sex organ, but since it is located in the genital area, we like to mention it.

The business of colouring the different parts like this works well because it gets everyone laughing and makes it easier to deal with the nervousness many of us feel when we talk about sex organs. But we also get the class to do it for another reason: we think it helps them to learn the names of these organs. If you just look at the drawing and see that this part is labelled *penis* and that part *scrotum*, it's all jumbled and doesn't stick in your mind. But if you spend a few moments colouring them, you have to pay attention and you'll remember better. These are important parts of the body, so it's worth the effort. If this book isn't yours and you can't colour in it, try making a tracing of these drawings and colouring them.

While everyone in my class is busy colouring pictures, we talk about slang words. People don't always use the scien-

---

testes (TES-teez) *pubic* (PEW-bik)
testicles (TES-ti-kuls) *faeces* (FEE-sees)
anus (AY-nus) *bowel* (BOW-ul)

tific names for these body parts. The kids in our classes came up with quite a list of slang words for the penis, scrotum and testicles.

SLANG WORDS FOR THE PENIS, SCROTUM AND TESTICLES

Penis			Scrotum and Testicles	
cock	john	codger	balls	rocks
dick	thomas	tool	nuts	sack
prick	rod	thing	eggs	goolies
willie	meat	banger		
pecker	pisser	donger		

Personally, I don't object to slang words, but some people do and they may get upset if they hear you using them. You may or may not care about upsetting people in this way, but you should at least be aware of the fact that there are people who find slang words offensive.

When we've finished colouring the male sex organs, we move on to the female sex organs. The genital organs on the outside of a woman's body are sometimes referred to as the *vulva*. The vulva has many parts. We usually start at the top with the fleshy mound called the *mons* and colour it with blue spots. Then we move towards the bottom of the mons where it divides into two folds, or flaps, of skin called the *outer lips*. Try colouring them with red stripes. In between the outer lips lie the *inner lips*. Try blue stripes for the inner lips. The inner lips join together at the top and there is a small, bud-shaped organ called the *clitoris*. Colour it red. Just down from the clitoris, between the inner lips, is the

mons (MONZ)   *clitoris* (KLIT-or-iss)

If you cut an apple in half, you would be able to see the seeds and core on the inside of the apple. This drawing, which shows the inside of an apple, is called a cross-section.

The drawing below is also a cross-section. It shows the inside of the penis and scrotum.

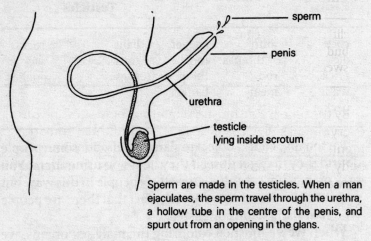

sperm

penis

urethra

testicle
lying inside scrotum

Sperm are made in the testicles. When a man ejaculates, the sperm travel through the urethra, a hollow tube in the centre of the penis, and spurt out from an opening in the glans.

Illustration 2. Cross-section of the penis and scrotum.

urinary opening, the opening through which urine leaves the body. Colour it blue. Below the urinary opening is another opening called the *vaginal opening*. It leads into the hollow pouch, or cavity, on the inside of our bodies called the *vagina*. Use your imagination – colour the vaginal opening red, blue, striped or whatever. Finally, we come to the anus; choose a colour and colour the anus.

While we're colouring in the female genitals, we also

vaginal (vah-JI-nul)   *urethra* (yur-EE-thrah)

make a list of slang words used to refer to this part of a woman's body.

SLANG WORDS FOR THE CLITORIS, VULVA AND VAGINA

Clitoris	Vulva and Vagina		
clit	cunt	beaver	snatch
bud	pussy	hole	slit
sweet-pea			

By the time we've finished colouring both these pictures, everyone has giggled off a good deal of their embarrassment. They have also got a pretty good idea of where these body parts are, which makes it a lot easier to understand how a man and woman make babies.

Sexual intercourse

When we tell the pupils in our classes what sexual intercourse means, they usually have two reactions. One is that they want to know just how a man's penis could get into a woman's vagina. We explain that sometimes the penis gets stiff and hard and stands out from the body. This is called an *erection*, and it can happen when a male is feeling sexual or is having sex with someone, and at other times too. (We'll say more about this in Chapter 8.) An erection happens because the spongy tissue inside the penis fills up with blood. Some people call an erection a 'hard-on' because the penis feels so stiff and hard.

erection (e-REK-shun)

While it is erect, the penis can slide right into the vaginal opening. The vagina isn't very large, but it's very elastic and stretchy, so the erect penis can easily fit in there.

In addition to wanting to know *how*, some of the kids in our classes want to know *why* anyone would want to do this.

People have sexual intercourse for all sorts of reasons. It is a special way of being close with another person. It also feels good, which some of the class find hard to believe. But these areas of our bodies have many nerve endings; if they are stroked or rubbed in the right ways, these nerve endings send messages to pleasure centres in our brains. When our pleasure centres are stimulated, we get pleasurable feelings all over our bodies. People also have sexual intercourse because they want to have a baby, but babies don't start to grow every time a man and woman have intercourse, just sometimes.

Making babies

In order to make a baby, two things are needed: a seed from a woman's body, which is called an *ovum*, and a seed from a man's body, which is called a *sperm*. You may have heard adults talking about an ovum and calling it 'a woman's egg' or talking about sperm and calling it 'a man's seed'. When the children in our classes hear the word 'egg', many of them think about the kind of eggs that chickens lay and that we eat at breakfast. When they hear the word 'seed', they think about the things we plant in the ground in order to grow flowers and vegetables. But the ovum and the sperm are not like these kinds of eggs and seeds. For one thing, an ovum is much smaller than the eggs we cook for breakfast — in fact, it is much smaller than the smallest dot you could

ovum (OH-vum)

make with the tip of even the sharpest pencil point. And a sperm is even smaller than an ovum.

Sperm are made inside the testicles, the two egg-shaped organs inside the scrotum. Sometimes, when a man and a woman are having sexual intercourse, the man *ejaculates*. When a man ejaculates, the muscles of his penis contract and the sperm are pumped out of the testicles through the *urethra*, a hollow tube in the centre of the penis, and spurt out through an opening in the centre of the glans, as shown in Illustration 2. A couple of spoonfuls of a creamy, white fluid, full of millions of tiny, microscopic sperm come out of the penis. This liquid is called *semen* or *ejaculate* or, in slang terms, 'come'.

ejaculates (e-JA-cue-lates)　　　　*semen* (SEE-men)
ejaculate (e-JACK-u-lat)

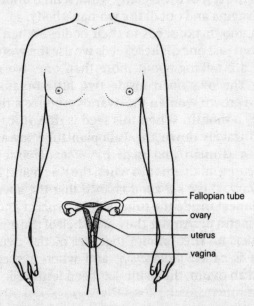

Fallopian tube
ovary
uterus
vagina

Illustration 3. The sex organs on the inside of a woman's body.

After the sperm leave the penis, they start swimming up towards the top of the vagina. They pass through a tiny opening at the top of the vagina that leads into an organ called the *uterus* (see Illustration 3). The uterus is a hollow organ and, in a grown woman, it's only about the size of a clenched fist. But the thick muscle walls of the uterus are quite elastic and, like a balloon, the uterus can expand to many times its original size. The uterus has to be able to expand because it is here, inside a woman's uterus, that a baby grows.

Some of the sperm swim up to the top of the uterus and into one of two little tubes, or tunnels, called the *Fallopian tubes*. Not all the sperm make it this far. Some drift back down the uterus and out into the vagina, where they join other sperm that never made it out of the vagina. These sperm and the rest of the creamy white semen dribble back down the vagina and out of the woman's body.

Women, too, make seeds in their bodies. When we are talking about just one of these seeds we use the word *ovum*. When we are talking about more than one, we use the word *ova*. The ova ripen inside two little organs called *ovaries*. In a grown woman the ovaries produce a ripe seed about once a month. When this seed is ripe, it leaves the ovary and travels down the Fallopian tube towards the uterus. If a woman and man have sexual intercourse around the time of the month when the ripe ovum has just left the ovary, there's a good chance that the sperm and ovum will meet inside the tube. When a sperm and ovum meet, the sperm penetrates the outer shell of the ovum and moves inside it. This joining together of the ovum and the sperm is called *fertilization*, and when a sperm has penetrated an ovum, the ovum has been fertilized.

uterus (YOU-ter-us)   *ova* (OH-vah)
Fallopian (fuh-LO-pee-an)   *ovaries* (OH-vah-reez)

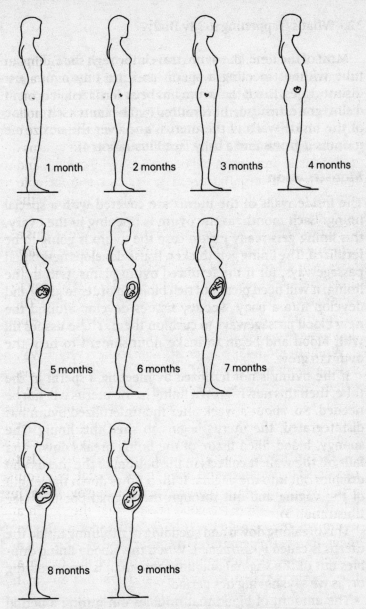

Illustration 4. Stages of pregnancy. A fertilized ovum plants itself on the inside wall of the uterus and over the next nine months it develops into a baby.

Most of the time, the ovum travels through the Fallopian tube without meeting a sperm and the tiny ovum just disintegrates. But if the ovum has been fertilized, it doesn't disintegrate. Instead, the fertilized ovum plants itself on one of the inside walls of the uterus, and over the next nine months it grows into a baby (see Illustration 4).

Menstruation

The inside walls of the uterus are covered with a special lining. Each month, as the ovum is ripening in the ovary, this lining gets ready just in case the ovum is going to be fertilized. The lining gets thicker. It also develops new blood passageways, for if the fertilized ovum plants itself in the lining, it will need plenty of rich blood in order to grow and develop into a baby. Spongy tissues develop around the new blood passageways to cushion them. These tissues fill with blood and begin to make nourishment to help the ovum to grow.

If the ovum is not fertilized by meeting a sperm in the tube, then this newly grown lining in the uterus will not be needed. So, about a week after the unfertilized ovum has disintegrated, the uterus begins to shed this lining. The spongy, blood-filled tissue of the lining breaks down and falls off the wall. It collects in the bottom of the uterus and dribbles out into the vagina. It then flows down the length of the vagina and out through the vaginal opening (see Illustration 5).

This breaking down and shedding of the lining inside the uterus is called *menstruation*. When the bloody lining dribbles out of the vaginal opening, a woman is menstruating or, as we say, having her period.

The amount of blood that dribbles out during a period

menstruation (MEN-stroo-ay-shun)
menstruating (MEN-stroo-ay-ting)

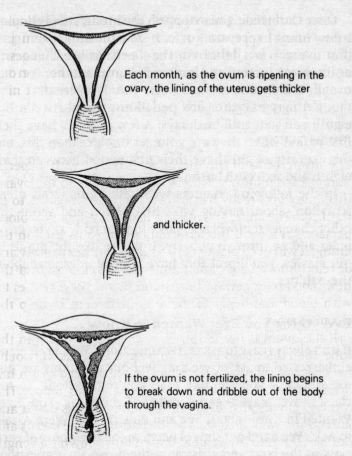

Each month, as the ovum is ripening in the ovary, the lining of the uterus gets thicker

and thicker.

If the ovum is not fertilized, the lining begins to break down and dribble out of the body through the vagina.

Illustration 5. Cross-section of the uterus. The shaded area is the lining of the uterus.

varies. Some of us have a couple of tablespoons, others have almost a cupful. The blood doesn't come out all at once, but dribbles out slowly over a number of days. Then it stops. It may take only a couple of days or it may take a week or so for all of the menstrual blood to empty out of your body.

Once the bleeding has stopped, the uterus starts growing a new lining in preparation for next month's ripe ovum. If that ovum is not fertilized, the newly grown lining will again break down and you will have another period, usually within a month or so after your last period.

A girl may have her first period any time between her eighth and sixteenth birthdays. A few girls will have their first period when they are younger or older than this, but the majority of girls have their first period between their eighth and sixteenth birthdays.

In the following chapters we'll talk more about menstruation, about having your first period and about the other changes that will take place in your body as you grow older and go through puberty. If you're like the pupils in our classes, you'll probably have a lot of questions about these things.

Everything You Ever Wanted to Know . . .

It isn't always easy to ask certain questions. We may feel too embarrassed to ask or we may feel our questions are just too stupid. If you feel like that, you're not alone. In my classes, we play a game called 'Everything You Ever Wanted to Know about Sex and Puberty, but Were Afraid to Ask'. We hand out slips of paper at the beginning of each class so the boys and girls can write down their questions and put them in a question box. They don't have to sign their names to the questions, and I'm the only one who gets to see them, so nobody can look at the handwriting and figure out who wrote the question. We also leave the locked box in place where people can get to it during the week in case they think of questions after class. At the end of each class we take the questions out of the box, read them out loud, and answer them as well as we can.

In writing this book we've tried to answer all the questions that have come up in our 'Everything You Ever Wanted to Know' game, but you may find that you have questions that we haven't answered. If so, perhaps your mother or father, the school nurse, one of your teachers or another adult can help you find answers to your questions.

Using this book

You may want to read this book with your parents, with a friend or all by yourself. You may want to read it straight through from beginning to end or you may want to jump around, reading a chapter here and there, depending on what you are most curious about. However you decide to go about reading this book, we hope that you'll enjoy it and that you'll learn as much from reading it as we did from writing it.

Chapter 2

Changing Size and Shape

If you notice that the jeans you bought just a couple of months ago are up around your ankles already or that your brand-new shoes are suddenly too small, it's probably because you are beginning to go through puberty. As you begin puberty, your body starts to grow at a faster rate.

The growth spurt

The sudden increase in the rate of growth at the start of puberty is called a 'growth spurt'. It happens at different ages for different girls and is more noticeable in some girls than in others. It usually starts before you begin to develop breasts or to grow soft nests of hair in the area between your legs.

Starting around the age of 2, the average girl grows about 50 mm (2 in) a year until she starts puberty. When puberty begins, she may start growing twice as fast, so that she grows 100 mm (4 in) that year instead of only 50 mm (2 in). Of course, not everyone is average, so you may grow more or less than this.

The growth spurt usually lasts less than a year, then the growth rate begins to slow down again. By the time you've had your first menstrual period, your growth rate has usually slowed back down to 25–50 mm (1–2 in) a year. Most girls reach their full adult height within one to three years after their first period.

Boys go through a growth spurt during puberty too, but they usually don't start theirs until a couple of years after girls start. This is why 11- and 12-year-old girls are often taller than boys their age. However, a couple of years later, when the boys start their growth spurt, they catch up with the girls and surpass them in height. Of course, some girls, the ones who are on the tall side, will always be taller than most of the boys. But often a girl who is taller than the boys she knows when she is 11 or 12 will find that the boys have caught up by the age of 13 or 14.

During puberty, as you are growing taller, your bones are, of course, getting longer, but not all the bones in your body grow at the same rate. Your arms and legs tend to grow faster than your backbone during puberty, so you may notice that your arms and legs are longer in proportion to the trunk of your body than they were during childhood or than they will be when you reach adulthood.

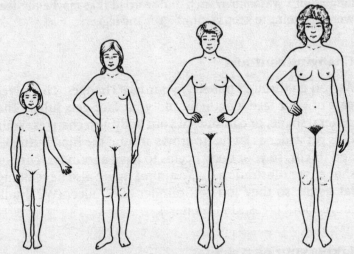

Illustration 6. Girls in puberty. As we go through puberty, our hips get wider. Fat tissue begins to grow around our hips, thighs, and buttocks, giving our bodies a curvier shape. Our breasts begin to swell, and soft nests of hair begin to grow under our arms and on our genitals.

The bones in your feet also grow faster than your other bones. So your feet reach their adult size long before you've reached your adult height. A number of the girls we talked to worried about this. As one girl explained:

I was just a little over 1.5 m (5 ft) tall when I was 11, but I wore a size 6 shoe. I thought, 'Oh, no, if my feet keep on growing, they're gonna be gigantic!' But I'm 16 now, and I'm 1.72 m (5 ft 8 in) tall, but my feet are still size 6.

In reaction to this, another girl said:

I'm sure glad to hear that. I wear a size 6½ now and I'm only 12 years old and 1.54 m (5 ft 1 in). People are always teasing me about my big feet. The last time I bought tennis shoes, the man in the shop made some big joke about how if my feet became any bigger, he'd have to sell me the shoe boxes to wear. I pretended to laugh, but I was embarrassed and worried that maybe my feet were just going to keep getting bigger and bigger.

Changing contours

As you go through puberty, your face changes. The lower part of your face lengthens and your face gets fuller. The general shape, or contour, of your body also changes. Your hips get wider as fat tissue grows around the hips, buttocks and thighs, so your body begins to have a rounder, curvier shape (see Illustration 6). Your breasts are also developing fat tissue, so they too get rounder and fuller. (We'll talk more about breasts in Chapter 4.)

Liking your own shape

Bodies come in all sorts of shapes and sizes – short and tall, thin and plump, narrow and wide, angular and curvy, straight and rounded. To some extent, you can change the shape of your body by diet and exercise. If you are thin, you can put on weight. If you are fat, you can diet so that your body loses some of its fat tissue. You can exercise to build up or slim down areas of your body. But you do have a basic shape to your body that can't be changed no matter how much or how little you eat or what kind of exercise you do.

If you aren't satisfied with your body and are under- or overweight, perhaps you need to see a doctor and start a diet and exercise programme to help you gain or lose weight. If you are not sure whether you're under- or overweight, your doctor can help you decide if your weight is within normal ranges for your height and body build. If you fall within these weight ranges and still aren't happy with the way your body looks, maybe you need to think about where you've got these ideas about how your body *should* look that are making you feel dissatisfied with the way you *do* look.

It would be nice if we could all look at our bodies without having to compare them to someone else's and just say, 'Hey, I like the way I look.' But we live in a society where there's a lot of competition between people, between companies and even between countries. We are always comparing and competing to see who's best. But who decides what's best?

Most of us get our ideas about what's the 'best' or 'most attractive' kind of female body from the women we see in magazines and television and in films. Right now these women might be mostly tall, thin, blonde, blue-eyed, white-skinned women with rosy cheeks, no spots or freckles, flat stomachs, tiny waists, long legs, big breasts, hairless legs and underarms, curvy hips and thighs – without a single unwanted bulge anywhere. As you may have noticed, there are few of us who actually look like this. For one thing, we aren't all white-skinned, blonde-haired and blue-eyed. And we aren't all thin with tiny waists and big

Illustration 7. We are different sizes, shapes and colours.

breasts. We come in a pleasing array of sizes, shapes and colours.

But when we are constantly bombarded with pictures of these glamorous skinny, blonde, blue-eyed women, it can make us feel that there is something about our hips, breasts, thighs, height, shapes, faces, skin or hair that is somehow not right. If we don't look like these women, we may be unhappy with the way we do look. In fact, people are often so unhappy about their looks that they spend millions of pounds each year on hair dyes, cosmetics, fad diets, leg and underarm hair removers, different slimming aids and on and on. Some people even have operations to make their breasts a different size.

With all the images of these 'perfect' women who seem

to be having glamorous lives and no problems at all, it's easy to begin thinking that their kinds of body actually *are* better or more attractive. If you feel that way sometimes, it might help you to remember that these bodies seem to be more desirable only because they are in fashion in our particular culture at this particular time. Being in fashion doesn't make a mini-skirt 'better' than a knee-length skirt, and being in fashion doesn't make one body type 'better' than another.

It helps, too, to remember that fashions change and that they vary from culture to culture. The drawings in Illustration 8 show bodies that have been in fashion in other times and in other cultures. The first drawing is a flapper in the

Illustration 8. Fashions in beauty: from left to right are a flapper, a sixteenth-century woman and a Polynesian woman.

1920s. During the 1920s curvy bodies and big breasts were definitely not in fashion. In fact, women with big breasts wrapped their breasts tightly, strapping them down, so that they wouldn't stick out. The second drawing shows a woman in the 1500s. Today she would be considered a bit chunky, but then her type of body was the 'best', 'most attractive' kind of body a woman could have. The third drawing shows a Polynesian woman. She doesn't match our culture's standard of beauty, but in her culture, she'd be considered a great beauty and her rounded body would be considered the 'best' and 'most attractive'.

Learning to appreciate yourself and to like your own body whether or not it matches what's in fashion is a big step in growing up. And if you can manage to find your own body attractive, other people will too, and it won't matter whether it's the so-called best or most attractive kind of body – not one bit. We guarantee it.

Chapter 3

Body Hair, Perspiration and Spots

For some girls, the growth spurt and the changes in the shape of their bodies are the first signs of puberty. For others, the first sign that puberty is beginning is that they start growing hair in new places on their bodies.

Pubic hair

Pubic hair is the name given to the curly hairs that grow in the area of our bodies where our legs join together. This area has many names, such as the vulva and the genital area. Some people call this area of the body the vagina. Actually, the vagina is inside your body, so it is not really correct to call it the vagina.

If you stand sideways in front of a mirror, you'll notice that there is a little mound of flesh in this area that protrudes (sticks out) a bit. This mound is called the *mons*, which is a Latin word that means little hill or mound. It is also called the *mons veneris*. *Veneris* is another Latin word, which refers to Venus, the goddess of love, so *mons veneris* means 'mound of Venus' or 'mound of love'. The mons is just one part of the vulva or genital area. We'll be talking about the other parts of the vulva later, but for now, let's concentrate on the mons.

The mons is a pad of fat tissue that lies under the skin. It cushions the pubic bone that lies beneath it. If you press

veneris (ven-AIR-iss)

down on the mons, you can feel the pubic bone under-neath. For this reason, the mons is also referred to as the *pubis*. Regardless of what you call it, sooner or later you will begin to notice curly hairs growing here.

If you look at your mons, you will notice that, towards the bottom, it divides into two folds or flaps of skin. These are the *labia majora*, or outer lips. In many girls, pubic hair first begins to grow on the edges of these lips. In others, it first begins growing on the mons itself.

FIVE STAGES OF PUBIC HAIR GROWTH

Doctors have divided pubic hair growth into the five stages shown in Illustration 9. You may be in one of these stages or in between one stage and another. See if you can find the stage you're closest to.

Stage 1 starts when you are born and continues through-out childhood. In this stage the mons and the lips are either hairless or they have a few light-coloured, soft hairs similar to the hair that may be growing on your tummy. There aren't any pubic hairs.

Stage 2 starts when you grow your first pubic hairs. If you have hairs growing on your vulva during childhood, you will be able to tell the difference between these childhood hairs and pubic hairs because the pubic hairs are longer, darker and curly. At first, they may be only slightly curly and there may be just a few of them. You may have to look very closely in order to see them.

In Stage 3 the pubic hairs get curlier and thicker, and there are more of them. They may get darker. They cover more of the mons and the lips than they did in Stage 2.

In Stage 4 the pubic hair gets still thicker and curlier, and it may continue to get darker. It also spreads out so it covers more of the mons and the lips.

pubis (PEW-bis)   *majora* (may-JOR-ah)
labia (LAY-bee-uh)

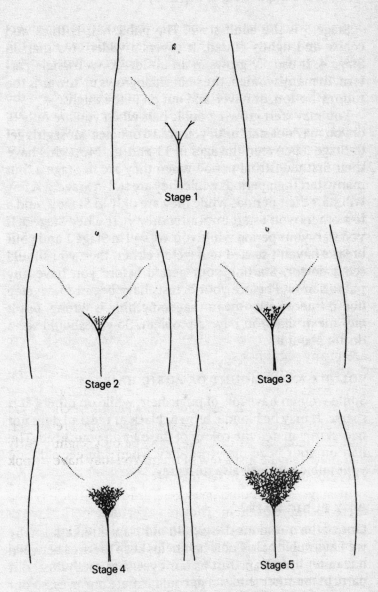

Illustration 9. The five stages of pubic hair growth.

Stage 5 is the adult stage. The pubic hair is thick and coarse and tightly curled. It covers a wider area than in Stage 4. It usually grows in an upside-down triangle pattern. In many women, the pubic hair grows up towards the tummy button, or navel, and out on to the thighs.

You may start growing pubic hair when you are only 8, or you may not start until you are 16 or older. Most girls get to Stage 3 between the ages of 11 and 13. Most girls have their first menstrual period when they are in Stage 4, but many start their periods while they are still in Stage 3. A few will start their periods while they are only in Stage 2, and a few others won't start until after they've reached Stage 5. If you start your period while you are still in Stage 1 and your breasts haven't started to develop either, then you should see a doctor. Starting your period before you have any pubic hair and before your breasts have begun to develop doesn't necessarily mean that something is wrong, but it *may* mean that you have a problem. So you should see a doctor about it.

COLOUR AND AMOUNT OF PUBIC HAIR

Some women have lots of pubic hair, while on others, it is sparse. It may be blonde, brown, black or red and does not necessarily match the colour of the hair on your head. The hair on your head may turn grey when you get old, and your pubic hair may also turn grey.

WHY PUBIC HAIR?

One of the questions the girls in our class often ask is why we have pubic hair. Pubic hair helps keep the area between our outer lips clean. Just as our eyelashes catch dust, dirt particles or other things that could irritate our eyes, so our pubic hair catches things that could irritate the sensitive area between our outer lips. During childhood we don't need the protection the pubic hair provides because this area is not as sensitive as it becomes during puberty.

FEELINGS ABOUT PUBIC HAIR

Some of the girls we talked to felt really excited about growing pubic hairs. Here's what one girl had to say:

One day I was taking a bath and I noticed three little curly hairs growing down there. I started yelling for my mum to come and see. I felt very grown up.

Other girls weren't sure what was happening. As one girl explained:

I saw these curly, black hairs and I didn't know what they were, so I got the tweezers and pulled them out. Pretty soon, they grew back, and then there were more and more of them. So I figured it must be OK.

Growing pubic hair can be rather alarming, especially if you don't know what's happening. A number of girls told us that they plucked their first pubic hairs. It's not really a very good idea to pluck your pubic hairs. For one thing, they'll just grow back. Also, plucking them could cause the skin to become irritated, sore or infected (not to mention the fact that plucking them could be very painful).

Although many of the girls we talked to felt excited about beginning puberty, not all of them were. Some of the girls didn't like the fact that they were growing pubic hair and going through the other changes of puberty. One girl had this to say:

I just wasn't ready. I remember when I first saw that my pubic hairs were growing. I thought, 'Oh, no, I don't want this to start happening to me yet.' Then I got breasts and it was like I suddenly started having this grown-up body, but I still felt like a kid inside.

Another girl said that she was excited and proud about her body maturing, but at the same time she was also uncertain:

I was afraid I was going to have to be all grown up and wear high heels all the time instead of being a tomboy and climbing trees. But, really, it turned out that I did just the same things I always did.

All the girls we talked to, whether they felt good or bad (or a bit of both) about the changes happening in their bodies, agreed that it helps to have someone to talk to about your feelings. Reading this book with someone might be a good way of starting to talk about those things.

Underarm hair

We also start to grow hair under our arms during puberty. Most girls don't start growing underarm hair until after they've started growing pubic hair or their breasts have started developing. Many don't grow underarm hair until after their first period. But for a few girls underarm hair is the very first sign that puberty is beginning. Although this is unusual, it's not abnormal and it doesn't mean there's anything wrong. The other changes, developing pubic hair and breasts and having your first period, will all happen eventually.

Other body hair

The hair on our arms and legs may get darker as we go through puberty, and we may have more of it than we did during childhood. Some girls notice that they begin to grow darker hairs on their upper lip as well.

Shaving

In some parts of the world women with lots of underarm and leg hair are considered more attractive or more womanly than women who don't have much hair on these parts of their bodies. In our country the opposite seems to be true, at least in many people's minds. Here it seems that women who don't have hair on their underarms or legs are considered more attractive. The pretty, glamorous women we see in magazines, on TV and in films have smooth, hairless legs and armpits. It's not that these women are somehow different from us and don't grow hair in these places. They are hairless because they shave their hair or remove it by some other means.

Boys start growing hair under their arms and on their legs during puberty too. When boys start growing hair in these places, they generally feel very proud. It is a sign that they are turning from boys into men. On men leg and underarm hair is considered attractive and manly. On women it is often considered unattractive and unfeminine, which doesn't make much sense if you think about it.

You'll have to decide for yourself whether or not you want to remove the hair from your legs and underarms. It's not always easy to make this decision on your own because of pressure from the people around you, as in this girl's case.

I wasn't going to shave my legs, but then my girl-friends started saying, 'Ugh, look at all the hair on your legs. Why don't you shave it?' So I started doing it even though I didn't really want to.

Some girls said that they wanted to remove the hair on their legs and underarms, but their mothers said they couldn't. If your mother doesn't want you to do this and you want to, that's something you and she will have to work out between you. Your decision should be your own, though, without pressure one way or another from someone else. (We hope this last statement doesn't get us in trouble with too many mothers.)

There are basically four ways of removing hair: by shaving with a razor, by using a chemical cream hair remover (a depilatory), by using a wax remover and by electrolysis.

You can use a razor to remove hair from your legs and underarms. But don't use a razor to remove hair from your upper lip, as this may eventually leave a stubble or darkened area on your lip. You can use an electric razor or a regular one to shave your legs and underarms. Make sure the blades are smooth and free of nicks, or you may cut yourself. A dull blade can pull, or 'drag', on your skin, so make sure you use a sharp one. It's difficult to cut yourself with an electric razor, but it's not at all difficult to cut yourself with a regular one, so be careful. Use soap or shaving cream and always shave in the direction of hair growth to reduce the pull or drag of the razor on your skin.

Depilatories kill the hair at the root. You put the cream on and leave it there for a certain length of time. When you wipe it off, the hair comes off too. Certain types of chemical removers can be used on your upper lip, but never use a depilatory intended for your legs on your face. It could badly irritate the facial skin. Also be sure to follow the directions and test the cream on a small area of skin for an allergic reaction before using it.

Another way of removing hair is to heat wax and spread it on the area where you want the hair removed. When the wax is cool, you pull it off and the hairs pull off with the wax. Wax kits are available from chemists. Some are designed for use on the legs, some for the face and some for the bikini line (see below). Still other kits are made to be used in all these areas. Read the instructions carefully and be sure you use the wax only on the area for which it is intended.

Electrolysis is a more permanent method of removing hair, although in most cases the hair does eventually grow back. Electrolysis involves the use of an electric needle to destroy the hair root. It is generally used for removing facial hair. Electrolysis should be done only by someone trained in the technique. Your GP may be able to help you find someone trained in electrolysis.

Since high-cut bathing suits and bikinis have become fashionable, many girls have asked us about the best way to remove pubic hair so that it won't show under these new-style swim garments. As we explained earlier, plucking pubic hair is *not* a good idea. Nor is it a good idea to use a chemical cream remover on this area of your body. You can shave your 'bikini line' with a razor, but do it gently, use plenty of shaving cream and always shave down, in the direction of hair growth. Even if you're careful, you may still find that shaving leaves unsightly red bumps and irritated skin. So if you want to shave your bikini line, experiment by shaving a small area and then wait at least twenty-four hours to make sure you won't have a bad reaction. There are also wax removers – 'bikini wax kits' – that can be used on this area of the body. However, make sure that the wax you use is intended for this area of your body and always follow the directions carefully.

Perspiration and body odour

Another change you may notice as you go through puberty is that you begin to have more perspiration (sweat) under your arms. This happens because your perspiration glands become more active during puberty. The odour of your underarm perspiration may also change, so that you have a more adult odour. You may also notice that other areas of your body, such as your feet, the palms of your hands or your vulva, have more perspiration and a new odour. Or you may notice that the palms of your hands, which also contain numerous perspiration glands, tend to perspire more or to get rather clammy from time to time.

Although these changes in perspiration and body odour are natural, healthy and another sign that you are growing up, some young people worry about the odour and the increase in perspiration. Actually, it's not so surprising that some young people worry about these things. Advertising agencies spend millions of pounds each year on commercials designed to make us worry about our body odours and whether or not we're 'dry' enough. But if you're healthy and eat properly, your body odour won't be offensive. Bathing or showering regularly and wearing freshly laundered clothes should keep you smelling clean and fresh. If you perspire quite a bit and this bothers you, you may find that wearing 100 per cent cotton undergarments will help. Cotton is more absorbent than synthetic (man-made) materials. Wearing outer clothes made of cotton or wool or other natural fibres may also help.

We all tend to perspire more when we're nervous. During puberty this tendency may be even more noticeable. Lots of teenagers get clammy hands or break out in a sweat when they become nervous. This is perfectly normal and usually lessens after you reach your twenties. If you have this problem, it helps to remember that it is normal. Sometimes just admitting to yourself 'Yes, I'm feeling really nervous (or embarrassed or uptight) right now' will help you to relax and perspire less.

DEODORANTS AND ANTIPERSPIRANTS

If you are bothered by the odour or amount of your underarm perspiration, you may want to use a deodorant and/or an antiperspirant. There are a number of these products on the market. They come in aerosol cans, nonaerosol sprays, sticks, creams, roll-ons – you name it. Some are 'unscented' and some have a scent added to cover up the smell of the product. Some are advertised as being 'a man's deodorant', but there generally isn't much difference between a so-called man's deodorant and a woman's deodorant.

Underarm deodorants are aimed at covering up your body odour with the supposedly more pleasant odour of the deodorant. Antiperspirants also have a substance to dry up perspiration. The most effective antiperspirants have a substance called aluminium chlorohydrate. Some people think that the aluminium can soak through your skin and get into your bloodstream, and that this may be harmful. Other people disagree. You'll have to decide for yourself whether you want to use this kind of product.

Whatever you decide, be sure to read the label. You may find that it is better not to put deodorant or antiperspirant on immediately after you come out of a hot bath or shower. If you are perspiring then, the deodorant/antiperspirant may just wash away. It might be better to let your body cool down a bit first.

With the way we've been going on about deodorants and perspiration here, you may be thinking, 'Oh, wow, I'd better run out and get some.' Please remember, though, that body smells are natural and normal, and unless your odour or the amount of perspiration bothers you, it's not really necessary to use anything.

While we're on the subject of body odour and deodorants, we want to say something about your vulva and about vaginal deodorant sprays. You have perspiration glands in your vulva and these too become more active during puberty. In addition, you have oil glands in your vulva, which also become more active. The increase of activity of these oil and perspiration glands may make your vulvar area feel more moist and have a different odour than when you were younger. Nowadays there are vaginal deodorant sprays made for use on your vulva, but we do not recommend them. They can be irritating to the vulva. Besides, unless you have an infection, your vulvar area shouldn't have an unpleasant smell. Daily washing with soap and water and wearing clean cotton underpants is all it takes to keep you smelling fresh. If you have a strong-smelling discharge from your vagina or your vulva smells bad, you may have an infection and should see a doctor rather than covering up the odour with a vaginal deodorant. (For more information on vaginal discharges and infections, see pages 101–2, 123–5 and the section on sexually transmitted diseases on pages 207–20).

Spots, acne and other skin changes

The oil glands in your skin become more active during puberty. Your skin becomes more oily and for many young people this leads to skin problems like spots and acne. Some young people have only mild problems with their skin; others have more severe problems; still others don't have any problems at all. But, eight out of every ten teenagers have at least mild skin problems.

Spots and other skin disturbances happen during puberty because your oil glands begin to make excess amounts of an oily substance called *sebum*. You have oil glands throughout your skin, all over your body. They are especially numerous on your face, neck, shoulders, upper chest and back. Sebum is made in the lower part of an oil gland and travels through the neck, or duct, of the gland to a pore, a tiny opening on the surface of your skin. Sebum helps keep your skin soft and pliable.

However, if you produce too much sebum, the pore may

sebum (SEE-bum)

become clogged and a blackhead may form. A lot of people think that blackheads are little particles of dirt trapped in the pores. This isn't true. Blackheads are black, not from dirt, but because the sebum and other substances produced by the glands sometimes turn black when they come in contact with the oxygen in the air.

Some young people get whiteheads, which are also the result of sebum. The sebum gets trapped just below the surface of the skin and forms the small, raised whitish bumps we call whiteheads.

If blackheads are not removed, the sebum may continue to fill the duct. This may cause pressure, irritation and inflammation. Germs can get in the duct and cause an infection. Whiteheads can also become inflamed and infected. Spots – red bumps that may be filled with whitish pus – may develop. If you have a serious case of spots, you have a problem called acne. Acne can be very troublesome and may cause pitting or scarring of the skin.

Spots and acne are often more of a problem for those who naturally tend to have more oily skin. The oiliness of your skin type plus the increased oil you produce during puberty combine to make you a candidate for these kinds of skin problems. If you have oily skin and acne during your teen years, you may find yourself wishing you had drier, less acne-prone skin. But when you're older, you may be glad to have oily skin, because this type of skin doesn't wrinkle as easily as dry skin does.

Acne also tends to 'run in families', so if your parents or older brothers or sisters had acne, you may be more likely to develop it. Many doctors believe that eating certain foods – chocolate, salty foods like nuts and crisps, greasy foods – make a person more susceptible to acne. However, some doctors disagree. In one study the amount of chocolate eaten didn't seem to have anything to do with

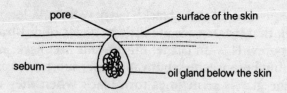

We have tiny oil glands just below the surface of our skin. These oil glands produce an oily substance called sebum.

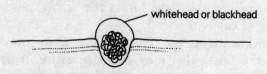

During puberty, our oil glands begin producing more sebum. If the pore, or opening, to the gland becomes blocked, a pimple may form.

Illustration 10. Oil gland.

acne. Still, if you find that certain foods give you spots, it's best to avoid them.

Stress may also be a factor in acne. A lot of teenagers find that they 'break out' – that is, get a lot of spots – just before an important event – a dance, a big date, a match – that they're particularly nervous or excited about.

Although sunlight may have a beneficial effect on acne and help to 'dry out' your skin, it may also aggravate the problem. In a hot dry climate the sunshine may be helpful. However, hot humid (moist) climates may make acne even worse. Some teenagers sit under a sun-lamp to help dry out their acne and/or to get a tan. This isn't always a good idea. For one thing, sitting under a sun-lamp can cause a severe sunburn, even if you sit there for only a minute more than the recommended time. While you're under the lamp it may not seem like much is happening, so it's tempting to stay longer. All too often this results in red, sunburnt skin the next day. If you use a sun-lamp, follow the instructions carefully. Another problem with sun-lamps and, for that matter, with prolonged sunbathing is that they can cause your skin to age before its time. People who have spent a lot of time in the sun or under sun-lamps may be wrinkly and look as though they're 50 or 60 by the time they're 30. Overexposure to sunlight also increases your chances of getting skin cancer later in life. So be sure to be careful with sun and tanning treatments.

Acne is most common between the ages of 14 and 17, although it also happens to older and younger boys and girls. Some teenagers are troubled by acne for only a year or two. Then their oil glands adjust themselves to the hormones, their skin becomes less oily, and their acne and spots clear up. Others have these problems throughout their teen years. For a few boys and girls, acne continues to be a problem even after their teens.

The pupils in our classes generally want to know if there is anything they can do to prevent spots or to cure acne. We explain that although there aren't any foolproof ways to prevent spots or any 100 per cent effective cures for acne, there are some things that help. Frequent shampooing will keep greasy, oily hair from adding to the oil on your skin. Washing the especially oily areas – your face, neck, shoulders, back and upper chest – at least once a day may also help prevent spots. Washing removes the oil from the surface of the skin and helps keep your pores open. Wash with hot water, which helps open your pores, and rinse with cold water to close the pores again. Wiping with a pad soaked in surgical spirit after you wash will remove any left-over oil and dirt. You can buy surgical spirit, which is very inexpensive, at a chemist's, and use cotton wool balls and pads. Be careful with the surgical spirit though. It can remove too much oil and leave your skin too dry.

If you have especially oily skin, you may want to wash

two or three times a day with ordinary soap. If you tend to get spots, one of the antibacterial soaps sold in chemists' may help. (Ask the chemist to recommend one.) If you have spots on your back, shower once or twice a day using an antibacterial soap and a back brush or loofah to scrub.

If you have blackheads, an abrasive soap or cleanser may help. (Again, ask your chemist to recommend one.) The abrasive in the soap often removes the blackheads and opens your pores. Be careful, though, because these soaps can irritate your skin. Don't use them more often than the instructions recommend. Black teenagers should *avoid* abrasives because their skin has a tendency to develop lighter or darker patches in the areas where the abrasives have been used.

Washing, even with antibacterial soaps or abrasives, isn't always enough to prevent spots and doesn't do much to help acne. Occasionally, mild cases of acne can be cleared up by using medicated acne lotions and creams that are sold without prescription. If these medications and the washing routines we've described don't take care of your problem and you're really bothered by acne, see your GP, who may then refer you to a dermatologist, a doctor who specializes in skin problems.

Very often, parents say, 'Oh, it's not that bad', or 'Leave it alone, you'll outgrow it.' But if you take the time to explain to your parents how much your skin problems bother you, they'll probably listen.

What can a dermatologist do for you? Well, that depends. If blackheads are a problem, the doctor can use a device called a *comedo* extractor to remove them. The comedo (comedo is the medical term for blackhead) extractor exerts pressure on the skin and causes the blackhead to pop out of the pore, thus unclogging the duct. The area around

comedo (KO-meh-dough)

the blackhead may be a little red for a while, but unlike squeezing or 'popping' your blackheads with your fingers, the comedo extractor won't leave scars. You should never pop your blackheads or spots because you might end up with permanent scars or pits. The extractor is used only on blackheads. Once you've got a spot, using the extractor may cause more harm than good.

The dermatologist can also prescribe drugs that are more effective than the medications you can buy without a doctor's prescription. For example, in certain cases the dermatologist may prescribe a drug called *tetracycline*. Tetracycline kills germs and can fight the infections that often start in clogged pores and lead to acne. This drug also cuts down on the amount of sebum your oil glands produce. For some teenagers tetracycline works miracles and completely cures their acne. However, you should use it only according to your doctor's orders because in some people it can cause problems, such as upset stomach and increased sensitivity to sunlight (sunburns). These and other side effects are usually pretty mild, but you must follow your doctor's orders carefully.

There are also other treatments a doctor can prescribe, so if you're troubled by skin problems, do see your GP.

Stretch marks

Some young people develop stretch marks, purplish or white lines on their skin, during puberty. This is fairly rare, but it does occur. It happens because the skin is stretched too much during rapid growth and it loses its elasticity, or stretchiness. (Other things, such as taking certain medications, being pregnant or gaining a lot of weight, can also cause stretch marks.) Many times these marks will fade to get less noticeable as a person gets older.

tetracycline (TET-rah-SIGH-clean)

Pubic hair, underarm hair, perspiration and skin changes are just a few of the changes you may notice in your body as you go through puberty. In the next chapter we'll be talking about yet another change – the change in your breasts.

Chapter 4

Your Breasts

Eskimos have over a hundred words for snow in their language because snow is such an important part of their lives. Judging from the number of words we have for breasts – the boys and girls in our classes came up with dozens – breasts must be an important part of our lives.

I no longer remember exactly when I first noticed that my breasts were beginning to develop, but I certainly remember the first time someone else noticed. I was baby-sitting for some friends of my parents who had 9-year-old twin girls. It was the first time I'd ever baby-sat for these girls. (It was also the last time. They dumped their pet goldfish in the toilet, 'so the goldfish would have more room to swim around'. While I was on my hands and knees fishing the goldfish out of the toilet bowl, they were down in the kitchen putting their tortoise into the toaster, 'to warm it up'.)

The evening got off to a bad start. They were nice as pie while their mum and dad were there, but as soon as the door closed behind their parents, they jumped on me, pulling open my blouse: 'Oh, you've got titties. Let's see, let's see', they demanded. 'We can't wait till we get titties.'

I managed to get the two of them off me and to button up my blouse, but I had never been so embarrassed in my life.

Regardless of whether you're as eager as those twins or as mortified as I was, sooner or later your breasts will begin to develop.

The breast during childhood

When we are children, our breasts are flat, except for a small, raised portion in the centre of each breast called the *nipple*. The nipple can range in colour from a light pink to a brownish black and is surrounded by a ring of flesh of about the same colour that is called the *areola* (see Illustration 11).

Sometimes, when our breasts are touched or stroked or when we are feeling sexual, our nipples may stand out a little more, and the areola may pucker up and get bumpy. Otherwise, during childhood our breasts are flat and smooth, and only the nipple stands out. During puberty the breasts begin to swell and to stand out more. The nipple and areola get larger and darker.

Inside the breast

In order to understand why your breasts are swelling and beginning to stand out, you have to understand what is

nipple (NI-pull)   *areola* (ah-REE-oh-la)

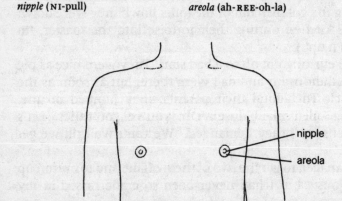

Illustration 11. The breast. In the centre of each breast is a small raised part called the nipple, which is surrounded by a ring of skin called the areola.

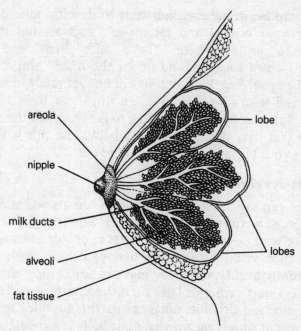

areola

lobe

nipple

milk ducts

lobes

alveoli

fat tissue

Illustration 12. Cross-section of an adult breast.

happening beneath the skin. Illustration 12 shows the inside of a grown woman's breast. A woman's breast is made up of fifteen to twenty-five separate parts, called *lobes*, although you can see only three of them in this picture. The lobes are like the separate sections of an orange, all packed together inside the breast. They are surrounded by a cushion of fat. Inside each lobe is a sort of tree. The leaves of these trees are called *alveoli*. When a woman has a baby, milk is made inside these leaves. The milk travels from the leaves, through the branches and trunk of the tree, which are called milk ducts, to the nipple. When a mother breast-feeds, the baby sucks on the nipple and out comes the milk.

alveoli (al-VEE-oh-lie)

As you begin puberty you start to develop milk ducts under your breasts and fat tissue forms around those ducts to protect them. These milk ducts and fat tissue form a small mound under the nipple and areola called a *breast bud*. Your breasts are not yet ready to make milk and won't be able to do so until you have had a baby. But your body is beginning to get ready for the time when you may decide to have a baby, and this is what causes your breasts to swell and stand out.

Breast development

No one can say for sure when a girl's breasts will start to develop. Sometimes it starts to happen when the girl is only 8 and other times not until after she is 16 or older. Most girls begin to develop breast buds between their ninth and fourteenth birthdays. But you may not be like most girls, so you may start earlier or later than this. Starting earlier or later than most girls does not mean there is anything wrong with you. It simply means that your body is growing at its own special rate.

Doctors have divided breast growth into five stages, which are shown in Illustration 13. You may be in one of these stages or in between one stage and another. See if you can find the stage you're closest to.

Stage 1 shows how the breasts look during childhood. The breasts are flat and the only part that is raised is the nipple.

Stage 2 is the breast-bud stage, when the milk ducts and fat tissue form a small, button-like mound under each nipple and areola, making them stick out. The nipple starts to get larger. This often happens just before the breast bud starts to form. The areola gets wider, and the nipple and areola become darker.

In Stage 3 the breasts get rounder and fuller and begin to stand out more. The nipple may continue to get larger and

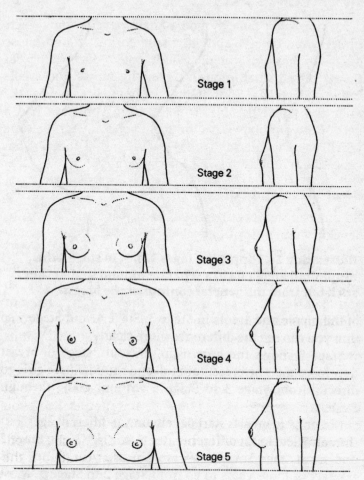

Illustration 13. The five stages of breast development.

the areola wider. Both may become darker in colour. The breasts are usually rather cone-shaped in this stage.

Stage 4 is a stage that many, but not all, girls go through. Girls who do go through it will notice that the areola and nipple form a separate little mound so that they stick out above the rest of the breast. Illustration 14 shows a close-up

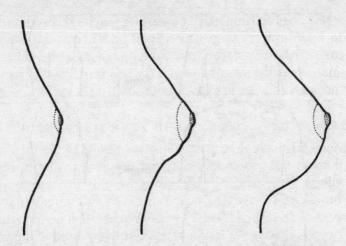

Illustration 14. Nipple in Stages 3, 4, 5. In stage 4 the nipple and areola form a separate mound so that they stick out from the general contour of the breast.

of the nipple and areola in Stage 3, Stage 4, and Stage 5 so that you can see the difference more clearly.

Stage 5 shows the grown-up, or adult, stage of breast development. The breasts are full and round. Some girls go directly from Stage 3 to Stage 5 without going through Stage 4.

Not only do breasts start developing at different ages, but they also develop at different rates. Some girls begin Stage 2 and are at Stage 5 within six months or a year. Other girls take six or more years to go from Stage 2 to Stage 5. Most girls take about four and a half years to go from Stage 2 to Stage 5, but once again, you may not be like most girls, so you may take a longer or a shorter time.

Starting early or starting late doesn't have anything to do with how fast you will develop. Some girls start early and grow very fast, while other early starters develop slowly. Some girls who start late grow slowly, but other late starters develop very quickly.

Nor does starting early or starting late have anything to do with how big your breasts will be when you are fully grown. An early starter may wind up having either large or small breasts. The same is true for late starters – they may end up with large breasts or with small ones.

BREAST DEVELOPMENT AND YOUR FIRST PERIOD

Most girls have their first menstrual period while they are in Stage 4 of breast development. However, a fair number will have their period while they are only in Stage 3, and some don't have their first period until after they've reached Stage 5. A few girls will have their first period while they are in Stage 2. If you have your first period while you are only in Stage 1 (before your breasts have begun to develop), you should see a doctor. Having your period before your breasts have begun to develop doesn't necessarily mean that something's wrong, but it *may* mean that you have a problem that needs a doctor's attention.

FEELINGS ABOUT DEVELOPING BREASTS

The mothers and daughters we talked to had different kinds of feelings about their breasts. Some girls were really excited when their breasts started developing, like this girl who told us:

I was so happy when my breasts started growing. First my nipples became bigger. Then my breasts started to stick out. I was so proud. I felt really grown up. I was always showing them off to my mum and my little sister.

Although many girls feel excited, they also worry about one thing or another. One girl said:

I was really upset. I had these little flat bumps under my nipples, and they hurt all the time, especially if they got hit or something. They were so sore. I thought maybe something was wrong.

One or both of your breasts *may* feel tender, sore or even painful at times. This is perfectly normal, and it doesn't mean that anything is wrong. Although it may be a bit uncomfortable, this soreness isn't anything to worry about. It's just part of growing up.

One question that regularly comes out of the class question box is 'Could a girl's breasts burst?' or, as one girl wrote, 'Could a girl's boobs pop like a balloon?' Each time we get one of these questions, we always answer, 'No, that can't happen', but secretly we've always wondered where in the world anyone could have got an idea like that. Then one day one of the girls came up after class and explained:

Grown-ups are always saying things like, 'Oh, you're really popping out', or 'You're really bursting out all over', and sometimes my breasts feel sore, like they really are about to burst, so I wondered.

This girl made us realize how confusing the things adults say can sound to children sometimes. If you've worried about this same thing, you can stop worrying. We can assure you that even though it may feel that way at times, your breasts won't pop or burst.

Other girls we talked to told us that they worried because both their breasts didn't develop at the same rate. One girl said:

One of my breasts was starting to grow and the other one was still completely flat. I was afraid that the other one would never grow and I was only going to have one breast instead of two.

Another girl explained:

Both of mine started growing at the same time, but one was a lot bigger than the other one and I was worried that I was going to grow up all lopsided.

It often happens that one breast develops before the other or that one seems to be growing at a much faster rate than the other. Even though one may start growing first, the other will eventually grow too. By the time a girl is fully developed, both breasts are pretty much the same size. Many grown women do notice that one breast is slightly larger than the other, but this difference in size is generally too small to be noticed by anyone other than the woman herself.

Some girls notice that tiny hairs begin to develop around the areola. One of the girls that this happened to told us:

I started growing these little hairs around my nipple, and none of my friends did. I thought I was odd, so I plucked them out with tweezers, but they just grew back.

Although most women don't grow hairs like this, many do. It's quite normal. Plucking these hairs doesn't usually get rid of them, for most of the time they just grow back. In fact, plucking them out could cause problems, for it might start an infection that could make your breast sore, red and painful.

'One of my nipples didn't stick out and the other did,' yet another girl told us. 'It sort of puckered in, and I wondered why.'

This girl had what is known as an inverted nipple. One or both nipples in some girls and women sink into the areola instead of sticking out. As a girl grows older, the inverted nipple may start to stick out. Lots of women have inverted nipples. They don't cause any problems. You may have heard that women with inverted nipples can't breast-feed their babies. This is simply not true. The only time that inverted nipples might be a problem is in an adult woman when if a nipple that wasn't inverted suddenly becomes inverted or vice versa. This doesn't necessarily mean that anything is wrong, but it is something to check out with your doctor.

Some girls we talked to worried because they noticed a little fluid coming from their nipples once in a while. This is normal. It is your body's way of keeping your ducts open. The fluid may be whitish or clear or slightly yellow or green. If there is a lot of it or if it is dark brown or has pus in it, see your doctor, for it may be a sign of an infection. (We'll talk more about inverted nipples and fluids coming out of the nipples later on when we talk about breast self-examination.)

As we said earlier, many of the girls we talked to felt excited and proud about developing breasts, but many also felt uncomfortable or embarrassed. A 22-year-old told us:

I was only 9 when I started developing, and no one else was. I used to wrap one of those bandages, the kind you put on a sprained ankle, around my chest to make me flat. I kept my coat on as much as I could and wore baggy clothes all the time. Now that I'm older, I can laugh about it, but back then it wasn't funny at all.

Many of the girls and women whose breasts started developing earlier than most talked about feeling embarrassed. Girls whose breasts began to develop late often had embarrassed feelings too. One woman, now in her thirties, told us:

I didn't start to develop until after my sixteenth birthday. Everyone, and I mean *everyone*, had breasts but me. They were all in their bras and there I was in my vest. I failed physical education in secondary school because I wouldn't take a shower. I was too embarrassed about my flat chest. Finally, my mum bought me a padded bra. My breasts did eventually start to develop, but I really felt badly about myself for a lot of years before they did.

Another woman told us:

I didn't start developing until I was 17. I thought there was something horribly wrong, like maybe I was really a man instead of a woman. Oh, and the teasing I had to endure! The boys used to call me 'ironing board' because my chest was so flat.

Even girls who were neither early nor late starters feel embarrassed. As one girl put it:

I started to develop when I was 11, just about the same time as everyone else. I was glad that I was getting tits, but I was embarrassed, especially at school.

Our parents, our brothers and sisters, our friends or people at school may tease us about developing breasts, and this may make us feel embarrassed at times. Even strangers, people on the street, may make comments on our changing bodies. Boys or men may whistle or make sexual remarks. Sometimes this attention is flattering. As one girl explained:

If I'm walking down the street and some guy says, 'Hey, there!' or whistles or something, I feel pretty good, like he's saying, 'Oh, you look good', especially if I'm with a girl-friend or a group of girls.

But a lot of girls and women don't like this kind of attention:

I hate when boys stare at my breasts or whistle or yell things at me. It makes me feel like a piece of metal and it makes me feel self-conscious and stupid. I mean, what can you do? Yell back at them? How would they like it if girls went down the street and stared at their crotches and yelled things like, 'Hey, that's a really big penis you've got there!' Boys do that. They say things like, 'Hey, that's a great set of tits!' I don't like it.

Often there isn't much you can do about this unwanted attention beyond simply ignoring it. But it may be helpful to talk about these experiences with other girls so that you can help each other deal with such situations.

Bras

We get a lot of questions about when a girl should start wearing a bra or if she even needs to wear one at all. There are no clear-cut answers to these questions: it's something you have to decide for yourself.

Some girls decide to wear a bra because they feel more comfortable having some support, so their breasts don't jiggle around when they walk, run, dance or play games. Others decide to wear bras because they feel self-conscious without one. Some girls wear bras because they've heard that your breasts will eventually begin to droop or sag if you don't wear a bra. Actually, though, you needn't worry about this type of drooping unless you are fairly large-breasted and/or you go without a bra for a number of years. One girl in our class had something interesting to say about this:

So what if your breasts droop? I mean, who says that breasts that don't droop are better than breasts that do? I don't care. I don't wear a bra and I'm not going to. I hate the way they feel, like I'm in a harness.

We should also mention that there are many girls who would like to wear a bra even though they aren't very developed and don't 'really need' one. One girl who wrote to us put it this way:

I'm 11 years old . . . I'm not very big. In fact, I'm kind of flat. Do you think it is silly for me to want a bra?

When girls tell us that they're worried about seeming silly, we try to make them see that there's nothing silly about wearing a bra, no matter how 'flat' you are. If the other kids or adults tease you about wearing a bra before you 'really need' one, you can always say something like, 'Oh, I'm just getting used to wearing one', 'I like them better than vests' or 'I feel more comfortable this way.'

Many girls have told us that they feel they'd like to start wearing a bra, but they're too embarrassed to ask their parents for one. We encourage girls who feel embarrassed asking for a bra to go ahead and ask anyhow. Many times, parents are waiting for you to bring up the topic yourself because they don't want to embarrass you! If you're embarrassed about asking for a bra, you might say, 'Would it be OK with you if I wore a bra?' or 'When do you think I should start wearing a bra?' Or you could write a note explaining how you feel. If your parent says something like, 'Oh, don't be silly, you don't need one yet', you could say, 'Well, maybe not, but I'd *like* one anyhow.'

BUYING A BRA

Bras can be purchased at almost any shop that sells women's clothing, and some shops have a special lingerie (underwear) section. The lingerie saleswomen, who have been trained to measure and advise customers, will usually be happy to help you determine your size and choose the style that's best for you.

Training bras are bras that have a flat or practically flat cup and are made to fit girls whose breasts haven't started to develop or whose breasts are just beginning to grow. There are also one-size-fits-all bras that have cups made of elastic material that stretches to fit your shape. However, if you are very large or very small, these one-size-fits-all bras may not work for you.

In addition to training bras and one-size-fits-all bras, there are also fitted bras, which come in various sizes. The size has two parts: a number, which represents the number of centimetres (or inches) around your chest, and a letter, which indicates the size of the cup. Cup sizes run from A through D or E. There are also double or triple As (AA or AAA) for very small breasts, and double Es (EE) for very large breasts.

In addition to different sizes, bra cups also come in different shapes and it is important to find a style that suits the shape of your breasts. That is why it is best, especially while your breasts are still developing, to try on a bra before you buy it.

You may have heard about padded bras and falsies. Padded bras have a pad of foam rubber inside the cup. When you wear a padded bra, it appears that your breasts are larger than they really are. Falsies are breast-shaped inserts that are worn inside the cup of a bra – again, to make it seem as if your breasts are larger than they actually are.

Breast size

When I was a girl, we used to do an exercise where we'd hold our arms at shoulder level, elbows bent, and jerk our elbows back to a one-two, one-two count. While we did this exercise, we chanted:

> We must, we must,
> We must increase our busts.
> It's better, it's better,
> It's better for the sweater.
> We may, we may,
> We may get big someday.

We hope girls no longer do this, not that there's anything wrong with the exercise. It's a good exercise for toning and firming the muscles of the chest wall. (It won't, however, make your breasts larger. Your breasts are composed of glands and fat tissue and no amount of exercise will enlarge them. If you do this exercise a lot, the chest muscles underneath the breast will get thicker and this will make your breasts stand out more.)

No, there's nothing wrong with the exercise itself, it's the chant that went along with it – all that business about 'we must increase our busts' and the emphasis on having big breasts, as if big breasts were somehow better than small ones. Breasts feel the same and can give us the same pleasurable feelings when they are stroked or touched regardless of their size. Small breasts do just as good a job of making breast milk as large ones. Still, with all the big-busted, glamorous women in advertisements, films and TV programmes, it's easy to get the idea that big breasts are more womanly or more sexy than small ones. But despite all the advertising, there are a great many people who find small breasts equally, if not more, attractive than large ones. And anyone who decides whether he or she likes you or not because of the size of your breasts probably isn't a person worth knowing anyhow.

Regardless of whether your breasts are large, small or medium sized, it's important that you learn how to examine them.

Breast self-examination

Doctors encourage women to examine their breasts to see if there are any lumps or other irregularities that might be signs of breast cancer. Not all breast lumps are signs of cancer. In fact, the vast majority of lumps that women find in their breasts are *not* cancerous; they are just simple cysts – collections of fluid. But since cancer can appear as a small lump in the breast, it is important to examine your breasts and have a doctor check any lumps you do find to rule out the possibility of breast cancer.

Each year more than 24,000 women in the United Kingdom get breast cancer. In some cases breast cancer can be cured by removing the lump. In others, it is necessary to remove the whole breast. Sometimes breast cancer can't be cured and the woman dies. If a woman discovers her breast cancer while the lump is small, she has a much better chance of being cured. That's why examining your breasts is so important. If a woman feels her breasts regularly, once a month, she has a better chance of being able to find the lump right away, before the cancer is so serious that it can't be cured.

Actually, breast examination is not so very important for teenagers because teenagers don't, as a rule, get breast cancer. (There have been a few young women who've had breast cancer, but it's very rare.) Many doctors tell women to start examining their breasts after they've reached their twenty-fifth birthdays, since breast cancer is rare before the age of 25.

We suggest that young women start examining their breasts as soon as they have had their first menstrual periods. We think this is a good idea for two reasons. First of all, it gets you started, while you're young, on what should become a lifelong habit. But perhaps more importantly, if you're examining your breasts regularly, it might get your mother, your older sisters or other women you may live with to do it too. Far too many women neglect this life-saving measure. Maybe your doing it will set an example for them. Why don't you and your mother or another adult woman try practising breast examination, which is described below, together?

You should examine your breasts about once a month. The best time is right after your menstrual period is over. Some women's breasts tend to be a little lumpy before or during their menstrual periods because the ducts and tissues of the breast swell a bit. If you are one of these women, you will find that your breasts are less lumpy just after your period, so it will be easier to examine them at that time.

Examine your breasts when you are relaxed and not feeling rushed. The examination consists of two parts: looking at your breasts and feeling them.

PART ONE: LOOKING (Illustration 15)

To begin, stand in front of a well-lighted mirror with your arms down at your sides and take a good look at your

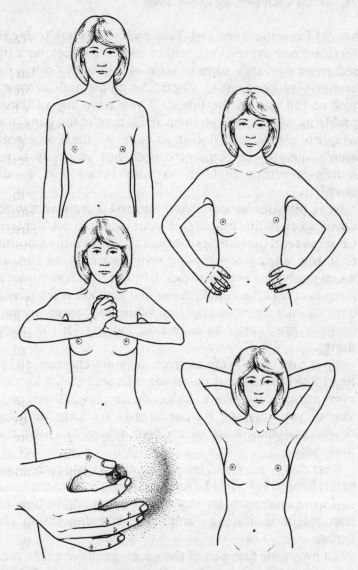

Illustration 15. Examining your breasts, Part One: Looking. Stand in front of a mirror and inspect your breasts in each of the four positions shown here. Finally, squeeze each nipple for signs of discharge.

breasts from the front and from each side. Look to see if there are any depressions, bulges, moles, dimples, dark or red areas, swellings, sores or areas of skin with a rough or orange peel-like texture. Check the nipple and areola as well as the skin of the breast. If you have any of these problems, keep an eye on them and if they're not gone in a couple of weeks, see a doctor. At your age, these problems aren't likely to be signs of cancer, but you may have a non-cancerous problem in your breast that needs attention.

Next, put your hands on your hips and press inwards and down so that the muscles of your upper chest tighten. Check to see if the muscles contract about the same amount or if any bulging or dimpling shows up on your breasts when you've got your muscles tight like this. Sometimes a lump that isn't noticeable in the first position will become obvious only when you tighten. While your hands are still on your hips, rotate to each side, looking for the same things.

Now put your arms in front of your chest at about heart level, press your palms together and check for uneven muscle contraction, bulges or dimpling. Check each side of your breasts. If your breasts are large or hang down, you may have to lift each breast to check the underside.

Next raise your arms, bend your elbows and place your hands behind your head. Once again, check from the front and from both sides for any signs of dimpling or bulging that might indicate a lump or thickening inside the breast.

To finish the first part of the exam, gently squeeze each nipple to see if you can get any fluid to come out. Fluid from the nipple is not necessarily a sign that something is wrong. But if there is a lot of it or if it is dark in colour or full of pus, see a doctor.

PART TWO: FEELING (Illustration 16)

This part is done lying down because when you lie down your breasts spread out and it will be easier to feel for lumps. Placing a small pillow or a large, folded towel under your shoulder will help distribute your breast tissue more

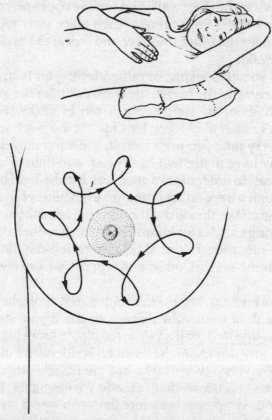

Illustration 16. Examining your breasts, Part Two: Feeling. Lie down with one hand behind your head. With your other hand, start on the outside of your breast and, using a circular motion, feel the entire breast. Repeat on the opposite breast.

evenly and make your exam easier. Lotion or oil will make your fingers more sensitive.

To begin, bend one arm and place your hand behind your head. Using the fatty pads of your fingers rather than your fingertips, start on the outside of your breast and use a circular motion to carefully feel each breast. Press all the way down to the chest wall. Also feel the upper part of your chest and under your armpit. Then place your pillow or towel under the other shoulder and repeat the process on the other side.

What you are looking, or rather, feeling for is any lump or thickening in the breast, the chest or under the armpits. This sounds pretty simple, but it can be tricky. For one thing, it's rather like feeling for a marble in a bag filled with jelly. Every time you press near it, the lump moves away. You may have to use two hands now and then to support your breast in order to get a good feel. It's also hard because most women have rather bumpy or even lumpy breasts. It's easy to mistake the ducts, the ribs, the breastbone or the underlying muscles for lumps. Once you have been doing it for a while, though, you'll be able to tell the difference between the normal lumps and bumps and any abnormal ones.

If you find any lumps, thickening, red spots, bulges or unusual fluid from your nipples, or if a nipple suddenly becomes inverted (or if an inverted nipple suddenly begins to stick out), *don't panic*. Remember, breast cancer in young women is very, very rare. But there are other, non-cancerous conditions that can affect young girls' breasts. So, if your symptoms last more than two weeks, get them checked out.

Chapter 5

Changes in the Vulva

The genital organs on the outside of your body, which are sometimes referred to as the vulva, also change as you go through puberty. The various parts of the vulva are easy to see if you hold a mirror between your legs as the girl in Illustration 17 is doing. The other drawings in Illustration 17 show how the vulva looks in a young girl, in a young woman going through puberty and in a grown woman.

The easiest way to learn about these organs and how they change during puberty is to use a mirror and compare your own body to these drawings. You probably won't look exactly like any of these drawings because each person's body is a little bit different. But if you looked at a drawing of a person's face with eyes, a nose, a mouth and so on, you could easily find the eyes, nose or mouth on your own face, even if the drawing didn't look *exactly* like your own face. In the same way, you can look at a drawing of a vulva and find the various parts on your own vulva. Of course, we're a lot more used to looking at faces than vulvas, but with a little practice, you can learn to see the features of your vulva as plainly as you can see the nose on your face.

Some people think that using a mirror to look at this area of their bodies, touching the various parts and learning their names is a great idea. As one girl in our class said:

Oh, I've looked at myself there lots of times. My mum got a mirror and showed me how to look at myself and how she looked so I'd know what I'll look like when I grow up. She taught me the names of everything and all that stuff.

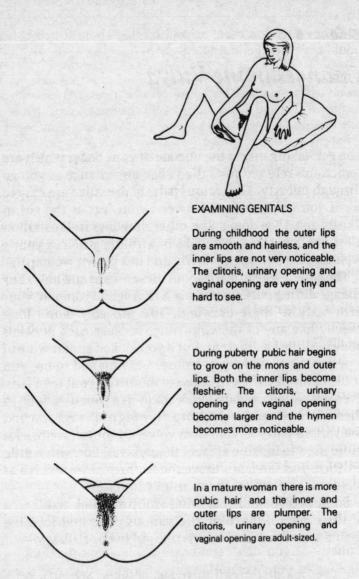

EXAMINING GENITALS

During childhood the outer lips are smooth and hairless, and the inner lips are not very noticeable. The clitoris, urinary opening and vaginal opening are very tiny and hard to see.

During puberty pubic hair begins to grow on the mons and outer lips. Both the inner lips become fleshier. The clitoris, urinary opening and vaginal opening become larger and the hymen becomes more noticeable.

In a mature woman there is more pubic hair and the inner and outer lips are plumper. The clitoris, urinary opening and vaginal opening are adult-sized.

Illustration 17. Examining the genitals.

Other girls don't feel as comfortable about touching or looking at their genitals. One girl in our class said:

I thought it sounded kind of strange, taking a mirror and looking at myself down there, but I was sort of curious, so I locked my bedroom door and took a good look. I'm glad I did, 'cause it made me feel like I know more about myself, like it wasn't such a big mystery.

Still another girl said:

Ugh, that's disgusting. I'd never do that. It's yucky down there.

This girl had been taught that her genitals were dirty and ugly and that it was shameful or wrong to look at or touch them. Even if no one has ever actually said to you that there is something wrong or dirty about your genitals, you may still feel uncertain about exploring them. People don't talk about genital organs very much and, as we all know, if something is too terrible to talk about, then it's probably really terrible!

But there is nothing terrible or wrong about this area of your body. People feel uncomfortable because it is a sexual part of the body, and people often feel uncomfortable about anything that has to do with sex. Some people get the idea that this part of the body is dirty because the openings through which urine and faeces leave our bodies are located here. Actually, this area of our bodies isn't any dirtier than, say, the inside of our mouths. (In fact, our mouths have more germs than this area of our bodies.)

In the following pages, we'll take you on a guided tour of the vulva and explain how your genitals change during puberty. If you don't feel comfortable about touching or looking at your genitals, that's all right. Just read these pages and look at the pictures. We wouldn't want you to do anything you don't feel like doing. If you'd like to, though, we think you'll find it helpful to keep a mirror handy so you can look at yourself as you read about these parts of your body. You may want to do this all by yourself, with a friend or with your mother. Do whatever feels most comfortable for you.

The mons

We'll start our tour at the top of the vulva, at the mons. As you may remember, the mons is a pad of fat tissue that covers the pubic bone. It is here, on the mons, that pubic hair begins to grow during puberty, and in grown women the mons is covered with curly pubic hair.

In addition to sprouting hair, the mons also gets fleshier during puberty so that it sticks out more. This is because the fat pad over the pubic bone is getting thicker.

The outer lips

As you move down along the mons, you will see that it divides into two separate flaps, or folds, of skin. As we told you earlier, these are the outer lips, or the labia majora. *Labia* is a Latin word meaning lips and *majora* means major, so they are sometimes called the major lips.

In a young girl the outer lips may be hairless or they may have a few light-coloured hairs. During puberty pubic hair begins to grow on the outer lips.

In young girls the lips are often separated. There may be space between them, so they may not actually touch each other. During puberty the lips get fleshier and they often begin to touch. In grown women the lips generally touch, but some women find that after they've had a baby, the lips are slightly separated again. In very old women the lips get thinner, less fleshy and may become separated again.

The lips are usually smooth in a young girl, but during puberty they may get sort of wrinkly. In grown women they tend to be wrinkly. Many women find that when they are old, the lips get smooth again.

The outer lips help protect the area underneath. The underside of the lips is hairless, in both young girls and grown women. In girls the underside of the lips is smooth, but as you go through puberty you may notice small, slightly raised bumps dotting the skin on the underside of the lips. These are oil glands. They make a small amount of oil that keeps the area moist so that it doesn't get irritated. Once you start puberty, you may notice a slight feeling of wetness in this area because of this oil. You may also notice a change in the way this area of your body smells. Again, this is because of the oil made by these glands.

During childhood this area may be light pink to red to brownish-black, depending on your skin tone. The colour is apt to change during puberty, getting either lighter or darker.

The inner lips

If you separate the outer lips, you will see two ridges, or folds, of skin called the *labia minora*, the minor lips or the little lips. During childhood the inner lips may not be very noticeable, but during puberty they grow and become more noticeable. Like the outer lips, they protect the area between them, and they too tend to change colour and get more wrinkly during puberty.

As you can see in Illustration 18, the labia look different in different women. In most women the inner lips are smaller than the outer lips, but in some women the inner lips protrude beyond the outer lips. The inner lips are

minora (mi-NOR-ah)

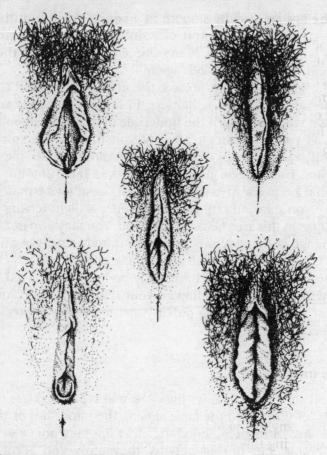

Illustration 18. The labia. The inner lips look different in different women.

usually about the same size, but some women notice that one is larger than the other.

The inner lips are hairless in both girls and grown women. They tend to be more moist as we grow older because they too have oil glands that begin producing more oil during puberty.

The clitoris

If you follow the inner lips up towards the mons, you will see that they join together at the top. In the area where the inner lips join together lies the tip of the clitoris, in slang terms, the 'clit'. In grown women the clitoris is about the size of the rubber on the end of a pencil. The way in which the inner lips join together is not the same in all women. In some women the inner lips come together forming a sort of hood that covers the clitoris. In other women the clitoris sticks all or part of the way out from the folds of the hood formed by the inner lips. When we are feeling sexual, the clitoris tends to swell and get larger for a while. It also grows permanently larger during puberty.

You may have to pull back the hood formed by the inner lips in order to see the clitoris; even then you can see only the tip of the clitoris. The rest of the clitoris lies buried under the skin. If you press down on the skin above the clitoris, you may be able to feel a rubbery cord under the skin. This is the shaft of the clitoris.

MASTURBATION

The clitoris and its shaft – in fact, this whole area of your body – is very sensitive. When you touch it, you may get an excited, tingly kind of feeling. Touching, rubbing, stroking or squeezing this area of your body so that you will have these feelings is called *masturbating* or *masturbation*. There are lots of slang words for masturbation, such as 'jerking off', 'playing with yourself' and 'jacking off'.

Sometimes when people masturbate, they get so excited that they have a shivery feeling that is called an *orgasm*. Having an orgasm is also called 'coming' or 'climaxing'. It's hard to explain exactly what an orgasm feels like, and

masturbating (MASS-tur-bait-ing)   *orgasm* (OR-gaz-um)
masturbation (MASS-tur-BAY-shun)   *climaxing* (KLY-max-ing)

orgasms probably feel different to different people, but most people agree that it is a good feeling.

Not everyone masturbates, but many if not most of us do at some time or other in our lives. Some women start masturbating when they are children and continue to do so all their lives. Some start during puberty; others don't start until they are grown women. Still others never masturbate. It's normal if you do it and normal if you don't.

Many men and boys also masturbate. They do so by touching or stroking their penises. (This is explained more fully in Chapter 8.)

Some people think that once a person starts having sexual intercourse or gets married, that person no longer masturbates. This isn't true. People who have sex regularly often continue to masturbate either alone or with their sexual partner.

You may have heard all sorts of strange things about masturbation. People used to think that masturbation would make you insane or make you go blind. These things simply aren't true. You may have heard that masturbation would cause you to grow hair on the palms of your hands, spots on your face, warts on your fingers or other terrible things. Again, none of this is true. You may have heard that masturbation will make you enjoy sex with another person less: also not true. Actually, most sex experts believe that masturbating is a way of rehearsing for your adult sex life, and that by learning how to give yourself pleasure sexually, you are taking the first step in learning how to have sexual pleasure with someone else.

One question that frequently comes up in our classes is whether or not masturbating 'too much' can hurt you in some way. The answer is no. Nothing bad will happen to your body regardless of how much you masturbate; masturbation is not harmful in any way. About the only thing that can happen is that your genitals might get a little sore if you are masturbating and rubbing them a great deal. Some people masturbate every day. Some masturbate many times in one day. Others only rarely masturbate, and still others never do. Remember, it's normal if you do it and normal if you don't.

Some people like to imagine things that make them feel more excited when they are masturbating. Imagining or pretending that something is happening is called day-dreaming or fantasizing. We day-dream and fantasize about all sorts of things. When our day-dreams are about sexual things, we call them sexual fantasies. Almost everyone has sexual fantasies. Fantasies can be a rich and varied way of experimenting with your sexual self, so our advice is relax and enjoy them.

For some people, having sexual fantasies and/or mastur-bating are in conflict with their religious or moral beliefs. These people feel that a person shouldn't allow him or herself to have such fantasies or to masturbate. For other people, having sexual fantasies and masturbating are not in conflict with their religious and moral beliefs. They think it's perfectly OK for a person to do these things. Personally, we tend to agree with this viewpoint and we think it's all right for a person to do these things. But if doing these things is in conflict with your beliefs, then you can decide not to do them. In any case, you should know that masturbation is not physically harmful in any way.

But let's leave the topic of masturbation and sexual fantasies and get back to the guided tour of your body.

The urinary opening

If you move down your clitoris in a straight line, you will come to the urinary opening. *Urinary* comes from the word *urine*. Urine is made inside our bodies. The food we eat and drink is broken down inside of us so that our bodies can use it. Not everything we eat and drink can be used by our bodies. After everything is broken down and used, some of the left-overs are in the form of the clear, yellowish, water-like liquid called urine. The urine collects in an organ inside our bodies called the *bladder*. The bladder is like a balloon or bag. It has a small tube at the bottom, which leads to the outside of our bodies. The urinary opening is the outside end of this tube. When our bladder is full, we press down, the tube opens up and the urine from the bladder runs down the tube and out through the urinary opening.

It may be difficult for you to see exactly where the urinary opening is. If you start at the clitoris and move downward in a straight line, the first dimpled area you come to is the urinary opening. It may look like an upside down V. During puberty the urinary opening becomes more noticeable than it is during childhood.

If you don't stay on a straight line down from the clitoris, you may mistake the opening to one of the two tiny glands also located in this area for the urinary opening. The opening to these glands are two little slits on either side of the urinary opening. Like the oil glands on the inner and outer lips, these glands make a small amount of oil that keeps this area moist. Some women have such tiny openings to these glands that they can't be seen; others have larger ones that can be mistaken for the urinary opening.

The vaginal opening

Now that you know where the urinary opening is, you'll be able to find the vaginal opening. As we explained earlier, the vagina is inside your body, so you won't be able to see the vagina itself, but you will be able to find the opening to it. If you move down from the urinary opening – again, in a straight line – you'll come to the vaginal opening.

Pictures of the vaginal opening are sometimes confusing since they make it look like a dark, gaping hole. It's not. The vagina itself is like a pouch. In young girls it's not very big. During puberty it starts to grow, but even in adult women, it's only about 75–127 mm (3–5 in) long. But the vagina is like a balloon and can expand to many times its size. It has to be able to expand like this so a man's penis can fit inside during sexual intercourse. Also, when a woman has a baby, the baby travels through the vagina on its way out of the mother's body.

Most of the time, though, the sides of the vagina touch each other. If you were to look into the opening of a collapsed balloon, you wouldn't see an empty space. You'd see the collapsed sides of the balloon all folded up and touching each other. The same is true of the vagina: when you look into the vaginal opening, you don't see a hole, you see the fleshy walls of the vagina up against each other.

The hymen

Just inside, the vaginal opening may be partly covered by a thin piece of skin called the *hymen*. Another name for the hymen is maiden-head. The hymen looks different in different women. It may be just a thin fringe of skin around the edges of the vaginal opening. It may stretch across the opening with one or more holes in it. Illustration 19 shows just a few of the ways the hymen may look.

In young girls the hymen may not be very noticeable. During puberty it usually gets thicker and more rigid and more noticeable. But not all girls have a noticeable hymen. A few are born without one. Others have such small ones that it's hard to see them. Also, it's possible for a girl to tear or stretch her hymen during vigorous exercise, such as

hymen (HI-men)

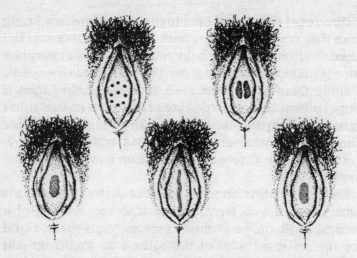

Illustration 19. The hymen. The hymen may have one or two large openings or several small ones.

horseback riding or gymnastics, though this is not common.

As strange as it seems, some people used to think that this tiny little piece of skin was *very*, *very* important. People thought that all women had the kind of hymen that has only a few holes and that stretches across the vaginal opening. They thought that the only reason a woman wouldn't have a noticeable hymen was because it had been stretched or torn by a man's penis during sexual intercourse. Today we know this isn't true, and that having a noticeable hymen or one that has not been stretched or torn doesn't necessarily have anything to do with whether or not a woman has had sex with a man. (In fact, some women have sex with men without their hymens stretching or tearing at all.)

But in the old days, people thought that if a woman didn't have an untorn, unstretched hymen covering her vaginal opening, this meant that she had had sex with a man and was not a virgin (a virgin is a person who has never had sex). People also thought that it was important for a woman to be a virgin when she married. Many people still feel this way, but back then a woman who was not a virgin when she got married could get into a lot of trouble. In some countries a woman could even be put to death if she wasn't a virgin when she married. In other countries young women were examined before marriage to see if they had a hymen. If they didn't, the marriage could be called off. In still other countries a bride was supposed to hang her bedsheets out the window the morning after her wedding night. Since her wedding night was the first time she was supposed to have sex, and since people thought the hymen would break and bleed only in sexual intercourse, the bride's bedsheets were supposed to have blood on them as proof to everyone that she had been a virgin before her wedding night.

You can imagine the problems all this fuss about the hymen made for those women who were born without one, for those whose hymens had been stretched or torn during childhood and for those whose hymens simply weren't very noticeable. Some were killed and others never married or lived their lives in disgrace. Not only that, but some women's hymens don't bleed very much when they are stretched or torn. So even those brides who were lucky enough to have hymens of the approved kind might not have had any blood on their wedding sheets. History is full of stories of clever brides who took a bit of animal's blood and poured it on the sheets to fool everyone. Still, it seems an awful lot of fuss about what is only a thin piece of skin.

People have, for the most part, changed their attitudes about the hymen. But in some parts of the world these ideas still persist and you may have heard some of these stories. If so, just ignore them. The appearance of your hymen doesn't necessarily have anything to do with whether or not you're a virgin, and neither a doctor nor anyone else can tell merely by looking at your hymen whether or not you've had sex.*

When your hymen is stretched or torn – whether it's during sex or while you're doing gymnastics or riding a horse or whatever – it may bleed a little, a lot or not at all. It may hurt a little, a lot or not at all. If it does hurt a lot or bleed a lot, you should, of course, see your doctor. But only rarely does a hymen bleed or hurt so badly that a doctor's care is needed. Most women never notice any blood or feel anything when their hymens are stretched or torn.

The anus

Although it is not really a sex organ, there is another opening in this area of the body. It is called the *anus*. You have probably heard some of the slang terms like 'arsehole', or 'shithole' that are also used to refer to it.

If you continue moving down from the vaginal opening, you'll come to the anus. It is the outside opening to the bowels, which are long, hollow tubes that are coiled up inside the body. The bowels are also called the *small intestines*.

Remember when we talked about how the food we take into our bodies is broken down and how urine is part of what is left over? Well, in addition to the watery urine, there are also more solid left-overs, which are called *faeces*. People sometimes use slang words like 'shit' or 'crap' to refer to faeces. The faeces travel through the bowels and

intestines (in-TES-tins)

*Specially trained doctors using special microscopes can, however, detect signs of the sexual crimes discussed on pages 225–9.

when we go to the lavatory and have a bowel movement, the faeces come out through the anus.

The skin around the anus, just like the skin of the labia, may change colour during puberty, getting a little darker. Pubic hair may also start to grow around the anus during puberty.

This completes the tour of the sex organs on the outside of your body. In the next chapter we will look at the inside of your body and still more changes that take place during puberty.

Chapter 6

Changes in the Reproductive Organs

The changes occurring outside your body during puberty – the breast buds, the pubic hair, the changes in your vulva – happen because other, even more dramatic changes are taking place on the inside. In order to understand puberty and menstruation, you have to have some idea of what's going on inside you.

Just as we have sex organs on the outside of our bodies, so we have sex organs on the inside. The sex organs inside our bodies are called reproductive organs because they are involved in the process of reproducing, that is, in having babies. Illustration 20 shows a side view of the reproductive organs – the vagina, uterus, Fallopian tubes and ovaries – in a young girl and in a grown woman. As you can see from these drawings, our reproductive organs also change as we get older. In this chapter we'll be talking about the changes that take place in these organs during puberty.

The vagina

In the last chapter you learned where the opening to your vagina is located. As we explained, the vagina itself is inside the body. The vagina is rather like a pouch tucked up inside us, which is very elastic, or stretchy, so that a man's penis can fit inside it during sexual intercourse. It is so stretchable that it can expand to allow a baby to pass from the uterus

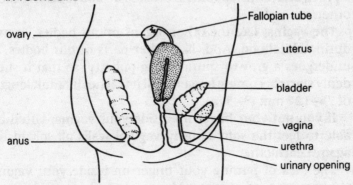

CROSS-SECTION OF REPRODUCTIVE ORGANS
IN YOUNG GIRL

ovary — Fallopian tube
— uterus
— bladder
— vagina
anus — urethra
— urinary opening

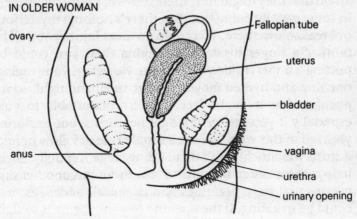

CROSS-SECTION OF REPRODUCTIVE ORGANS
IN OLDER WOMAN

ovary — Fallopian tube
— uterus
— bladder
anus — vagina
— urethra
— urinary opening

Illustration 20. Cross-section of the reproductive organs. Our reproductive organs change as we get older. They grow larger and also change positions as they grow. Note that the uterus is almost vertical in a young girl, but is usually tilted forward in a woman.

and through the vagina during childbirth. Most of the time, though, the vagina is like a collapsed balloon without any air in it, and its inside walls are folded up and touching each other.

The vagina, like the other organs in our bodies, grows during childhood. And, like other parts of our bodies, it undergoes a growth spurt during puberty, so that it suddenly starts becoming longer until it reaches its adult length of 75–127 mm (3–5 in).

If you put your finger up inside your vagina, you'll be able to feel the soft, squishy vaginal walls all folded up against each other.

The idea of putting your finger up inside your vagina might seem a little strange. Many girls, and women too, are afraid that they might hurt themselves or injure themselves in some way by doing this. But there's nothing mysterious or breakable in there. You could no more injure yourself by putting a finger inside your vagina than you could by putting a finger inside your mouth. However, your vaginal opening and hymen may be rather small and tight, so it's possible that it might feel a bit uncomfortable to you, especially if you are feeling a bit nervous about exploring yourself in this way. There's a simple rule to follow here: if it hurts too much, don't do it. Using some K-Y Jelly might help make it easier, but don't use body lotions or other skin creams that have perfumes and chemicals added, as they could be irritating. If the opening to your vagina is so tight and small that it's hard to get your finger in there, you might want to slowly stretch the opening over a period of a few weeks or months. Running your finger around the opening from time to time (while you're taking a hot bath is a good time) will help stretch it.

If you press upwards, just inside the vaginal opening you'll feel a bone covered by a soft bulge of tissue. It may feel rather sensitive, for underneath this bulge lies the urethra, the tube that runs from the bottom of the bladder to the outside of your body. Pressing upwards in this manner may give you the feeling that you have to urinate because the bladder lies quite near the vagina (see Illustration 21), and any pressure on the bladder can give you the feeling that you have to pee.

If you press down on the vaginal walls, you may feel some lumps. This is because the lower part of your bowels lie just under the vagina, so you may be able to feel lumps of faeces in the lower bowel.

If you slide your fingers more deeply into the vagina and press on the vaginal walls, you may notice that only about the first third of the vagina is very sensitive to your touch.

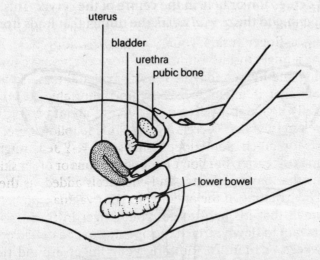

Illustration 21. The vagina. If you press up towards the mons, you may feel the pubic bone and the urethra, the tube through which urine travels from the bladder. If you press down, you may feel lumps of faeces in the lower bowel.

The upper portion of the vagina is not as sensitive because it has fewer nerve endings.

The cervix

At the top of the vagina you may be able to feel a firm, round knob. This is the *cervix*, the lower part, or neck, of the uterus, and it protrudes into the vagina (see Illustration 22). Like the vagina, the cervix grows larger during puberty. In grown women it is about 25–50 mm (1–2 in) in diameter.

It is not always easy to feel the cervix, since it is at the top of the vagina, but if you bear down as if you were making a bowel movement you should be able to feel it. It feels rather firm, like the tip of your nose. You may be able to feel a small depression or hole in the centre of the cervix. This is the opening to the *cervical canal*, the tunnel that leads from

cervix (SIR-vicks)   *cervical* (sir-vi-cul)

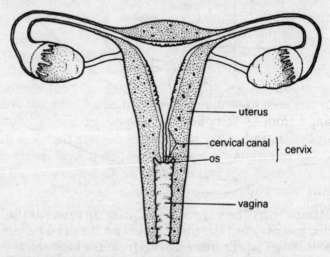

Illustration 22. The cervix. The cervix is the lower portion of the uterus and protrudes into the vagina.

the vagina into the uterus. This opening is called the *os*. It is no bigger around than the head of a kitchen match. Sperm pass through the os on their way to meet the ova. Menstrual blood passes through here when you are having your period. When a woman is having a baby, the cervical canal, like the vagina, stretches so the baby can pass through.

Your cervix and the walls of your vagina may feel wet, especially when you are sexually excited, for there are glands in here that make fluids that lubricate the vagina when we are sexually excited. Even if you are not feeling sexually excited, your vagina may feel rather wet. Like the skin on the outside of your body, the skin on the inside of the vagina is continually shedding old, dead cells. During puberty the vaginal walls begin to shed cells at a faster rate than during childhood, and the vagina begins to make a small amount of fluid to wash these cells away. A year or two before your first menstrual period, you may start to notice a clear or milky-white, watery discharge from your vagina. It may leave a yellowish stain on your underpants when it dries. This discharge is made up of dead cells and fluid from the cervix and vaginal walls. This discharge is perfectly normal, just another of the signs that puberty is beginning. If, however, the discharge has a strong, offensive odour; causes itching or redness on your vulva; is brown, green or a colour other than clear or white; or if it changes from a watery liquid to a liquid with small, whitish chunks in it (rather like watery curd cheese), then you may have an infection in your vagina. Such infections are not usually serious, but you should see a doctor so you can get them cleared up.

While we're on the subject of vaginal discharges, we want to mention one other important fact. Once you have begun to have your monthly menstrual periods, you may

os (OSZ)

notice that at certain times of the month you have more vaginal discharge than at other times. You may also notice that the appearance (the colour and consistency) of your vaginal discharge is different on different days. This is perfectly normal and natural. It happens because, as you go through puberty, special glands in your cervix begin to produce a mucus that mixes with the old cells and the cleansing fluids produced inside your vagina and adds to your vaginal discharge. On certain days of the month these glands in your cervix are very active and produce one kind of mucus. On other days these glands are less active and produce a different mucus. Therefore, your vaginal discharge may be noticeably different on different days of the month. For more information on the monthly changes in your vaginal discharges, be sure to read the section called 'Cervical Mucus Changes' in the next chapter (pages 123–5).

The ovaries

The ovaries also get larger during puberty, but there is an even more dramatic change that takes place in them: it is during puberty that one of your ovaries will produce its first ripe ovum.

Unlike a male, who constantly makes a new supply of sperm in his body, a female is born with all the ova she will ever have. There are hundreds of thousands of ova in a girl's ovaries, but only eight or nine hundred of them will ever fully ripen.

The ripening process begins in the brain. When a girl is about 8 years old, a part of her brain called the *pituitary* begins to send out substances called *hormones*. Hormones are made in one part of our bodies and travel to another

pituitary (pih-TYUO-eh-tair-ee)   *hormones* (HOR-moans)

part to act on an organ there so that it develops or behaves in a particular way. Our bodies make hundreds of hormones. You could go crazy just trying to remember all their names. But in this book we'll discuss only the hormones that are important in reproduction and puberty.

One of the hormones made by the pituitary during puberty is *FSH*, which is short for 'follicle stimulating hormone'. During puberty the FSH from the pituitary starts to get into the bloodstream and travels to the ovaries. It travels deep inside the ovary where the tiny ova lie. Each ovum is encased in a tiny sac called a *follicle*. The follicle stimulating hormone, as its name implies, stimulates some of the follicles and their ova to grow and develop. It also causes the follicles to make yet another hormone, called *oestrogen* (see Illustration 23).

As a girl is going through puberty, her pituitary makes increasing amounts of FSH, which causes the follicles in the ovaries to make more and more oestrogen. The oestrogen also gets into the bloodstream and travels to other parts of the body. It is oestrogen that causes many of the changes we notice during puberty. For example, oestrogen travels to our breasts and causes the milk ducts and fat tissue to develop so that our breasts begin to swell and stand out. It causes fat tissue to develop on our hips, thighs and buttocks, giving us a more curvy, womanly shape. Oestrogen also causes pubic and other body hair to grow.

As the follicles in the ovary are developing and making increasing amounts of oestrogen, they are also travelling towards the surface of the ovary. When they reach the surface, they press on the outer skin of the ovary, forming tiny bubbles that look like blisters. One follicle grows larger than all the others.

Finally, when a girl is making a sufficient amount of

follicle (FOL-eh-kul)　　　　*oestrogen* (EES-tro-jen)

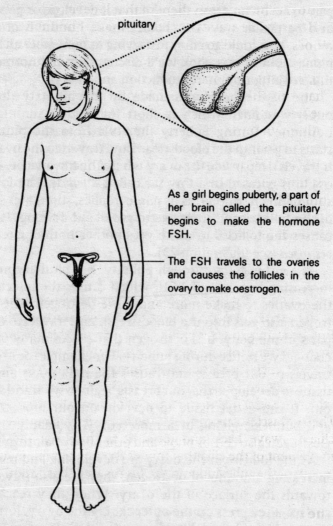

pituitary

As a girl begins puberty, a part of her brain called the pituitary begins to make the hormone FSH.

The FSH travels to the ovaries and causes the follicles in the ovary to make oestrogen.

Illustration 23. Hormones. The oestrogen that a girl's ovaries begin to make during puberty travels throughout her body, causing many changes, including the growth of pubic hair, swelling of the breasts and development of fat tissue around her hips.

oestrogen, her pituitary gland slows down its production of FSH for a while and starts making another hormone, called *LH* or '*luteinizing* hormone'. The LH travels to the ovary and causes the largest bubble on the surface of the ovary to pop, and the ripe ovum bursts off the ovary. *Ovulation* is what we call this process of the ovum popping off the ovary (see Illustration 24).

Although some girls feel a slight twinge or a dull ache or even a strong pain when ovulation happens, most of us never feel the ovum popping off. A girl may ovulate for the first time when she is as young as 8 or she may not ovulate until she is 16 or older.

After ovulation, the fringed ends of the Fallopian tube reach out to grasp the ovum and draw it into the tube.

The Fallopian tubes

The Fallopian tubes, through which ova travel on their way to the uterus, also grow longer and wider during puberty. But even in grown women, they are no thicker around than a strand of spaghetti. By the time we are grown women, each tube is about 100 mm (4 in) long. The insides of the Fallopian tubes are lined with tiny hairs, called *cilia*, which are attached to the muscles of the walls of the tubes. These muscles can contract and release, causing the tiny cilia to wave back and forth. It is this back-and-forth movement of the cilia that moves the ripe ovum down the length of the tube and into the uterus (see Illustration 25).

The uterus

Like the other reproductive organs, the uterus also changes as we go through puberty. It too grows larger, but even in

luteinizing (LOO-tin-eyes-ing)　　　*cilia* (SIL-ee-uh)
ovulation (oh-vu-LAY-shun)

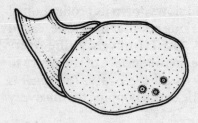

FSH from the pituitary causes some of the follicles in the ovary to develop and to make oestrogen.

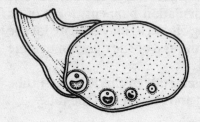

As more and more FSH reaches the ovaries, the follicles make increasing amounts of oestrogen and move towards the surface of the ovary.

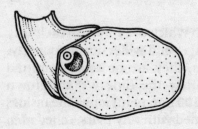

One of the follicles reaches the surface and presses on the outer skin of the ovary, forming a bubble.

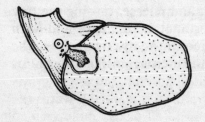

When a girl is making enough oestrogen, the pituitary slows down its production of FSH and makes LH. The LH travels to the ovary, causing the follicle to burst and release its tiny ovum.

Illustration 24. Ovulation.

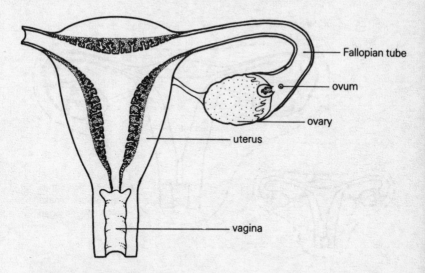

Illustration 25. The ovum. The ovum travels through the Fallopian tube to the uterus.

grown women it is only about the size of a clenched fist. The drawings in Illustration 26 are life-size drawings of the uterus and ovaries in a typical 11-year-old girl and in a grown woman. Try tracing them, cutting them out and holding them up to your body. Doing this will help you to understand the size and location of these organs and how they change as you go through puberty.

As you can see from Illustration 20 at the beginning of this chapter, the uterus not only grows larger, it also changes position during puberty. In a young girl the uterus is in an upright, almost vertical position, but as she grows older, it begins to lean forward, so it is tilted towards the bladder. This doesn't happen to all of us. Some women have what is called a tilted uterus (see Illustration 27), which means that the uterus has remained in its nearly upright position or has tilted in the other direction. It was once thought that having a tilted uterus might make it

cut along dotted line

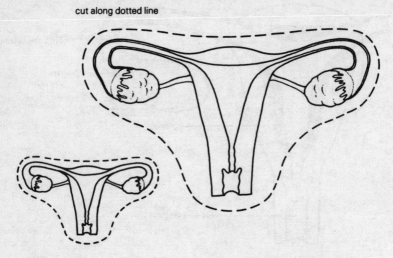

Illustration 26. The uterus and ovaries. Approximate drawings of uterus, Fallopian tubes and ovaries in a typical 11-year-old girl and a grown woman.

difficult for a woman to have a baby. All manner of backaches and problems were blamed on the tilted uterus. Doctors even performed operations to tilt the uterus forwards. We now know that having a tilted uterus has nothing to do with how likely you are to get pregnant or with any other sort of problem.

THE ENDOMETRIUM

The lining of the uterus is called the *endometrium*. During childhood it is very thin, but during puberty it too changes. When the ovaries begin to make enough oestrogen, the lining starts to grow thick with new blood vessels and spongy, cushioning tissues. By the time the LH from the

endometrium (en-doe-MEE-tree-um)

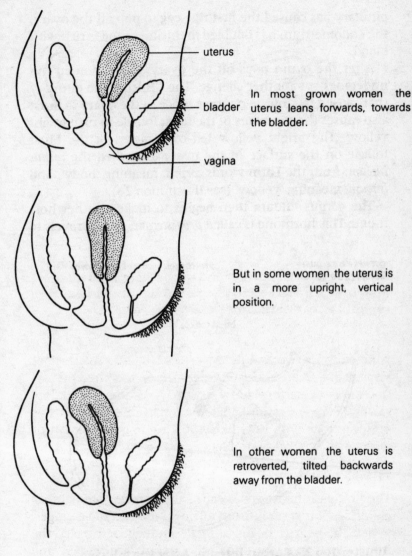

uterus

In most grown women the uterus leans forwards, towards the bladder.

bladder

vagina

But in some women the uterus is in a more upright, vertical position.

In other women the uterus is retroverted, tilted backwards away from the bladder.

Illustration 27. The position of the uterus.

pituitary has caused the first ripe egg to pop off the ovary, the endometrium has doubled in thickness and is rich with blood.

After the ovum pops off the ovary, the endometrium undergoes yet another change. The LH from the pituitary that caused the follicle on the surface of the ovary to burst also causes the remnants of the burst follicle to turn bright yellow. The bright yellow left-over pieces of the burst follicle on the surface of the ovary are called the *corpus luteum*, from the Latin words *corpus*, meaning 'body', and *luteum*, meaning 'yellow' (see Illustration 28).

The corpus luteum then begins to make another hormone. This hormone is called *progesterone*, and it travels to

corpus (KORE-pus)
luteum (LOO-tih-um)

progesterone (pro-JES-teh-rown)

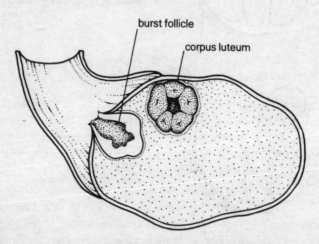

burst follicle

corpus luteum

Illustration 28. Corpus luteum. After the follicle containing the ovum has burst open, the remnants of the burst follicle turn bright yellow. These remnants are referred to as the corpus luteum.

the uterus and causes the endometrium to grow still thicker and to make nourishing substances that can help a fertilized ovum develop and grow into a baby.

If the ovum has been fertilized and the woman is going to have a baby, the corpus luteum keeps on making progesterone for a while, so that the endometrium will continue to secrete the nourishment the baby will need. If the ovum hasn't been fertilized, the corpus luteum stops making progesterone and disintegrates within a few days. Without the help of the hormone progesterone, the lining of the uterus begins to break down. The spongy tissue and blood of the lining fall off the wall of the uterus, collect on the bottom of the uterus and dribble through the cervical canal and out through the os into the vagina. (See Illustration 5 on page 33). From there, the blood and tissues trickle down the vaginal walls and out through the vaginal opening, and a girl has her menstrual period. The bleeding continues for a few days and then stops.

The menstrual cycle and the menopause

After a girl has had her first period, she continues ovulating (popping a ripe ovum off her ovary) and having her period (bleeding for a few days) about once a month for many, many years. This monthly process of ovulating and menstruating is called the *menstrual cycle*. Although the menstrual cycle repeats itself for many years, it does not continue for ever. When a woman reaches a certain age, usually between 45 and 55, her ovaries stop producing a ripe ovum each month and she no longer has her monthly bleeding period. Just as we have the word *puberty* for the time in a young woman's life when she first *starts* ovulating and menstruating, so we have a word for the time in an older woman's life when she *stops* ovulating and menstruating. This time in a woman's life is called the *menopause*.

The menopause may happen very abruptly. A woman may have her period one month, then the next month she doesn't have her period and never has one again. Or it may happen gradually. A woman may skip one, two (or more) periods, and then have one or two (or more periods), skip some and then have her period again for a while, and so on, until she finally stops altogether.*

As a woman is going through the menopause, her body is making less of the hormones oestrogen and progesterone. Most women adjust to this change in their body chemistry with no problems. Some women have hot flushes, brief episodes in which their body heats up and they may perspire profusely, as they are going through the menopause. For most women, hot flushes, although bothersome, are not so severe that they need a doctor's care, but a few women have such severe and frequent hot flushes that they need medical care for help in controlling them.

Just as there are many myths and misconceptions about hymens and about masturbation, so there are many myths about the menopause. Women going through the menopause, or the 'change of life', as it is sometimes called, supposedly are prone to fits of depression, anxiety or strange behaviour. People used to think that a woman going through the menopause would suddenly grow old, develop wrinkles, get fat and feel less sexual desire. Today we know that the menopause doesn't really cause any of these things. But there are many people who still have misconceptions about the menopause, so you may hear some of these things. If so, just ignore them.

menopause (MEN-O-pause)

*The menopause is not the only reason women skip menstrual periods; see pages 146–7 for more details.

But the menopause is many years away for you. You're probably more interested in learning about how menstruation works and about having your first period, and we'll be talking about these things in the next chapter.

Chapter 7

The Monthly Miracle:
The Menstrual Cycle

Once a month, deep inside our bodies, the ovary begins, ever so slowly, to turn. The bubble on its surface contains the one ovum that has, for some mysterious reason, been chosen from all of the hundreds of thousands of ova to be released that month. The funnel-like opening at the end of the Fallopian tube, lined with thousands of undulating cilia, turns to meet the ovary.

Suddenly, the bubble bursts. Triggered by a spurt of luteinizing hormone, the chemical messenger from the pituitary, the ovary contracts sharply and the ripe ovum bursts forth. The fringed ends of the Fallopian tubes reach out like fingers to grasp the ripe ovum and draw it into the narrow tunnel of the tube. In a dream-like, slow-motion ballet the tiny cilia caress the ripe ovum and gently move it along on its 100-mm (4-in) journey to the uterus, a journey that takes five to seven days.

As the ovum is moving through the tube towards the uterus, the lining of the uterus is preparing itself. The blood vessels in the area swell, flooding the uterus with a rich supply of blood to nourish the soft, spongy tissue of the uterine lining, which will cushion the ovum when it arrives. Glands in the uterus pour forth a banquet of nutrients that will nourish the developing ovum. The lining of the uterus has thickened to twice its normal depth – a luxuriously rich topsoil in which the ovum, if fertilized during the journey through the tube, will implant.

For the first few days after its arrival, the tiny ovum floats freely within the plush uterus. If fertilized, it will embed itself in the uterus on the seventh day. Meanwhile, on the surface of the ovary, the remnant of the burst bubble, the corpus luteum, which has turned a bright yellow after its explosive spasm, awaits a message from the uterus.

If in the upper reaches of the dark, narrow Fallopian tube no sperm meets and fertilizes the ovum, the ovum will not implant in the lining of the uterus. Then the corpus luteum begins to disintegrate. The chemical messages it's been transmitting to the uterus via the hormone progesterone cease. The levels of progesterone in the bloodstream drop. Without the continued supply of progesterone from the corpus luteum, the swollen network of blood vessels shrinks, restricting the flow of blood to the lining. This deprives the newly grown tissues in the lining of their support and nourishment. Over a period of days the lining falls away in small pieces. Within hours the now weakened blood vessels of the lining open, a few at a time. Each tiny vessel empties its droplets. More and more droplets are released and the flow of menstrual blood empties the uterus of the no-longer-needed tissues.

After some days of bleeding, the lining is emptied out and this process begins all over again. The uterine lining starts to grow rich and thick again, and more ova begin to move towards the surface of the ovary. Another ovum is released at ovulation, and if the woman is not going to have a baby, then her period begins again about two weeks after ovulation.

The menstrual cycle

The time from the first day of bleeding of one menstrual period to the first day of bleeding of the next period – the menstrual cycle – takes about a month. The menstrual cycle may last for twenty-one to thirty-five days. The average is about twenty-eight days. But there are very few women who actually have their periods regularly, every twenty-eight days, like clockwork throughout their entire lives. Most of us are somewhat more irregular than this. For example, in the last year, my periods went like this: my first three periods of the year were very regular. I began to bleed once every twenty-nine days and the bleeding lasted for five days each time. My fourth period came twenty-seven days after my third and lasted for only four days. Then I didn't have a period again for thirty days and when I did have it, it lasted for six days. My next period came thirty-one days later and lasted for five days. Then I started having my periods more regularly again, once every twenty-nine days and I bled for five days each time.

Each of us has her own pattern. Some are more regular than others. We may be very regular and suddenly get irregular, as one woman explained:

I was very regular when I was younger. I could set my watch by it, once every twenty-six days. Then, when I turned 30, I became very irregular – once every twenty-two days, once every twenty-six, once every thirty. Now, I'm more regular again.

On the other hand, some women are very irregular and then suddenly their periods start to become regular. No one is exactly sure why some women are regular and others irregular or why our patterns may change. But we do know that travelling, emotional ups and downs, illness and such things can affect our menstrual periods, making them start earlier or later than usual. There is an old-wives' tale that says that women who live together, who spend a lot of time with each other or who are close friends tend to have their periods around the same time, which might also account for why our patterns change. 'That's certainly true for me,' one woman told us:

I've always menstruated about the same time as the other women I'm around. When I lived at home, my sisters and I always had our periods together at the beginning of each month. When I went away to college, I found that my periods changed. I started menstruating around the middle of the month, same as my room-mates.

As it turns out, this old-wives' tale may have a great deal of truth to it. Scientific studies have shown that women who are close do often have their periods around the same time.

Young women who've just started having their periods are particularly likely to have irregular periods. It takes a while for our bodies to adjust to menstruating. You may have your first period and not have another one for six months. Or you may have your second period two weeks after your first one. It often takes two or three years to develop anything near a regular pattern and some of us never become very regular.

LENGTH OF YOUR PERIOD/AMOUNT AND TYPE OF BLOOD FLOW

Your period may last from two to seven days. The average is about five days. Some of your periods may last longer than others, so one month you may bleed for only two or three days, and the next time you may bleed for five or six days. Or you may be one of those women who bleeds for exactly five days each time. Here again, each of us has her own pattern, and our patterns may change over the course of our lives.

Athough it may seem as if a lot of blood comes out of the uterus, it isn't really that much. The amount of blood may vary from one tablespoon to one cup. Women have different patterns in this too. Some of us always have heavy periods, about eight tablespoons each time; others always have light periods, only one tablespoon each time. Still others vary between having heavy and light periods.

Some of us tend to bleed most heavily on the first day or two, gradually trickling off until there is only a light flow of blood on the last day. Others start off lightly on the first day, then get heavier. Still others will bleed for a number of days and stop or slow down to only a trickle for a day or so, then bleed more heavily again. All these patterns, and any combination of them, are normal.

The blood and tissue that comprise the menstrual flow may be thin and watery or the flow may have thick clumps, called clots. You may be more apt to notice clots in the morning when you get up, for the blood has been pooling and congealing in the top of the vagina while you've been lying down asleep.

The blood may be bright red to brown. It is especially likely to be brownish at the very beginning or toward the end of your period. Blood tends to turn brown the longer it sits. If your blood has been slow in moving out of your body, it may take on a brownish colour.

THE FOUR PHASES

Regardless of whether your periods usually come every twenty-one days or every thirty-five days, whether they're regular or irregular, light or heavy, the menstrual cycle works in essentially the same way in all of us. The menstrual cycle can be divided into four parts, or phases.

Phase 1

The first phase of the menstrual cycle is the bleeding phase, when you are actually having your period. During this phase the uterine lining is breaking down and being shed. We call the first day of bleeding Day 1 of your menstrual cycle. As we said, the bleeding phase may last for one to seven days, but it usually lasts about five days. So, for

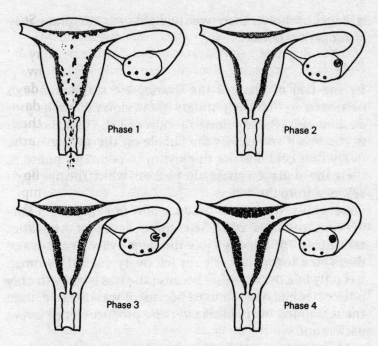

Illustration 29. The uterus in the four stages of the menstrual cycle.

the purposes of this discussion, we'll call Day 1 to Day 5 the first, or bleeding, phase of the cycle (see Illustration 29).

Phase 2

During this phase the pituitary gland is making FSH, which causes the follicles in the ovary to make oestrogen and to move towards the surface of the ovary. The oestrogen also causes the lining of the uterus to develop new blood passageways and spongy tissues to cushion them.

In a woman with a twenty-eight-day cycle who bleeds for five days this phase would start on about Day 6 and would continue until Day 13 or so. Of course, if your cycle is longer or shorter than twenty-eight days, this phase may be longer or shorter.

Phase 3

By the end of Phase 2 the ovaries are making enough oestrogen so that the pituitary gland slows down its production of FSH and releases a spurt of LH. The LH travels to the ovary and causes the bubble on the surface of the ovary that contains the ripe ovum to pop. This phase is, then, the ovulation phase, the phase in which the ripe egg is released from the ovary.

Generally, the ovaries produce only one ripe ovum during each menstrual cycle. Scientists believe that the ovaries take turns. During one cycle the right ovary ovulates and during the following cycle the left ovary does. If a woman has only one ovary, either because she was born with only one or has had one removed because it was diseased, then the remaining ovary takes over and produces a ripe ovum each month.

Most women don't feel anything when the bubble bursts and the ripe ovum pops off the ovary; however, some women do know when they are ovulating because they feel a cramp or a pain. Some women have a dull achy feeling for a day or so around the time they are ovulating. Others have a sudden sharp pain that passes very quickly; still others experience just a mild twinge that is hardly noticeable. But for most of us ovulation happens without our being aware of it.

In a woman with a twenty-eight-day cycle ovulation usually occurs on Day 14; however, it may happen one or two days earlier or later than this – that is, any time from Day 12 to Day 16.

Most books that describe the menstrual cycle talk about a twenty-eight-day cycle and explain that ovulation occurs about half-way through the cycle, on Day 14. Women who have longer or shorter cycles often assume that they too will ovulate at the half-way point of their cycles. Thus, many women think that ovulation would occur half-way through a thirty-two-day cycle, on about Day 16, or half-way in a twenty-two-day cycle, on Day 11. This is not true. Ovulation occurs about fourteen days (give or take one or two days either way) before the first day of bleeding of the next period. So, if a woman has a thirty-two-day cycle, she probably ovulates around Day 18 (32 − 14 = 18), and if she has a twenty-two-day cycle, she probably ovulates around Day 8 (22 − 14 = 8).

A woman can get pregnant only during the ovulation phase of her menstrual cycle, when her ovary has just recently released the ripe ovum. It would be nice if we could predict exactly when a woman is going to ovulate. That way, a woman who wanted to get pregnant could have sexual intercourse at a time when her chances of getting pregnant are highest, and a woman who didn't want to get pregnant could avoid having intercourse at this time. But it doesn't work that way. One month a woman might have a twenty-eight-day cycle, so she'd ovulate around Day 14. But the next month she might have a thirty-five-day cycle, so she'd probably ovulate around Day 21. The following cycle might only be twenty-one days long, so she'd ovulate around Day 7.

Therefore, attempting to prevent pregnancy simply by counting the days of your cycle and avoiding sex around ovulation doesn't work very well. (For more information on preventing pregnancy, see pages 183–203).

Phase 4

As this phase begins, the ripe ovum is in the Fallopian tube, travelling towards the uterus. The corpus luteum, the remnants of the burst follicle on the surface of the ovary, has turned bright yellow and is making progesterone. The

Summary of the four phases of the menstrual cycle

PHASE 1

- The uterine lining is being shed; the woman is having her period.
- The pituitary and the ovaries are making only small amounts of hormones.

PHASE 2

- The pituitary is making FSH.
- The ovaries are making oestrogen.
- The follicles in the ovary are moving towards the surface of the ovary.
- The uterine lining is starting to thicken.

PHASE 3

- The pituitary releases a spurt of LH.
- The ripe ovum bursts from the ovary and moves into the Fallopian tube.

PHASE 4

- The remnants of the burst follicle become the corpus luteum and begin to make progesterone.
- The progesterone makes the uterine lining grow even thicker.
- If fertilization occurs, the corpus luteum keeps making progesterone; if not, the corpus luteum disintegrates.
- Without progesterone from the corpus luteum, the uterine lining breaks down and is shed. The first day of bleeding is Day 1 of the next cycle.

progesterone is causing the lining of the uterus to get even thicker and to secrete nutrients.

If a sperm manages to make its way into the Fallopian tube at this time, there's a good chance that fertilization will take place. The sperm penetrates the outer shell of the ovum and the fertilized seed then travels to the uterus. It plants itself in the rich uterine lining.

If fertilization takes place, the corpus luteum continues to produce progesterone for some time so that the uterine lining will provide nutrients to nourish the fertilized ovum. But most of the time fertilization doesn't happen. The ovum disintegrates. Because fertilization hasn't happened, the corpus luteum also disintegrates and stops producing progesterone.

At this point in the menstrual cycle there is very little oestrogen and very little progesterone being made in our bodies, so the lining of the uterus starts to break down and is shed. As the lining is being shed, the pituitary starts making more FSH. In turn, the ovaries start making more oestrogen. As soon as the lining is shed, a new lining begins to thicken and the menstrual cycle starts all over again.

In a woman with a twenty-eight-day cycle Phase 4 would run from about Day 15 (just after ovulation) until Day 28. On the twenty-ninth day the bleeding would start again and thus would be Day 1 of the next cycle.

Cervical mucus changes

In addition to the menstrual cycle changes there are other important cyclical changes that take place in your body each month. As you may recall from the last chapter, your cervix has certain glands that produce mucus (see page 102). This mucus mixes with the old cells and cleansing fluids in your vagina to make up your vaginal discharge. The amount and type of mucus produced by these glands varies depending on the phase of the menstrual cycle.

These changes in the amount and type of your cervical mucus (and, therefore, in your vaginal discharge) may not be as noticeable in teenagers as they are in older women. The cervical mucus cycle may also follow a somewhat different pattern in different women, and for some women these changes may be more noticeable than in others. In general, however, the pattern of cervical mucus changes goes something like this: on the days immediately following a woman's menstrual period the glands in the cervix are not very active. They don't produce much mucus, so there is usually less vaginal discharge at this time and the vagina and vaginal lips are apt to feel rather dry.

After a few days the glands start to become more active, so there is an increasing amount of vaginal discharge and the vagina and vaginal lips are noticeably 'wetter'. The mucus produced by the glands on these days may be clear to white to yellowish in colour. It may be thin and watery or rather thick, pasty and sticky.

During the ovulation phase of the menstrual cycle the glands in the cervix are very active and usually produce more mucus than at any other time in the cycle. The mucus on these days tends to be clear and quite slippery. If you were to put some of this mucus between your thumb and forefinger, you would be able to stretch the mucus in long, shimmery strands. This type of mucus is called fertile mucus because it appears at the time of the month when a woman is ovulating and is therefore most fertile and most likely to get pregnant. The mucus produced at other times of the month has a chemical make-up and structure that is hostile to sperm and helps prevent them from passing through the cervix and into the uterus. But this fertile mucus has a different chemical make-up and structure that actually helps sperm on their journey and increases a woman's chances of getting pregnant.

In a few women the fertile mucus may be accompanied by some red or brownish colour in the vaginal discharge. This slight staining is unusual, but it is perfectly normal and natural, just a bit of bleeding that some women have at ovulation.

Within one to about three days after ovulation the fertile mucus disappears. Some women don't have much mucus or discharge on these days. From this point until their next period their vagina and vaginal lips again feel rather dry. Other women continue to have some discharge and a feeling of wetness, but the mucus on these days tends to be rather sticky and pasty, quite different from the fertile mucus. Still other women alternate between dry and wet days.

Menstruation – when?

The girls in our classes always ask 'When will I have my first period?' Unfortunately, we can't answer that question. Each of us has her own timetable. No one can say exactly when it will happen, but we *can* give you an idea. A girl may have her first period any time between her eighth and sixteenth birthdays. But very few girls have their periods when they are as young as 8, and the vast majority have theirs before they are 16. In fact, most girls have their periods between their eleventh and fourteenth birthdays. Still, there are plenty of girls who have their periods when they are only 8 or 9 and plenty who don't have theirs until 15 or 16. If you reach the age of 16 and have not started menstruating, it's a good idea to discuss this with your GP. Not menstruating by the age of 16 isn't necessarily a sign that there's something wrong. There have been cases of perfectly normal girls who didn't start to menstruate until their twenties, but it's a good idea to see a doctor to rule out the possibility that you have a medical problem that is keeping you from menstruating. Your GP may refer you to a gynaecologist, a doctor who specializes in women's health care.

Even though it's impossible to say exactly when any particular girl will have her first period, there are some clues. One thing that may give you a clue as to when you'll start is when your mother started. Daughters often have their first periods around the same age that their mothers did. This is not a hard-and-fast rule, but it is at least a clue. Ask your mother if she can remember exactly when she started.

You might want to use the chart on page 127 to keep track of your progress through puberty. Perhaps keeping a chart like this is something you and your mother, a girl-friend or another person you feel close to could do together, and it might be fun to share this chart with your daughter if some day you become the mother of a girl.

Start by filling in the first section of the chart. Every three months or so fill in a new section. (Make more chart pages as you need them.) Begin by writing in the date and recording your height and weight. If you have not yet begun your growth spurt, you may notice a dramatic increase in your height and weight as time passes and you fill in more sections on the chart. If your growth spurt has already started, you'll probably notice a more gradual increase in your height and weight.

On the next line, where it says 'Stage of pubic hair development', write the numeral 1, 2, 3, 4 or 5 to indicate which stage of pubic hair development you are in now. It might be helpful to turn back to Illustration 9, on page 45, which shows the five stages of pubic hair development. If you don't have any pubic hairs at all, you would write the numeral 1 on that line of the chart. If you have at least a few pubic hairs, you would write the numeral 2 there. If your pubic hair looks more like the drawing of Stage 3, write a 3, and so on. If you are between stages, you might want to write something like 'between Stages 2 and 3' or 'between Stages 3 and 4'.

On the next line, the one that says 'Stage of breast development', write the stage you are closest to right now.

PUBERTY CHART

Date:
Height: Weight:
Stage of pubic hair
    development:
Stage of breast
    development:
Other changes:

Date:
Height: Weight:
Stage of pubic hair
    development:
Stage of breast
    development:
Other changes:

Date:
Height: Weight:
Stage of pubic hair
    development:
Stage of breast
    development:
Other changes:

Date:
Height: Weight:
Stage of pubic hair
    development:
Stage of breast
    development:
Other changes:

Date:
Height: Weight:
Stage of pubic hair
    development:
Stage of breast
    development:
Other changes:

Date:
Height: Weight:
Stage of pubic hair
    development:
Stage of breast
    development:
Other changes:

Date:
Height: Weight:
Stage of pubic hair
    development:
Stage of breast
    development:
Other changes:

Date:
Height: Weight:
Stage of pubic hair
    development:
Stage of breast
    development:
Other changes:

It might be helpful to look at Illustration 13 on page 65. Again, if you're between stages, you might want to make a note of this.

If you notice other changes – for example, underarm

hair, dark hair on your arms and legs, more perspiration, spots, a change in the appearance of your vulva, a vaginal discharge – note these things on your chart in the space after the words 'Other changes'. Any time you notice something new, fill in another section of the chart, even if it hasn't been three months since your last entry. Of course, when you first menstruate, mark that on the chart too!

Keeping a chart like this of the stages of pubic hair and breast development can give you some idea of when you'll start to menstruate. Doctors have studied groups of girls going through puberty to see what stages of breast and pubic development girls were in when they started to menstruate. The following table shows the results of these studies.

WHEN GIRLS STARTED TO MENSTRUATE

Stage	Percentage* of Girls Who Started to Menstruate in Each Stage of Breast Development	Percentage* of Girls Who Started to Menstruate in Each Stage of Pubic Hair Growth
1	0	1
2	1	4
3	26	19
4	62	62
5	11	14

*Percentage means part of 100. If we say 62 per cent of all girls menstruate when they are in breast Stage 4, we mean that of a group of 100 girls, 62 of them will have their first period while they are in Stage 4 of breast development.

As you can see from this table, most girls (62 per cent) start to menstruate when they are in Stage 4 of breast development. Also, most girls (62 per cent) have their first periods in Stage 4 of pubic hair development. So if your puberty chart shows you've reached Stage 4 of breast and pubic hair development, you can expect to start menstruating in the near future. However, as you can also see from the table, 11 per cent of girls don't have their periods until Stage 5 of breast development and 14 per cent don't start until Stage 5 of pubic hair development. Moreover, a fair number of girls, 26 per cent, start their periods while they are in breast Stage 3, and 19 per cent start while they are in pubic hair Stage 3.

None of the girls studied started to menstruate while they were in breast Stage 1 and only 1 per cent (1 out of 100) started in pubic hair Stage 1. So if you are still in Stage 1, you probably won't start menstruating until you've moved to a more advanced stage of breast and pubic hair development.

Breast development and pubic hair development don't always go together. So you may be in one stage of breast development and in another stage of pubic hair development. For example, one of the girls in our class had her first period when she was in Stage 4 of breast development and Stage 3 of pubic hair development.

Another question that often comes up in our classes is 'How long does it take to go through the various stages?' Again it's hard to answer this question exactly, but we do know how long most girls take to go through them.

As you can see from the table on page 130, most girls spend about eleven months in Stage 2 of breast development. In other words, it takes eleven months to get from the beginning of Stage 2 to the beginning of Stage 3. Some girls take as little as two and a half months and some as long as twelve months. There are a few girls (about 5 per cent) who will take either a shorter or longer time than this.

Likewise, reading across the second line of the table will tell you that most girls spend about eleven months in breast

LENGTH OF TIME THAT GIRLS REMAIN IN VARIOUS STAGES

Stage	Most Girls	95 per cent of all Girls
Breast 2	About 11 months	About 2½ to 12 months
Breast 3	About 11 months	About 4 to 26 months
Breast 4	24 months	About 1 month to 7 years
Pubic Hair 2	About 7 months	About 2½ to 15½ months
Pubic Hair 3	6 months	About 2½ to 11 months
Pubic Hair 4	About 15½ months	About 7 to 29 months

Stage 3. Some girls take as little as one month to get through Stage 3 and some take as many as twenty-six months. Ninety-five per cent of us will take somewhere between one and twenty-six months; most of us will take about eleven months.

Your first period

These charts and tables are fun to fill in and they can give you some idea of when you can expect to start menstruating, but no one can predict the exact day of your first period and this worries many girls.

'What'll I do if it happens when I'm at school?' is a question that often comes up in our classes. Luckily, there are usually some girls in our classes who've already started to menstruate and can share their experiences with the other girls. Here's what one of them had to say:

I got my first period during history class. I wasn't sure if it was happening, but I thought it might be. So I raised my hand and said I had to go to the lavatory. Sure enough, there was blood on my knickers. Luckily, I had my purse with some change in it, so I got a sanitary towel out of the machine and pinned it to my knickers and just went back to class.

Sanitary towels are pads of soft cotton wool that are used to absorb the menstrual flow. This girl was lucky. There was a towel machine in the girls' lavatory and she had some change with her. Another girl wasn't so lucky:

I got my period at school, too. I knew right away what it was, but I went to the lavatory to check. There weren't any towels in the machine, so I just wadded up some loo paper and went to the nurse's office. She was real nice and gave me a clean pair of knickers and a sanitary towel.

A number of girls said that they'd gone to the school nurse, to their gym teachers, to the secretary in the school office or to a woman teacher for a sanitary towel. If their underpants were bloody, sometimes the nurse or whoever had a spare pair. At other times, they'd just ignored the blood or they'd just rinsed their pants out with cold water and put them on while they were still damp or waited until they dried.

One girl told us that she'd been prepared:

I knew I was getting old enough, so at the beginning of the school term, I put a sanitary towel in my bag in those special carrying cases they give you. And I just kept it there so I'd be ready. The school I was going to didn't have a school nurse, and the towel machines were always broken or empty. I didn't want to have to go into the office and say I was having my period and needed a towel. There were always a lot of people in there. I would have been too embarrassed.

Another girl told us that she, too, had been prepared:

I had that towel in my bag for almost a year. I thought I was so smart – being ready and all.

Then I'm walking down the hall one day and my girl-friend says, 'Hey, you have blood on your skirt.' I almost died. 'Stand in back of me,' I said, and she walked down the hall right behind me so no one could see. I took my coat from the cloakroom and put it on and went to the office. I told the secretary I was ill and had to go home.

Most girls notice a feeling of wetness before the blood soaks through their underpants and on to their clothes. And most girls don't bleed enough right at first to have it show through on their clothes. But some girls had embarrassing stories to tell about how the blood had soaked through their clothes, making a spot. If you're feeling worried about your first period, why not talk it over with your mother or someone else who might have some helpful hints. Finding out what has happened to other people or just talking about your worries can help a lot.

Sanitary towels and tampons

You can have your period any time, night or day, at home, at school or anywhere else you happen to be. Regardless of where or when it happens, you'll want to have some way of absorbing the menstrual flow.

In the past women have used everything from grass to soft cloths and sponges to catch their menstrual flow. Nowadays we have all sorts of menstrual products, so many that it may be hard to choose which one you want to use. You might ask your mother or another woman which she prefers and why. You can also try the various products yourself until you hit on the one you like best.

SANITARY TOWELS OR PADS

Sanitary towels come in different sizes and thicknesses and can be bought in supermarkets and chemists. They are made of layers of soft cotton wool. Most of them have a piece of plastic lining to prevent the blood from soaking through the pad (see Illustration 30).

Some sanitary towels are made to be worn with a belt.

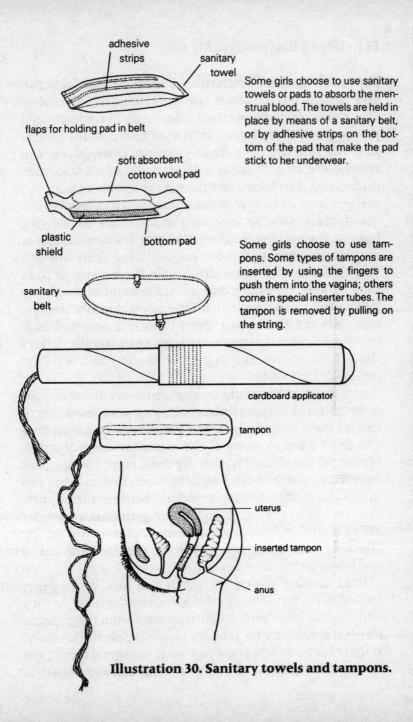

adhesive strips

sanitary towel

Some girls choose to use sanitary towels or pads to absorb the menstrual blood. The towels are held in place by means of a sanitary belt, or by adhesive strips on the bottom of the pad that make the pad stick to her underwear.

flaps for holding pad in belt

soft absorbent cotton wool pad

plastic shield

bottom pad

sanitary belt

Some girls choose to use tampons. Some types of tampons are inserted by using the fingers to push them into the vagina; others come in special inserter tubes. The tampon is removed by pulling on the string.

cardboard applicator

tampon

uterus

inserted tampon

anus

Illustration 30. Sanitary towels and tampons.

The towel fits to the belt, which is worn around the waist. You can also pin the towel to your underpants with safety pins. Some sanitary towels are made so that you don't need pins or a belt. They have a strip of adhesive on the under- side. The adhesive is covered by a strip of glossy paper. You remove the strip of paper and press the towel into your underpants. The adhesive will hold the towel in place.

If you have a heavy menstrual flow, you may need to use the thickest pads, at least on the days you are flowing heavily. If your flow is lighter, you may want to use one of the thinner pads, which are not as bulky. There are also very thin pads that some girls use on the last day or so of their period if they have only a small amount of blood.

Wearing a pad for the first time can feel rather strange, especially the thick ones. Even though it may feel as if everyone can see that you're wearing a pad, it really doesn't show. Look for yourself in the mirror and you'll see – the pad really isn't visible.

Sanitary towels should be changed every three or four hours to avoid soaking through the pad. It's a good idea to change them frequently even if you have a very light flow and don't have to worry about soaking through the pad. Menstrual blood itself is perfectly clean and odourless, but once it comes into contact with the germs in the vagina and in the air, it does develop an odour, because germs grow very rapidly in the rich blood. These germs aren't necess- arily harmful, but they can cause an unpleasant odour. By changing your pad frequently you won't give the germs and odour a chance to develop.

Used sanitary towels should be put in a waste-paper basket or dustbin. Don't flush them down the toilet, as they will clog the plumbing. Public lavatories often have special disposal containers for sanitary towels beside the lavatory. If there isn't one and you don't want to come waltzing out of the toilet in front of everyone with a bloody towel in your hand, fold the towel in half and wrap it in toilet paper. Then, when you leave the lavatory, just toss it into the nearest dustbin. It's a good idea to wrap them up like this even when you're at home, for it will cut down on odour from the pad.

TAMPONS

Another way of catching the menstrual flow is to use a tampon. Women have been using tampons since the dawn of time. They made small rolls of absorbent grass or cloth and put the roll inside the vagina to absorb the blood. Nowadays, we have tampons made of absorbent cotton wool that usually have a string attached to the end so they can be easily removed. Some tampons come in an applicator to make it easier to insert the tampon into the vagina.

The girls in our classes usually have a lot of questions about tampons. First of all, they want to know if a tampon can 'go up inside you'. The answer is no. The tampon goes through the vaginal opening into the vagina, but it can't get up into the uterus. The passageway between the vagina and uterus, the cervical canal, is too small. The opening to the cervical canal, the cervical os, is no bigger around than the head of a matchstick. It's simply not possible for a tampon to get into the uterus.

The girls in my class also want to know whether a tampon can 'get lost' in the vagina, usually because they've heard some story about a woman who had to go to the doctor because her tampon 'got lost'. A tampon can't really get lost in the vagina, but what can happen is that the string that is attached to the end of the tampon may get drawn up into the vagina, or the tampon may get so far into the vagina that the woman can't feel the string and thinks it's lost. If this should happen to you, relax – it's a simple matter to get it back out again. Just reach your fingers up inside your vagina and pull the tampon out. If it's way up inside there, you may have to squat or bear down as if you were making a bowel movement. This will push the tampon down lower so you can reach it. Most of the time the tampon string dangles out of the vaginal opening and you just pull gently on the string to remove the tampon.

Girls also want to know whether a virgin, a person who has never had sexual intercourse, can use a tampon. The answer is yes. A girl can use a tampon regardless of her age and whether or not she's a virgin. It may be more difficult to use a tampon if you're young or if you have only small openings in your hymen. But your vaginal opening and your hymen are stretchy. If you have trouble getting the tampon in, try using your finger gently to stretch the opening. After a couple of months of gently stretching yourself a few times a week, you should be able to get the tampon in.

The girls in our classes always want to know in exact detail how to get the tampon in. Since the instructions that come with most tampons are not very detailed, we always spend some time talking about how to insert a tampon.

Some women like to insert their tampons while they are standing up; others do it lying down; still others do it in a sitting position. Regardless of which position you use, it helps if you remember that the vagina doesn't go straight up and down, but angles toward the small of the back. If you don't insert the tampon at a slight angle, it's going to hit against the vaginal walls and will be much harder to insert.

Make sure, too, that you're using the right size tampon. Tampons, which can also be purchased in supermarkets and chemists, come in three or four sizes. The smaller sizes may be called mini or regular and the largest is called super. If you're just starting out, you will want the smallest, thinnest tampon, as it will be easier to insert.

If you're using a tampon with an applicator, spend a few minutes experimenting with one of the applicators so you'll know how it works. If your vaginal opening is dry, you might want to lubricate the tampon with a little saliva or K-Y Jelly. Don't use hand or body lotions or face creams to lubricate the tampon; they may contain chemicals that could irritate your vulva and vagina.

It's important to relax because if you are tense, your muscles will tighten up and your vaginal opening will contract.

Be sure to remove the outer wrapping, then gently push the end of the tampon and applicator into your vagina to a depth of 12–25 mm (½–1 in). You may have to hold one portion of the applicator while you push on the plunger of the applicator. Some tampons come on a stick. You push the tampon up into the vagina with the stick. Others don't have any applicator at all; you just push the tampon up inside with your finger.

Now here's the part they never tell you in the instructions. If you don't push the tampon in far enough, it's going to feel uncomfortable. If you put a finger inside your vagina and tighten the muscles in the area by pulling in and up, you'll feel the muscles just inside your vaginal opening tighten. You'll want to get the tampon up above the point where those muscles tighten. Otherwise, the tampon is caught between the muscles and it will feel uncomfortable. If a tampon is inserted properly, you won't be able to feel it once it's in place. And there is no danger of the tampon falling out because the muscles just inside the vaginal opening will prevent it from doing so.

If it hurts to insert the tampon, then use a sanitary towel and try gently stretching your opening with your finger as we explained above. Then try a tampon again.

Like sanitary towels, tampons should be changed every three or four hours. The tampon itself can be flushed down the toilet, but the applicator should be thrown in a rubbish bin, as it could clog the toilet.

Tampons are so comfortable to wear that women sometimes forget they're there and may neglect to remove the last one at the end of their periods. This will eventually cause a foul odour and maybe a discharge, but after you remove the forgotten tampon, this should clear up.

Toxic shock syndrome

While we're on the subject of towels and tampons we should mention *toxic shock syndrome* (TSS for short), which is a disease that has been associated with articles put into the vagina such as tampons, diaphragms, caps and contraceptive sponges, although it can also occur in women who don't use these articles, and in men and children too.

TSS is an infection. It is caused by bacteria that make a poison, or toxin, that gets into the bloodstream. In women the bacteria that cause TSS usually enter the bloodstream through a tiny scratch or abrasion on the wall of the vagina. The disease usually starts with a sudden fever, vomiting and diarrhoea. Sometimes there is an accompanying headache, sore throat or achy muscles. Within forty-eight hours, there may be a dramatic drop in blood pressure so that the person becomes very weak and groggy. A red rash that peels like sunburn may develop.

TSS is very rare and no one in Britain has ever died of it. Although no one is certain what tampons have to do with the disease, most of the women who've contracted it were using tampons at the time.

If you do use tampons, change your tampon every three to four hours. Always change it before you go to bed and first thing when you wake up or, better still, use a sanitary towel at night. If you do develop a sudden fever (over 38.9°C 102°F) and are vomiting, remove the tampon and see your doctor right away.

Is it all right to . . . ?

The girls in our classes always have questions about whether it is all right to do certain things while they're having their periods: is it all right to take a bath or a shower? To wash my hair? To go riding? To take a gym class? To have sexual intercourse? To drink cold drinks or eat cold food?

The answer to all these questions is yes. You can do anything you'd do at any other time of the month. Of course, if you're going swimming during your menstrual period, you'll want to use a tampon instead of a sanitary towel.

You may have heard that you shouldn't shower or bath during your period, but this simply isn't true. In fact, you are apt to perspire more heavily while you're menstruating, so a daily shower or bath may be especially important. You may have heard that cold food or drinks or strenuous exercise would cause a heavier flow, cause your period to last longer or give you period pains. Again, none of this is true. In fact, exercise can sometimes help to relieve period pains.

Douching

Douching is a way of cleansing the vagina by flushing it out. Either water, water and vinegar or a commercial douche preparation can be used to flush the vagina. Some women use a syringe-type douche, which has a nozzle on one end and a bulb, or container, on the other end that holds the water or douche solution. The woman places the nozzle in her vagina and squeezes the bulb so water or douche solution is forced into the vagina. Some women use a bag-type douche, which has a nozzle and a tube that leads

douching (DOOSH-ing)

to a bag (resembling a hot-water bottle), which holds the water or douche solution. When a clip is released, the water or douche solution runs through the tube and into the vagina.

Although some women do douche, it's really not a good idea. For one thing, it isn't necessary. The vagina is self-cleansing. As we've explained elsewhere, the vaginal walls secrete fluids that rinse your vagina and keep it clean naturally. These fluids are slightly acidic, which prevents germs from growing. Douching can change the acid level of your vagina and encourage infections. Commercial douche preparations can irritate your vaginal tissues. Moreover, there's always the chance of introducing germs into the vagina by means of the douche equipment. Excessive force could push germs from the vagina up into the sterile uterus, causing an infection. For these reasons it is not a good idea to douche. Occasionally, a doctor will recommend douching with certain medications as part of the treatment for a vaginal infection. Other than this, though, douching is not recommended.

Period pains

Almost every woman has period pains at some time in her life. They may happen before or during menstrual periods. The pains may be just a mild achy feeling or they may be sharp and severe. Most women have only mild pains and they have them only once in a while. A few women get very severe pains every time they menstruate.

No one knows why women have menstrual pains, but there are a number of theories. One theory holds that pains happen because the uterus contracts rhythmically while we're having our periods to help expel the menstrual blood. Women who are particularly sensitive may feel these contractions as period pains. Another theory holds that the pains are caused by excessive amounts of hormones called *prostaglandins*. Prostaglandins help the uterus contract, and women who have problems with period pains often have more prostaglandins in their bodies than women who aren't troubled by pains.

The theories go on and on. One particularly popular theory says that the pains are 'all in your head'. This theory is often held by doctors, most of whom are men, so maybe it's not surprising that they think 'it's all in your head'. There are plenty of women who believe this theory too, but if you've ever had severe menstrual pains, you know it's not in your head – it's in your abdomen and it hurts.

If you are troubled by period pains, there are some home remedies you can try. Exercises like the ones in Illustration 31 have proved helpful for many women.

Masturbating until you have an orgasm may be helpful, for after you have an orgasm, the blood vessels in the area are less congested and blood flows more freely. Likewise, massaging your lower abdomen or using a heating pad or hot-water bottle may be helpful.

If none of these remedies brings relief, you might try aspirin or one of the non-aspirin (paracetamol) pain relievers. Aspirin may be more effective than a non-aspirin pain reliever because aspirin is an antiprostaglandin, which means it acts against the prostaglandins. There are also aspirin-type medications made especially for menstrual pain. These medications usually contain some caffeine (the stimulant in tea and coffee) as well. Sometimes this combination works where plain aspirin has failed.

If you've tried all these things and are still troubled by period pains, you should see a doctor. Severe pains are sometimes a sign of some underlying medical problem. Also, a doctor can prescribe stronger pain relievers

prostaglandins (prost-uh-GLAN-dins)

EXERCISE 1

Lie flat on the floor with your face forwards and your arms by your sides.

Gradually raise your head and chest without using your arms until your torso is off the floor.

Using your arms, raise your torso further so that your back is arched. Repeat several times.

Illustration 31. Exercises for period pains.

EXERCISE 2

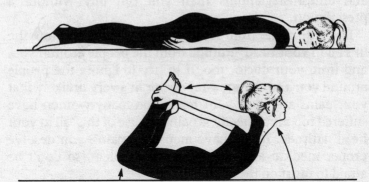

Begin by lying on your stomach. Grab your ankles with both hands, pulling forwards towards the back of your head. Gently rock back and forth. Repeat several times.

EXERCISE 3

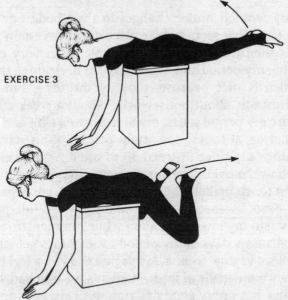

Lie on a coffee table or platform about 0.5–1 m (2–3 ft) off the ground, as shown here. Place your hands on the ground in front of you. Bend your knees and pull your ankles in towards your buttocks. Then, in one smooth, continuous motion, kick your legs out again. Continue until you gradually build up to do it for six minutes.

and antiprostaglandins than you can buy without a prescription.

If you do suffer from severe pains, you may run into the 'it's all in your head' attitude from the people around you, and from your doctor too. If so, try to ignore the people around you and change your doctor. It's very unlikely that your pains are all in your head. Too many women have suffered too much needless pain because of this 'all in your head' attitude. If you have menstrual pains, you deserve proper medical attention for your problem, so don't be afraid to insist on it.

Menstrual changes

Many women notice changes in their bodies or in their emotions that seem to take place during a certain phase of their menstrual cycle. For example, I get very energetic during my period and often have fits of cleaning the house (which is nice because, most of the time, I'm not too enthusiastic about housework). About a week and a half before my period starts, my breasts swell a bit and get very tender or, at times, downright painful. (This started happening only since I turned 30.) I often notice a change in my bowel movements during my period. Sometimes I get a slight touch of diarrhoea; other times I'm constipated for a day or so. I sometimes have mild pains or a full, pressured feeling in my lower abdomen while I'm menstruating. On the first few days of my period I sometimes get what I call the 'lead vagina' feeling. My vagina and vulva feel heavy, as if they were made of lead. (Well, it's not that bad, but 'lead vagina' is a pretty good description.) I always know when I'm about to ovulate because I feel very sexual.

Many of the girls and women we talked to also noticed emotional and physical changes that seemed to be related to their menstrual cycles. Most of these changes happen during their periods or in the week or so before their periods. These are some of the changes you may experience while you are menstruating or just before your period starts.

extra energy
lack of energy or a tired, dragged-out feeling
sudden shifts in moods
tension or anxiety
depression
feelings of well-being
bursts of creativity
a craving for sweets
spots, acne or other skin problems
a particularly clear and rosy glow to the skin
heightened sexual feelings
headaches
vision disturbances
diarrhoea
constipation
swelling of the ankles, wrists, hands or feet
swelling and tenderness of the breasts
swelling of the abdomen
bloated feeling
temporary weight gain (usually 1.5–2.5 kg/ 3–5 lb)
decreased ability to concentrate
increased ability to concentrate
increased appetite
increased thirst
period pains
increased need to urinate
urinary infections
a change in vaginal discharge
nausea
runny nose
sores in the mouth
backache

In some women these changes are very noticeable; in others, they are hardly noticeable at all; and some women don't notice any changes in their bodies or their feelings over the course of their menstrual cycles.

Pre-menstrual tension

Some women regularly experience one or more of the negative menstrual changes listed above during the twelve to sixteen days preceding their menstrual period. Such women are said to have pre-menstrual tension, or PMT. No one is sure what causes PMT. Some doctors think that it is related to vitamin and nutritional deficiencies; others think that it is caused by a hormone imbalance.

Mild forms of PMT are quite widespread. As many as 40 per cent of us experience some PMT symptoms at some time in our lives. It is not unusual, for example, for a woman to have a bloated feeling, spots, swelling of the breasts or other PMT symptoms in the week or so before her period.

If you have mild PMT symptoms, you may find that eliminating sugar, coffee and chocolate from your diet, eating balanced meals with foods rich in vitamin B_6 and magnesium (green vegetables, whole grains, nuts and seeds) and taking a vitamin supplement that includes the B complex vitamins will help alleviate symptoms. Some doctors use hormones to treat PMT, but others are not convinced that hormone treatments are really effective.

If you think you have PMT, you should see your GP to discuss your condition.

Missing a menstrual period

If a woman gets pregnant, she stops having her menstrual period for the nine months that she is pregnant. If she is not breast-feeding she may start having her period again within a month or so after the baby is born, or it may take several months before she starts menstruating again. Women also miss periods as they are going through the menopause. But the menopause, pregnancy and childbirth are not the only reasons why a woman sometimes misses periods.

As we explained earlier, young women who've just started menstruating sometimes skip one or more periods on a regular basis. Even after a woman has been menstruating regularly for a number of years, she may occasionally skip one or more menstrual periods. This is quite normal and isn't anything to worry about.

Crash dieting, extreme malnutrition and anorexia (a condition that affects mainly young women and stops them from eating enough if at all) can also cause missed periods. If you haven't had sexual intercourse with anyone and you miss three periods in a row, it's a good idea to see a doctor. Missing three periods in a row doesn't necessarily mean that there is something wrong with you, but may be a sign that you have a medical problem that needs a doctor's attention. If you have had sexual intercourse and you miss a period, see your doctor *right away*, for you may be pregnant.

Not all women have menstrual periods every twenty-one to thirty-five days. Some women have their periods only once or twice a year; that's just the way their bodies work. But sometimes missing your periods is a sign that something is wrong.

Other menstrual irregularities

There are also other menstrual irregularities that happen from time to time. As we explained earlier, some months your period may be heavier than others. This is quite normal, but sometimes the bleeding is excessive. If you are soaking through a pad or tampon (and we mean literally soaking through, so it's drenched with blood) every hour for an entire day, then it's a good idea to see your doctor.

Sometimes a woman's period doesn't stop. If your period continues for more than a week without showing any signs of slowing down or letting up, once again, you should see your doctor. If you've been having your period for seven days and you're still trickling out a bit of blood, that's nothing to worry about, but if the blood is still coming out as heavily as it was in the beginning of the week, you may have a problem.

Sometimes a woman's periods come too close together. As we explained earlier, travelling, illness, emotional ups and downs can all make your period come earlier or later than usual. But if your period is less than eighteen days or more than thirty-five days apart for three menstrual cycles, it's a good idea to see your doctor.

Some women experience what we call *spotting* between their periods. Spotting is a day or two of very light bleeding. It's not unusual for a woman to spot for a day or two around the time of ovulation. You can figure out whether your bleeding is related to ovulation by keeping track of your menstrual periods (see below) and noting the days when spotting occurs. Count back two weeks from the first day of bleeding of the next cycle. If the spotting occurs around two weeks before each period, it's probably related to ovulation and isn't anything to worry about. If the spotting occurs at other times and continues for more than three cycles, again, consult your doctor.

These are just guidelines to help you decide when to see your doctor about menstrual irregularities. If you feel there's something abnormal about your periods or if you are uncertain, don't hesitate to consult your doctor. Most menstrual irregularities are not serious, but sometimes they can indicate an underlying problem that needs attention, so don't hesitate to get any problems that are bothering you checked out.

Keeping track of your menstrual cycle

It's a good idea to keep a record of your menstrual cycle. That way, you'll learn how your own pattern works and will know about when to expect your next period.

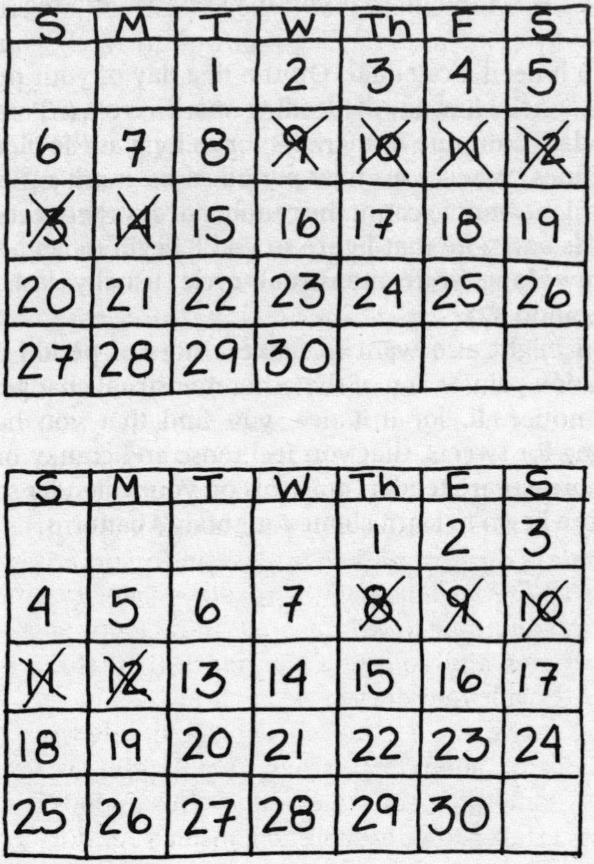

Illustration 32. Recording your periods. To keep track of your periods, use a calendar like this. This girl had her first day of bleeding on the ninth and she continued to bleed for five more days, so she marked these days with Xs. The next cycle began on the eighth of the following month and her period lasted five days, which are marked with Xs. By counting the number of days between the Xs that mark the first day of bleeding, you can determine the length of your cycle. This girl's cycle was twenty-nine days long.

(Remember, though, that you may not be very regular at first.)

You'll need a calendar. On the first day of your period, that is, on the first day of bleeding, mark a cross (X) on your calendar. Continue to mark Xs for as long as the bleeding continues. When your next period starts, mark a X again. You might want to count the number of days between your periods and note that figure so you'll begin to get an idea of how long your menstrual cycle usually lasts (see Illustration 32).

You might also want to make a note of period pains, ovulation pain or any of the other menstrual changes you may notice. If, for instance, you find that you have a craving for sweets, that you feel tense and cranky or that your breasts are tender, note this on your calendar so that you can begin to learn about your body's patterns.

Chapter 8

Puberty in Boys

This book was written for girls, to help them understand how puberty happens in their bodies. But puberty doesn't happen only to girls; it happens to boys, too. Since most girls are curious about boys' bodies, we decided to include a brief chapter on how puberty happens in boys (see Illustration 33).

In some ways puberty in boys is similar to puberty in girls. In both sexes there is a sudden growth spurt and a change in the general shape of the body. Both boys and girls begin to grow pubic hair and other body hair. Girls produce ripe ova for the first time and boys begin to make sperm, the male counterpart of ova. The genital organs of both sexes begin to develop and grow larger. Both boys and girls begin to perspire more and tend to get spots at this time in their lives.

But boys and girls are different, so puberty is a bit different in boys than it is in girls. For one thing, the puberty growth spurt usually happens earlier in girls. The average girl starts the growth spurt about two years before the average boy. But as we have seen, not everyone is average. Some girls start earlier than average, some later. The same is true of boys; some boys will even start the growth spurt before some of the girls their age.

Because boys and girls are different, some of the things that happen in a girl's body during puberty don't happen to boys and vice versa. Obviously, boys don't start having menstrual periods. And some things that happen to boys, such as a deepening and a lowering of the voice, don't happen to girls.

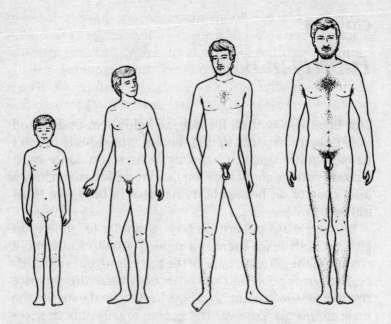

Illustration 33. Boys in puberty. Like girls, boys too go through puberty. They get taller, their shoulders get wider, their bodies more muscular, their genital organs develop and they begin to grow hair on their chests, arms, legs, genitals, underarms and faces.

Circumcision

Illustration 1 on page 23 shows the sex organs on the outside of a man's body. You might want to take another look at that picture before reading this chapter so that you'll remember the names of the various parts of the male genitals.

Illustration 34 on page 154 shows a penis that has a foreskin. The foreskin is a flap or sheath of skin that covers the glans of the penis. The foreskin is loose and can be stretched or slid down the shaft of the penis so that the glans is exposed. Some males do not have a foreskin because they've been *circumcised*. *Circumcision* is an operation in which the foreskin is cut away. In Western countries, when a boy is circumcised, the operation is usually done shortly after birth, but it may also be done when he is older. When an older boy or a man is circumcised, it is usually because of a medical problem. For example, in some males, the foreskin becomes adherent, or 'stuck', and must be circumcised.

Sometimes a boy is circumcised at birth for religious reasons. For instance, some Jewish and Muslim parents have their boy babies circumcised because it is a custom in their religions. In the past some doctors felt that males who weren't circumcised would be more likely to get certain diseases, so they circumcised all baby boys, even if it wasn't a custom in their parents' religion. Nowadays we know that this isn't true. So unless there are religious reasons, most male babies are not circumcised.

The only difference between circumcised and uncircumcised males is that circumcised males don't have a foreskin; otherwise, their penises look, feel and work the same way.

The penis and scrotum

The penis is made of spongy tissue. There is a hollow tube, the urethra, that runs down the inside of the penis. When a male urinates, the urine passes through the urethra and comes out through the opening at the tip of the glans. Sperm travel through this same tube and come out at this same opening when a man ejaculates (a valve on the bladder prevents sperm and urine from coming out at the same time).

Underneath the penis lies the scrotum, the skin sac that

circumcision (sir-come- SIH-zhun)
circumcised (SIR-come-sized)

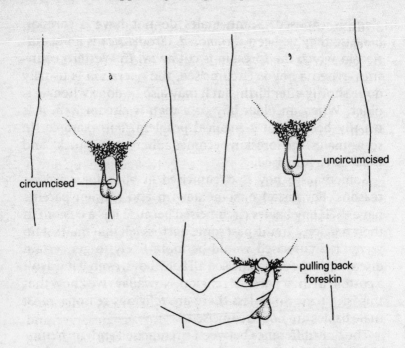

Illustration 34. Circumcised and uncircumcised penis.

holds the two testicles. The testicles are very sensitive and it can be very painful if they are hit.

Five stages of genital development

The appearance of a boy's penis and scrotum changes as he goes through puberty. During childhood a boy's scrotum is drawn up close to his body. As he goes through puberty the scrotum begins to get looser and to hang down. When a man or boy is cold or frightened or feeling sexual, his scrotum may get tighter and draw up close to his body for a while. The penis and scrotum also get larger as a boy goes through puberty and pubic hair begins to grow around the genitals.

Just as doctors have divided the breast and pubic hair development of girls into five stages, so they have divided the growth of male genital organs into five stages (see Illustration 35).

Stage 1 starts at birth and continues until the boy starts Stage 2. The penis, scrotum and testicles don't change very much during this stage, but there is a slight increase in overall size.

In Stage 2 the testicles start to grow and to hang down more. One testicle may hang lower than the other. The skin of the scrotum darkens and gets rougher in texture. The penis gets somewhat larger.

During Stage 3 the penis gets longer and somewhat wider. The testes and scrotum continue to get larger, and the skin of the penis and scrotum may continue to get darker.

By Stage 4 the penis has become considerably longer and wider. The testes and scrotum have also become larger, and the skin of the penis and scrotum may still be getting darker.

Stage 5 is the adult stage in which the penis has reached its full width and length, and the testicles and scrotum are fully developed.

A boy's genitals may start developing when he is as young as 9 years of age, but some boys don't start until they are 15 or older. The average boy starts puberty after his eleventh or twelfth birthday. But, of course, not all boys are average, so some start earlier and others later. Most boys take about three or four years to go from Stage 2 to Stage 5, but some boys take less than two years, and others take five or more years. Starting early or starting late doesn't have any effect on how long it takes a boy to go through these stages. Some early starters develop quickly, others grow slowly. The same is true for late starters: some grow quickly, others slowly. Starting early or starting late doesn't

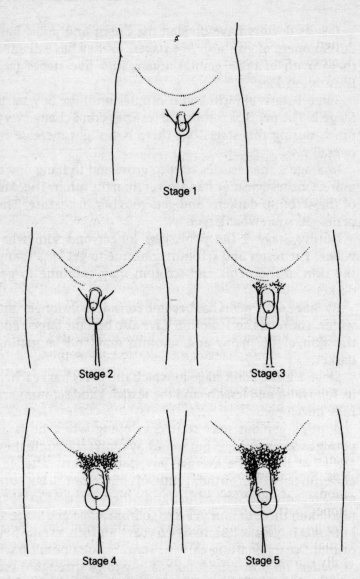

Illustration 35. The five stages of male genital development.

Stage 1

Stage 2

Stage 3

Stage 4

Stage 5

have anything to do with how large a boy's penis will be when he's fully grown. Late starters may end up with either large or small penises, and the same is true for early starters. Just as breast size doesn't have anything to do with how feminine or womanly a female is, so penis size doesn't have anything to do with how masculine a male is.

Pubic hair and other body hair

Boys also start to grow pubic hair as they go through puberty. Boy's pubic hair is similar to girl's pubic hair. At first there are only a few, slightly curly hairs, but as puberty continues, the hairs get curlier and darker, and there are more of them. The pubic hair first starts to grow around the base of the penis. Then a few hairs begin to grow on the scrotum. As a boy gets older, pubic hair starts to grow on his lower belly and up toward his tummy button, or navel. It may also grow down around his anus. It may start growing out onto his thighs. The pubic hairs usually don't start to grow until after the testes have started developing.

Boys also start to grow hair in their armpits during puberty. This usually happens about a year or so after the pubic hair has started growing, but some boys start growing hair under their arms before they have any pubic hair.

During puberty boys also grow hair on their faces. The hair usually starts growing on the corners of the upper lips. Sideboards may start to grow at the same time. The moustache continues to grow and then hair grows on the upper part of the cheek and just below the middle of the lower lip. Finally, it grows on the chin. Hair doesn't usually start growing on the chin until a boy's genitals are fully developed. For most boys, facial hair starts growing between the ages of 14 and 18, but it may start earlier or later.

The hair on a boy's arms and legs tends to get darker and

thicker during puberty. Some boys grow hair on their chests and back too. Some develop quite a bit of hair on their chests; others have very little.

Changing shape and size

Girls' bodies get curvier during puberty and boys' bodies get more muscular. Their shoulders get broader and their arms and legs get thicker. Boys also have a growth spurt during puberty. Their growth spurt is more dramatic than girls'. It lasts longer and, on the average, boys grow taller than girls. It usually happens about two years later than girls' growth spurt. Generally, it doesn't happen until their penises have started to grow.

Skin changes

Like girls', boys' skin also begins to change during puberty. The oil glands become more active and most boys develop some spots. Boys, too, begin to perspire more heavily during puberty and their perspiration may have a different odour. Like girls, some boys develop purplish marks on the skin that usually appear on the hips and buttocks. As they grow older, these marks usually fade.

Breasts

Boys' breasts don't, of course, go through the same kind of changes that girls' do during puberty, but a boy's areola does get wider during puberty. Most boys' breasts swell a bit during puberty and, like girls, boys sometimes notice a feeling of tenderness or soreness in their breasts at this time. This swelling usually starts during Stage 2 or 3 of genital development. It may happen to both breasts or to only one. It may last only a few months or a year, but it may continue for two years or even longer. Eventually, though, it goes away.

Voice

Boys' voices change during puberty, getting lower and deeper. While their voices are changing, some boys' voices have a tendency to 'break', to shift suddenly from a low pitch to a high, squeaky pitch. This breaking may last for only a few months, but sometimes it goes on for a year or more.

Erections

In Chapter 1, on page 27, we talked about erections. When a man or a boy has an erection, blood rushes to the penis and fills up the spongy tissues there. Muscles at the base of the penis tighten up so the blood stays in the penis for a while, making it feel hard. During an erection the penis gets longer and wider and, usually, darker, and it stands erect, away from the body as in Illustration 36.

Males get erections throughout their lives, even when they are tiny babies. Stroking or touching the penis or scrotum can cause an erection. Getting sexually excited and having sexual fantasies can cause an erection. Males can also get erections even if the penis and scrotum aren't being touched or rubbed and even if they aren't feeling or thinking about anything sexual. Some males wake up in the morning with erections. Having to urinate will cause erections sometimes.

During puberty boys are apt to get erections more frequently. As they go through puberty, most boys start to experience what we call 'spontaneous erections'. Spontaneous erections are erections that happen all by

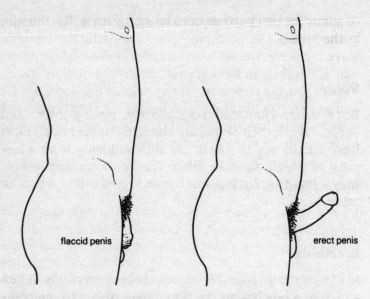

flaccid penis

erect penis

Illustration 36. Flaccid and erect penis. When a man or boy has an erection the soft, spongy tissue inside the penis fills with blood. The penis gets stiff and hard and stands out from his body.

themselves, without the penis or scrotum being touched, and even if a boy isn't having sexual thoughts or feelings.

Spontaneous erections can be very embarrassing for a boy. They may happen when he is in school, at home, walking down the street or just about any time or place. It's a popular myth in our society that girls are much more embarrassed by the changes that happen in their bodies during puberty – growing breasts, having their periods and so on – than boys. But the boys in our classes had a lot of stories to tell about getting spontaneous erections and worrying that the people around them would notice the bulge in their trousers from the erection.

When a male has an erection, one of two things may

happen. The erection may go away all by itself. The muscles at the base of the penis may relax, allowing the blood to leave the penis, so that it gets smaller and soft again. Or he may masturbate or have sexual intercourse until he has an orgasm. During an orgasm the muscles of the penis release and contract rhythmically, and shortly after the orgasm the muscles at the base of the penis relax, allowing the blood to leave and the penis to get soft again.

Sperm and ejaculation

Like girls, boys begin to make their first ripe seeds, the sperm, during puberty. The cross-section in Illustration 37 shows the inside of the penis and scrotum. The sperm are made inside tiny little tubes that are coiled up inside the testicle. They then travel through these tubes to the *epididymis*, which is a sort of storage area or compartment. The sperm spend about six weeks in the epididymis, where they finish ripening. They travel from the epididymis through a tube called the *vas deferens* to another set of storage compartments located outside the testicle. These storage compartments are called the *ampulla*.

Just at the lower end of the ampulla the vas deferens connects to the *seminal vesicles*. A fluid called seminal fluid is made in the seminal vesicles. Seminal fluid and sperm mixed together make semen. The seminal fluid enriches the sperm, enabling them to swim faster. The prostate gland also adds some fluid to the mixture. When a male ejaculates, muscles of the vas deferens and prostate gland contract to force the semen out of his body through the urethra. Urine from the bladder also travels down this tube, but urine and semen can't travel through the urethra at the

epididymis (eh-pih-DIH-dih-miss)   *ampulla* (am-PUL-ah)
vas (VAZ)   *seminal* (SE-min-ul)
deferens (DEAF-eh-renz)   *vesicles* (VE-seh-kuls)

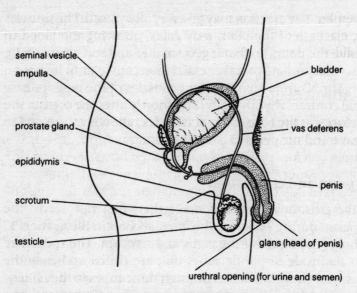

seminal vesicle

ampulla

prostate gland

epididymis

scrotum

testicle

bladder

vas deferens

penis

glans (head of penis)

urethral opening (for urine and semen)

Illustration 37. Cross-section of the penis, scrotum and testicle.

same time. There is a little valve on the bladder that closes off the bladder any time the semen is about to come out. Just as having her first menstrual period is a landmark for a girl going through puberty, so having the first ejaculation is a landmark for a boy.

A boy may have his first ejaculation while he is masturbating. Many of the boys in our classes had their first ejaculations in this way. Others have their first ejaculation in their sleep. This is known as having a wet dream. The boy wakes up and finds one or two tablespoonfuls of creamy, white liquid on his stomach or his bedclothes. If he hasn't been prepared for it, having a wet dream can come as quite a surprise.

Wet dreams are one of the male body's ways of relieving the testicles of a build-up of sperm. If a boy masturbates, then he may not have wet dreams, for masturbating until he ejaculates is another of the body's ways of relieving the build-up of sperm in the testicles.

Testicular self-examination

Before we end this chapter, there's one other topic we'd like to mention — testicular self-examination. Just as it's important for females to examine their breasts regularly for signs of cancer or other medical problems, so it's important for males to regularly examine their testicles for signs of cancer or other medical problems.

Since you're a female and don't have testicles, you won't, of course, have to practise testicular self-examination. But we've included the explanation of testicular self-exam in Illustration 38 because you may want to share this information with your brother, father or grandfather and encourage him to examine his testicles. And if some day you marry or have a regular sexual partner, you can encourage your loved one to practise this important habit.

As you will learn in reading the caption to Illustration 38, a testicular exam involves feeling the testicles for the presence of lumps or other abnormalities. It's important to note that, just as most lumps that females discover while examining their breasts are not cancerous, so most of the lumps males discover while examining their testicles are not cancerous. Most lumps in the scrotum are the result of non-cancerous cysts, that is, collections of fluid. Some of these non-cancerous cysts will go away by themselves; others require an operation. Even though most lumps are not cancerous and even though some will go away by themselves, it's important that any male who discovers a lump, bump or other abnormality in his testicles or scrotum sees a doctor *right away* in order to have the problem evaluated.

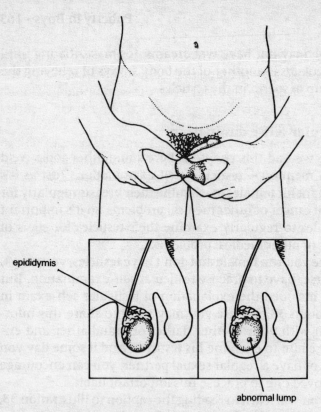

epididymis

abnormal lump

**Illustration 38. Testicular self-examination. Most testicular
cancers are discovered by men themselves. Since testicular
cancers found early and treated promptly have an excellent
chance for cure, learning to examine your testes properly can
help save your life. It doesn't take much effort and you have to
do it only once a month.**

It's best to examine your scrotum immediately after a hot
bath or shower. The scrotal skin is most relaxed at this time and
the testicles can be felt more easily. Examine each testicle
gently with the fingers of both hands. Put your index and
middle fingers on the underside of the testicle and your thumb
on the top. Roll your testicle gently between your thumb and
fingers, feeling for a small lump about the size of a pea. Repeat
this procedure with the other testicle.

You should learn what the epididymis feels like at the back of
the testicle so that you won't confuse it with an abnormality. If
you do find anything abnormal, it will most often be a firm area
on the front or side of the testicle.

Since cancer is easier to cure when it's discovered in its earliest stages, testicular examination, like breast examination, is an important and even life-saving habit. Unfortunately, very few boys or men examine their testicles regularly or even know about it.

Of course, it may be somewhat embarrassing to talk to your father, grandfather or brother about testicular examination. But by showing him Illustration 38 and asking him to read this important information, you might just be saving a life. So even if you feel a bit embarrassed or shy about it, we'd none the less encourage you to share this information with your loved ones.

Chapter 9

Sexual Intercourse, Reproduction, Contraception, Sexually Transmitted Diseases and Other Health Issues

The changes that take place in your body during puberty happen because your body is getting ready for a time in your life when you may decide to have a baby. Of course, just because you're physically able to reproduce (that is, to make a baby) doesn't mean you're mature enough to become a parent yet. But your body is getting ready for the time when you may want to start a family of your own.

Because puberty is a time when the body is preparing itself for reproduction, topics like pregnancy and childbirth naturally come up in our classes. Since human beings reproduce by sexual intercourse, intercourse is another subject that we always spend a good deal of time talking about in class. When we start talking about reproduction and intercourse, the boys and girls always start asking questions about *contraception* (birth control), sexually transmitted diseases (STDs, also called *venereal* diseases or VD) and other reproductive health matters. In fact, the young people in our classes have *lots* and *lots* of questions about all of these subjects. You may have many of the same questions, so in this chapter we're going to talk about these

contraception (KON-tre-SEP-shun)
venereal (veh-NEAR-eh-ul)

things and try to answer your questions. Unfortunately, there just isn't room in this book to cover these topics fully or answer all your questions. However, we'd like to say at least a bit about each of these subjects and to answer some of the most commonly asked questions. And at the end of the chapter we'll suggest some ways in which you can go about finding answers to any other questions you may have.

Sexual intercourse

This is a subject about which the boys and girls in our classes are *very* curious. We explained a bit about sexual intercourse back in Chapter 1, on pages 27–8. You may want to take another look at those pages before reading the questions and answers in this section. Because they are, quite naturally, curious about sexual intercourse, the young people in our classes ask questions like the ones listed in the next few pages.

I don't quite understand how the penis fits into the vagina when a man and woman have sex. Could you explain or show us a picture?

There's an old saying that, 'A picture is worth a thousand words', and we agree. So we've included Illustration 39, which shows an erect penis fitting into the vagina in just one of the many positions a couple may use for intercourse.

What's the first thing you should do when you have sex? Could you explain to us, step by step, what people do when they're having sex?

Sexual intercourse isn't something that has specific rules you have to follow. When children go out to the playground after school, they don't have a specific set of directions. No one tells them that first they must take five

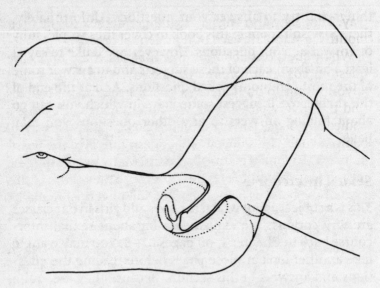

Illustration 39. Penis in vagina.

steps, then do three somersaults, then swing on the swing for five minutes, then climb to the top of the bars. They just go out there and play and do whatever they feel like doing.

By saying this, we don't mean to suggest that having sexual intercourse is like going out to play (although there can be a certain playfulness when two people are having sex). The point we're trying to make is that there aren't any specific rules or instructions or a 'right way' to have sexual intercourse.

Some people like to hug and kiss a lot first. Some like to French kiss (put their tongues into each other's mouth while kissing); others don't like this. Touching, kissing and hugging usually give people warm, excited, sexual feelings. The couple may then touch, rub or caress each other's genitals or breasts before intercourse, which is called foreplay. They may also engage in oral-genital sex (using their mouths to stimulate each other's genital organs).

When questions about oral-genital sex come up in the question box, many young people say, 'Ugh, why would anyone want to do that?' We explain that many couples find this a very pleasurable way of enjoying each other's bodies and a special way of being close. It's also a way of being sexual with someone that doesn't involve the possibility of the woman getting pregnant. Many people find the idea of oral-genital sex revolting because they think of this area of the body as being 'dirty' or full of germs. Actually, though, this area of our bodies isn't any dirtier or more germ-laden than other parts.

Another thing that bothers some young people when they hear about oral-genital sex is that they think it's something you have to do when you have sex. This isn't true. Some couples enjoy oral-genital sex and often include it in their love-making. Others have religious or moral objections to it or don't feel comfortable with it, so they rarely or never do it. When you grow up, you may decide that it's something you'd like to try or you may decide it's not something you ever want to try. It's normal if you do and normal if you don't. Like everything else about sex, you're the one who decides.

Is sex painful for women?

No, sex isn't painful for women or for men either. In fact, sex usually feels quite wonderful, provided of course that the two partners are considerate of each other's feelings.

As we've explained, the penis gets thicker and wider when it's erect, and the vagina is a very stretchy, elastic organ and easily expands to accommodate an erect penis. When a man is sexually aroused ('turned on'), his penis produces a small amount of lubricating fluid. When a woman is sexually aroused, her vagina also produces lubricating fluid. These fluids help the penis slide into the vagina comfortably. In addition, the upper portion of a woman's vagina also 'balloons out', or expands a bit, when she's sexually aroused, so there's no discomfort when the penis goes into the vagina.

If, however, a couple try to have sex before the woman is fully aroused and her vagina has begun to lubricate and expand, having sex could be uncomfortable. Trying to force a penis into a dry, unlubricated vagina can, in fact, be painful. Since men sometimes become aroused more quickly than women, it's important for the couple to make sure that the woman has enough foreplay so she is also ready and well-lubricated before the man puts his penis into the vagina. If necessary, a couple can use K-Y Jelly to increase lubrication and make sex more comfortable.

Although sex isn't usually painful, when a woman has sex for the first time (or for the first several times), she sometimes experiences some discomfort or pain. This may happen for any number of reasons. One reason is that she may be nervous, which makes her tighten her vaginal muscles and decreases the lubrication in her vagina. Another reason is that the couple may be nervous and unsure and may be rushing things, trying to put the penis into the vagina before the woman is lubricated enough. Also, when a woman is a virgin (a person who's never had sex), her vaginal opening or the opening in her hymen may be rather small and tight. If the couple don't take their time, don't go slowly and gently, but force things, the hymen or vaginal opening can be painfully stretched or torn. This is why it is important for a couple to begin their sex lives in a relaxed, slow and gentle manner.

How does it feel to have sex?

We get asked this question a lot and to tell you the truth, we find it hard to answer. It's very difficult to explain in words how it feels. Also, sex feels differently to different people. But if people are considerate of each other's feelings, if they are relaxed and take their time, if they tell or show each other what kind of touching and rubbing feels good to their bodies, then sexual intercourse feels good. In fact, most people agree that it feels wonderful.

Of course, how it feel depends a lot on the situation. If you're having sex with someone you love and the two of you both feel comfortable about what you're doing, then sex can bring pleasure, fun, passion and joy. There's a rush of good feeling when you share a good sexual experience with someone you truly care about. Sex can be a very special way of being close with someone and of discovering more about each other. But sex can also bring sadness and emotional pain. If you don't truly care about each other or you don't feel it's right for you to be having sex, intercourse may not be a pleasant feeling at all. So, as we say, it depends a lot on the situation. If you're wondering about how you'd know if it was right for you, you might be interested in reading the section called 'Making decisions about how to handle your sexual and romantic feelings' in the next chapter.

Pregnancy and childbirth

Whenever we discuss sexual intercourse, questions about pregnancy and childbirth naturally come up. Here are just some of the questions we've been asked.

Are there only certain times of the month when a girl can get pregnant and if so, when?

A woman's ovum can be fertilized only during the twenty-four hours (sometimes experts say forty-eight hours) immediately after she's ovulated. It's only in this first day or so after the ovum has popped off the ovary that the ovum is at the exact ripeness to allow for fertilization. After that, the egg is 'overripe' and cannot be fertilized. Within a few days, it will break down and disintegrate completely.

Because there's only, at most, forty-eight hours during which a woman's ovum can be fertilized during each menstrual cycle, it would seem to be a pretty easy thing to avoid getting pregnant: just don't have sex during those forty-eight hours. Unfortunately, it's not that simple. First of all, sperm can stay alive in the woman's body for three to five days. So let's say a woman ovulated on the tenth day of the month. If she'd had sex on the seventh and the man had ejaculated, the sperm could still be in her body, alive and well, waiting for the ovum when it popped off the ovary on the tenth.

Also, there's no way to predict exactly when a woman is going to ovulate. A woman usually ovulates twelve to sixteen days before the first day of bleeding of her next menstrual period. So we can count backwards and get an idea of when she ovulated in the previous cycle. But we can't tell when she'll ovulate in the next cycle because, as we've explained, women's menstrual cycles aren't always regular. One month a woman's cycle may last twenty-eight days, the next month thirty-two and the next twenty-one. Even women who have fairly regular periods – say every twenty-seven or twenty-eight days – will occasionally have longer or shorter than usual periods. There's just no way of telling ahead of time exactly when a woman will ovulate. So, even though there are only certain times of the month when a female can get pregnant, it's impossible to tell exactly when that time will come.

I heard that if you have sex only during your period, you won't get pregnant; is this true?

No, this isn't true. Females can and do become pregnant from having sex while they're having their menstrual period. A female whose period lasts for longer than seven days is more likely to get pregnant from having sex during her period. But even a female whose period lasts seven days or less could get pregnant from having sex during this time.

Here's an example of how this might work. Say Mary starts her period on 3 June. She bleeds for seven days, until 9 June. She has sex on 8 June, while she's still bleeding. Her next period starts on 24 June. Altogether, twenty-one days have elapsed between the first day of bleeding of her period on 3 June and the first day of bleeding for her next period on 24 June. By counting back twelve to sixteen days from 24 June, we can figure that she probably ovulated between 8 and 12 June. Mary was still bleeding on the 8th; she may have ovulated on the 8th; she had sex on the 8th. So, there's a good chance she'd get pregnant even though she was having her period.

Even if Mary didn't ovulate until the 9th or 10th, she still might get pregnant because the sperm can stay alive for at least three days. And if the experts who say sperm can stay alive for five days are right, she might have got pregnant from having sex on the 8th even if she didn't ovulate until the 12th.

Or, to take another example, let's say Susan has a period on 1 August. She bleeds for seven days, until 7 August. She has sex on the seventh day, on 7 August, while she's still bleeding. Her next period starts on 28 August, which would mean she'd had a twenty-seven-day cycle. So she may have ovulated as early as 12 August. She stopped bleeding on the 7th. But if the experts who say that sperm can stay alive for five days are right, there might still be some live sperm in her body from the time she had sex on 7 August. Therefore, when Susan ovulated on 12 August, she could become pregnant from having had sex on the 7th while she was still bleeding.

It is, then, possible for a female to get pregnant from having sex during her menstrual period.

How old does a girl have to be before she can get pregnant? Could a girl get pregnant before she's even had her first period?

When a girl reaches puberty and begins to ovulate and menstruate, she is physically capable of becoming pregnant. It would be next-to-impossible for a girl to get pregnant *before* she'd ever had her first period. The only way this could occur would be if a girl happened to have sexual intercourse around the time that her ovary was getting ready to release its very first ripe ovum. The ovum could be fertilized by a sperm and, instead of having her first period two weeks later as she normally would, the girl could be pregnant.

But even if a girl did have sex right round the time of her first ovulation, it is highly unlikely she'd get pregnant because a girl's first ovum is really a sort of 'practice' ovum. It isn't usually fully mature, so it probably couldn't be fertilized. Thus, although it's possible, it's *highly unlikely* that a girl could get pregnant before she's had her first period.

Can a girl get pregnant the first time she has sex?

A lot of young people think that a girl can't get pregnant the first time she has sex. This is not true. Once a girl has begun to ovulate, to produce a ripe ovum each month or so, she can get pregnant, even if she's had sex only one time.

Does a girl have to have sex to get pregnant?

If a sperm meets an ovum and fertilizes it, a girl (or woman) can become pregnant. The most common way that a sperm and an ovum meet is when a couple has sexual intercourse round the time of ovulation and the male ejaculates sperm into the vagina. But if the sperm were ejaculated even near the opening of the vagina, it would be possible for a sperm to swim into the vagina, up into the uterus and to the Fallopian tube, where it could fertilize the ovum. Even if a male were to pull his penis out of the vagina and ejaculate in such a way that none of the sperm got into the vagina or near the vaginal opening, pregnancy might still occur. As a male gets sexually aroused and his penis gets erect, a couple of drops of fluid may appear at the tip of his penis. This fluid may contain some sperm, and these sperm could cause pregnancy.

We should also mention that a female can't get pregnant from kissing, masturbating herself, swimming in a pool, sitting on someone's lap or sitting on a toilet seat.

With the exception of special medical procedures doctors use to help women who are having problems getting pregnant, there are no ways in which a female can become pregnant other than the ones we've mentioned here.

How old is a woman before she's too old to have a baby?

Women stop having babies when they've gone through the menopause. The menopause is a time in a woman's life when her ovaries stop producing a ripe ovum each month and she stops having her menstrual periods. The menopause usually happens between the ages of 45 and 55, although it does happen earlier or later than this for some women.

As far as we know, the oldest woman who ever had a baby was a 56-year-old grandmother from Glendale, California. Although her periods were coming only once in a while, the woman had not yet gone through the menopause. She had sexual intercourse and, much to her surprise, became pregnant. She gave birth to a normal, healthy baby.

Why are some babies girls and some boys?

The sex of the baby depends on the father's sperm. Some sperm have what scientists call an 'x factor', which means they are capable of uniting with an ovum and making a female baby. Other sperm have a 'y factor', which means that they are capable of uniting with an ovum and making a male baby. If a y-factor sperm fertilizes the ovum, the baby will be a boy. If an x-factor sperm fertilizes the ovum, the baby will be a girl.

How long is a woman pregnant before she has a baby?

A woman is usually pregnant for about nine months. However, sometimes pregnancy can last for a little longer or a little less than nine months. If the baby isn't born by the end of nine months, the doctor will carefully watch the woman for a few weeks or so. If the baby still isn't born, the doctor may give the woman some medication that will make her have the baby because it isn't healthy for the baby to stay in the uterus too long. But this is unusual and most babies are born by the end of, at most, ten months.

Sometimes a pregnancy will last for less than nine months. If the baby is born at the end of only eight months or earlier, we say it is 'premature' or 'pre-term'. Premature babies sometimes need special medical care, and if a baby is born too prematurely, before six months or so, its chances of surviving are much lower.

What happens when a baby is born?

When a baby is ready to be born, the mother goes into what we call 'labour'. During labour the muscles of the mother's uterus begin to contract rhythmically and the mother feels a cramping sensation. At first the contractions aren't very strong and come only once in a while. As labour continues, the contractions become stronger and stronger and come more often. At some point during labour or childbirth the *amniotic* sac, the bag of fluids inside which the baby grows, breaks open and the woman feels a gushing or leaking of fluid from her vagina. This is often called the 'breaking of the waters'. If the amniotic sac doesn't break on its own, the doctor will break it.

During labour the cervix begins to dilate (open up). When the cervix is fully dilated and the contractions are strong and regular, the force of the contractions begin to push the baby out of the uterus, through the cervix, through the vagina and out through the vaginal opening. Most babies are born head first, but some babies come out feet first or with some other part of the baby coming first.

The average length of time for labour with a woman's first baby is about twelve to fourteen hours, and about seven hours with her subsequent pregnancies. However, some women have shorter or longer labours than this. Doctors usually tell women to come to hospital when the contractions are coming regularly, every five minutes. Once the contractions are coming this regularly, it will usually be at least several more hours before the baby is born, but some women have very short labours and occasionally you will hear of a baby being born in a car on the way to the hospital. Sometimes, a woman will have some contractions in the week or so before the baby is born, but this is pre-labour and isn't considered real labour.

For some women labour and childbirth are very painful; for others there is little or no pain. For most women there is some discomfort, for the contractions have to be very strong in order to push the baby out. Some women practise

amniotic (AM-knee-OT-ik)

certain exercises during pregnancy and use breathing techniques during labour that help control the pain. If the pain is too intense, the woman may choose to have an anaesthetic that numbs her from the waist down so she doesn't feel the pain.

Once labour has progressed to the point where the cervix is fully dilated (opened to about 100 mm/4 in), the 'pushing stage' begins. During this stage the mother, if she hasn't been anaesthetized, can help to bring the baby out by pushing along with the contractions. Even if she can't help push, the contractions alone are usually enough to push the baby out into the world. This pushing stage usually lasts for one to three hours with a first pregnancy and for about half an hour with subsequent pregnancies, but it may be shorter or longer than this.

During the pushing stage, the baby begins to move out of the uterus and through the cervix into the vagina. When the entire top of the baby's head is visible at the vaginal opening, it usually takes only a few more contractions to push the baby entirely out into the world.

When a baby is born, it has a cord, known as the *umbilical cord*, attached to its tummy. The other end of this cord is attached to the *placenta*. The placenta is a special organ that develops inside the uterus during pregnancy to bring blood and nourishment from the mother to the baby. The placenta usually comes out within a half-hour after the baby. The doctor then cuts the cord and disposes of it and the placenta. The cord is cut within a short distance of the baby's tummy and is clamped or tied. By the time the baby is a couple of weeks old, the cord above the clamp or knot will have dried up and fallen off by itself.

After the birth, the doctor or nurse checks the baby and may clean it up a bit before giving it to its mother to hold.

umbilical (um-BILL-i-KUL)   *placenta* (pla-SEN-ta)

The boys and girls in our classes get a big kick out of hearing about their own births. You might ask your mother to tell you about her labour with you.

What is a Caesarean section?

If for one reason or another a baby can't be born in the normal way, the doctor does an operation called a *Caesarean section*. The woman is anaesthetized so she can't feel anything from her waist down. Then the doctor makes an incision in her abdomen and uterus and removes the baby from her body by lifting it out through the incision. Afterwards, the incision is sutured shut. Babies born by Caesarean section are usually perfectly healthy.

There are a number of reasons why a baby might have to be born by Caesarean section. For example, labour may be taking so long that the baby is getting worn out and its heartbeat is slowing down. Or the baby might be in a position that would make normal delivery difficult or impossible. The woman's cervix might not be dilating properly or her contractions might be too weak to push the baby out. For these or other reasons the doctor might need to do a Caesarean section.

What is an embryo? What's a foetus?

After an ovum has been fertilized and plants itself in the uterus, it begins the nine-month-long process of developing into a baby. For the first three months it is referred to as an *embryo*. After three months, it is called a *foetus*.

What is a miscarriage? What is a still birth?

When an embryo or foetus dies, it is expelled from the mother's uterus and this is called a miscarriage. Most

Caesarean (si- ZAIR-ee-an)   *foetus* (FEE-tus)
embryo (EM-bree-oh)   *miscarriage* (miss- CARE-ij)

miscarriages happen during the first three months of pregnancy. It is unusual for a woman to miscarry after three months, but it does happen. Doctors aren't always sure why a miscarriage has happened, but usually the embryo or foetus has a defect or problem in its development that makes it impossible for it to survive. Having a miscarriage doesn't usually affect a woman's chances of having a normal baby in the future.

Still birth means that the baby is born dead. In some cases the baby has died during the birth process; in other cases the baby has died in the womb before birth. Sometimes the doctor can pin-point a defect in the baby that caused the death, but at other times the reason for the still birth remains a mystery. Fortunately, miscarriages after the third month of pregnancy and still births are rare. Most women have normal pregnancies and give birth to healthy babies.

What are birth defects and why do they happen?

Sometimes babies are born with physical problems or handicaps, such as blindness, brain damage, heart or lung problems or deformed limbs. Because these problems are present at birth they are called birth defects. They may be caused by such things as defects in the ovum or sperm, problems inherited from the mother or father, the mother being exposed to harmful drugs or X-rays during pregnancy, a disease the mother has during pregnancy, premature birth or problems with the baby not getting enough oxygen immediately after birth. There are also other, less common causes, and sometimes the cause of a birth defect is not known. Fortunately, birth defects are rare. Most babies are born completely healthy.

With all this talk about miscarriage, still births and birth defects, you may be feeling a little worried, especially if your mother or someone else you know is pregnant. But, as we explain to the boys and girls in our classes, the chances of these things happening is *very* small. A pregnant woman and her baby would be *much* more likely to be injured in a car accident than to have any of these problems. So, please relax, knowing that pregnancy and childbirth are normal, natural events, that they almost always go perfectly well and that babies are almost always born perfectly healthy!

How do twins happen? Why don't twins always look alike? If a woman has twins, do they both come out at the same time?

Twins can happen in one of two ways: either there are two fertilized ova or there is one fertilized ovum that splits into two (see Illustration 40).

Usually a woman's ovaries produce only one ripe ovum a month. Occasionally, though, a woman will produce two ripe ova at the same time. If both of these ova are fertilized and plant themselves in the lining of the uterus, the woman will have twins. Twins that grow from two separate ova, fertilized by two separate sperm, are called *fraternal* twins. One may be a boy and one a girl, or they both may be the same sex. They won't necessarily look alike.

fraternal (frah-TUR-nul)

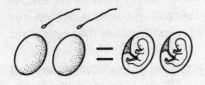

Sometimes a woman will produce two ripe ova the same month. If each of these ova is fertilized by sperm, the woman will have fraternal twins.

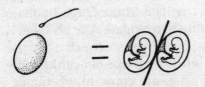

At other times, a sperm may fertilize a single ripe ovum. Then, after fertilization, the ovum splits into two, and the woman will have identical twins.

Illustration 40. Twins.

The other type of twins are called *identical* twins. Identical twins happen when the fertilized ovum splits into two shortly after fertilization. No one knows why this happens. Twins that come from the same ovum and sperm look almost exactly alike and are always the same sex.

When twins are born, one comes out first and the other comes out within a few minutes. In some cases it takes more than a few minutes for the second twin to be born; there have been times when it took a whole day. But, usually, twins are born within a few minutes of each other.

What about triplets?
What are the most babies a woman ever had at one time?

Triplets (three babies), quadruplets (four), quintuplets (five), sextuplets (six), septuplets (seven) and octuplets (eight) happen much less frequently than twins.

Once you start getting more than three babies at a time, the chances of all the babies surviving is lower. Because there are so many of them, they're smaller than average and they're usually born prematurely; that is, before they've had a chance to develop fully. As far as we know, the largest number of babies born at one time is twelve, but not all of them survived; the largest number that ever lived was eight or possibly nine.

We're not sure of the exact number because it is always changing. Nowadays there are drugs, called fertility drugs, that doctors give to women who haven't been able to get pregnant because they don't ovulate. These drugs stimulate the ovary and cause the woman to ovulate. The problem is that they can stimulate the ovaries so much that the woman produces not one but several ripe ova at the same time. Newer and stronger drugs are constantly being developed. As a result, the number of babies born to a woman at any one time has been increasing. However, nowadays multiple births should not result from careful use of these drugs.

Contraception (birth control)

Contra means 'against' and *ception* refers to conception, the process whereby an ovum is fertilized by a sperm, implants in the uterus and begins to grow into a baby. So *contraception* means preventing pregnancy. There are a number of different methods of contraception. If a male and a female want to have sexual intercourse, but *they* don't want to become pregnant, *they* need to use a method of contraception. (Notice that we emphasized the word 'they' in this last sentence. Even though the female is the one who actually becomes pregnant, she doesn't become pregnant by herself. We say 'they' because *both* males *and* females are involved in every pregnancy and *both* must be responsible for contraception and unplanned pregnancies.)

Contraception, which is also called birth control and family planning, is a topic that we spend quite a lot of time discussing in our classes. If, like most of the boys and girls in these classes, you haven't started having sex, you really don't need to think about contraception yet. But even though it may be some years before you need to think about this, it still might be a good idea to learn about contraception in preparation for the time in your life when you do start having sex. Besides, like many boys and girls, you may be curious about it.

Young people often have mistaken ideas about contraception and pregnancy. For instance, some of them think that a female can't get pregnant if she has sex only during her period, that she can't get pregnant the first time she has sex or that she can't get pregnant if her partner pulls his penis out before he ejaculates. But, as we explained earlier, these things are just *not true!* It's also *not true* that jumping up and down after sex to shake out the sperm or that bathing or showering after sex will prevent pregnancy. Nor will douching (pouring water or mild solution into the vagina) after sex prevent pregnancy. In fact, a flow of liquid may help push the sperm through the cervix into the uterus.

Some young people who've had sex without using contraception and who haven't become pregnant develop a false sense of confidence. They figure that since they've got away with it so far, they'll continue to get away with it. This is also *not true*. In fact, the longer a person continues to have sex without using contraception, the greater the chances of a pregnancy. Other young people think 'It can't happen to me', that pregnancy is something that happens only to other people. Again, *not true*. Anyone who has sex without using contraception risks becoming pregnant, and most of them do sooner or later. Still other young people think that because they've had sex in the past without using contraception and haven't become pregnant, this means that they are infertile or sterile and can't make babies. Once again, this is *not true*. Even if you've got away with it in the past, this doesn't mean you're infertile – it just means you were lucky!

Now that you know some things that aren't true, perhaps you'd like to learn some of the facts about contraception.

Most methods of contraception work by stopping a woman from ovulating (that is, from releasing a ripe ovum from her ovary) *or* by preventing the sperm from reaching the ovum *or* by disturbing the lining of the uterus in such a way that a fertilized ovum cannot successfully grow there. There are several methods, including: the pill; the female barrier methods – the diaphragm, the cap, the female condom and the contraceptive sponge; the male barrier method – the condom (sheath); the intra-uterine device (IUD); spermicides – sperm-killing substances that come in the form of contraceptive creams, jellies, C-films, pessaries and foams; Natural Family Planning (NFP); the injectable contraceptive; the 'morning after' pill and sterilization.

With the exception of sterilization, an operation that makes a person unable to reproduce, these methods of contraception are all temporary methods: once a couple stops using the method, they can become pregnant. Sterilization, however, is considered a permanent method because once a man or woman is sterilized he or she can't ever make a baby again.*

Some of these methods – such as the pill, the IUD, the injectable contraceptive and the 'morning after' – require a doctor's prescription. Some – like the condom, the sponge, contraceptive foam and other spermicides – can be purchased at a chemist's without a doctor's prescription. Others, like the cap and diaphragm, can be purchased at a chemist's without prescription, provided a doctor has previously fitted the woman for one and she knows her size.

The chart on the next several pages describes each of the major methods. You might find it helpful to read the chart before reading the rest of this section and the questions and answers that follow.

METHODS OF CONTRACEPTION

The pill
Also called birth control pills and oral contraceptives, this method requires a woman to take a monthly series of pills that contain hormones like the ones naturally made in a woman's body to control the menstrual cycle. This method works by preventing a

---

* People sometimes change their minds after sterilization and decide they do want to have children after all. In such cases, it is sometimes possible to have an operation to reverse the sterilization, but such operations are only rarely successful. Therefore, only people who are absolutely sure that they don't want to have children in the future should have a sterilization operation.

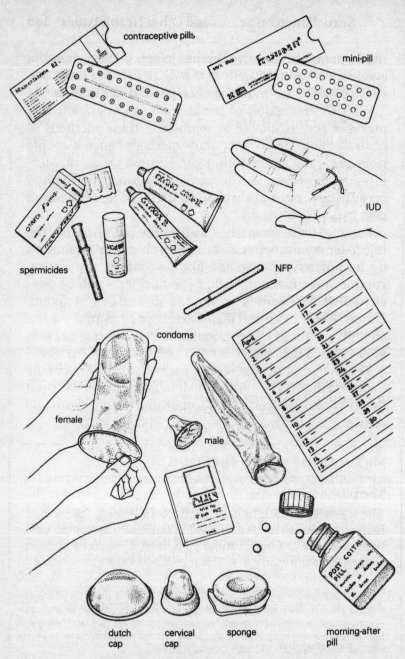

Illustration 41. Methods of contraception.

woman from ovulating, by causing changes in her uterus so a fertilized ovum can't implant there and/or by altering the mucus secreted by her cervix so that sperm can't pass through the cervix into the uterus.

There are basically two types: the combined pill, which contains the hormones oestrogen and progestogen; and the mini-pill, which contains only progestogen. With most types, the woman takes one pill a day for twenty-one days and then has seven 'off' days. During these off days, no pill is taken and the woman has her period. Other types are taken every day, even during the period.

The pill provides protection against pregnancy even on the 'off' days, but the whole series must be taken on schedule in order to work. Missing even one pill can lead to pregnancy.

The female barrier methods:
cap, diaphragm, contraceptive sponge and female condom

There are four barrier methods. All four are devices that are placed in the top of the vagina, in front of the cervix prior to intercourse. They work by acting as a barrier to prevent the sperm from passing through the cervix into the uterus.

The cap and *diaphragm* are circular rubber domes. Caps are shaped like thimbles and fit over the cervix. Diaphragms, which look like rimmed caps, are larger. They fit over the cervix on one side and tuck under the pubic bone on the other. They are both used with spermicides, which are put inside the device before it is placed in the vagina. The diaphragm or cap may be placed in the vagina up to twenty-four hours prior to intercourse. However, if more than three hours elapse before intercourse, additional spermicide must be added. The device must be left in place for at least six hours after intercourse. If the couple wishes to have intercourse again during this time, the device *must not* be removed, but more spermicide must be put directly into the vagina. After use, the device is cleaned and stored for further use.

diaphragm (DIE-ah-fram)

The sponge looks like a powder puff and contains a spermicide, which is released when the sponge is moistened. After moistening it, the woman places the sponge in the top of her vagina before having sex. The sponge must be left in place for at least six hours after intercourse to make sure all the sperm are dead. After use, the sponge is thrown away. Unfortunately, the sponge isn't highly effective at preventing pregnancy, and therefore is not a recommended contraceptive method.

The female *condom* is a polyurethane bag with a ring at each end. The ring at the closed end of the bag fits inside the vagina and covers the cervix; the ring at the open end of the bag covers the vulva and prevents the condom from being pushed inside the vagina during intercourse. It is discarded after use. The female condom has been available only for a short time, so experts have not yet been able to assess how effective it is.

The condom

This method is also called the male barrier method, the sheath, prophylactics, 'johnnies', 'jolly bags', 'French letters', 'Durex' (one of many brand names) and preventives. The condom fits on the erect penis in much the same way that a glove fits over a finger. The condom is placed over the erect penis prior to intercourse. (This must be done *before* the penis enters the vagina.) When the male ejaculates, the sperm are trapped in the condom so they don't enter the vagina. After intercourse, before the penis becomes soft again, the condom is held firmly at the base of the penis (to avoid spilling sperm) and the penis and condom are withdrawn from the vagina. After use, the condom is discarded.

The intra-uterine device (IUD)

The IUD is also called the coil or loop. It is a plastic and copper device between 20 and 40 mm (about 1–1½ in) long that is inserted into a woman's uterus by a doctor. When in place, it can't be felt. It protects against pregnancy as long as it remains in

condom (KON-dom) *intra-uterine* (in-treh-YOU-tur-in)

the uterus. Depending on the type used, the IUD may be left in place for three to five years. A woman can't remove an IUD herself; her doctor must both insert and remove it. Although no one is entirely certain how it works, it is thought that the copper on the IUD inhibits sperm movement, preventing them from reaching the ovum, and that the presence of an IUD makes it impossible for a fertilized ovum to plant itself in the uterus.

Spermicides

These are sperm-killing chemicals that come in the form of creams, jellies, C-films, pessaries and aerosol foams. They are placed in the top of the vagina shortly before intercourse and work by killing sperm before they can get through the cervix into the uterus. Some types of creams and jellies are used with caps and diaphragms, others are made to be used alone. However, when used alone they aren't very effective at preventing pregnancy and therefore are not recommended methods.

Contraceptive foam is more effective, especially when used with a condom. A special applicator is used to insert the foam into the top of the vagina, which may be done as many as three hours prior to intercourse. If more time elapses before intercourse, if a couple decides to have sex a second time or if the woman gets up and walks round, allowing the spermicide to drip out, more foam must be added before intercourse. The foam works by acting as a barrier as well as by killing or stunning the sperm.

Natural Family Planning (NFP)

NFP is also called fertility awareness. It involves a woman learning to tell when during each menstrual cycle she is most likely to be fertile (that is, capable of becoming pregnant) and refraining from sexual intercourse at that time. People who use NFP have three techniques for determining when the woman is fertile:

1. daily observations of the mucus secreted by her cervix (certain changes in the mucus indicate fertile times); this is called the cervical mucus (Billings) method;

2. charts of her daily body temperature (slight changes in body temperature indicate when the fertile time is past);

3. keeping track of the days of the cycle on a calendar to predict fertile times.

Using techniques 1 and 2 together is called the sympto-thermal method and is the most effective means of NFP. Using *only* the calendar technique is called the rhythm method. The rhythm method alone is not a very effective method of preventing pregnancy and therefore is not recommended. NFP should be taught by a qualified NFP teacher; it cannot be learnt from a leaflet or book.

The injectable contraceptive

This method, which is also called the 'jag' or 'jab', is not as widely used as some of the others and is not a first-choice method. It involves an injection of large amounts of a hormone similar to the hormone used in the mini-pill. It prevents pregnancy in the same manner as the mini-pill. The hormone is injected into the woman's muscle and is then released into the woman's body slowly over a period of months. A single injection usually protects against pregnancy for two to three months.

The 'morning-after' pill and IUD

Considered emergency methods, these methods are used only in cases where a woman fears she might become pregnant because she hasn't used birth control, she's used her method improperly or she thinks that her method might not have worked properly. The morning-after pills contain a high dose of hormones like the ones in combined birth control pills, and must be taken within seventy-two hours of unprotected intercourse in order to work.

Inserting an IUD within 5 days of unprotected intercourse will also prevent pregnancy, although this is usually done only in cases where the woman plans to go on using the IUD as her regular method of contraception and where it is medically suitable to do so.

Sterilization

Sterilization involves a surgical operation, which is called vasectomy in men. Vasectomy is a minor operation that can be done in a doctor's surgery under a local anaesthetic, but is also often carried out in a clinic or hospital under a general anaesthetic. The vas deferens are cut, sealed or otherwise blocked so that sperm can no longer travel from the testicles to the penis. Female sterilization is a more involved operation, done under a general anaesthetic and usually requires at least a short stay in hospital. The Fallopian tubes are cut, sealed or otherwise blocked so that ova can no longer travel through them, and therefore can't be fertilized by sperm.

Sterilization is a permanent method, so it is only for people who are sure they won't want children in the future. After the operation, a man still ejaculates, but there are no sperm in his semen. After sterilization men still produce sperm in their testicles and women still produce ripe ova, but the sperm and ova are reabsorbed by the body. Only one member of a couple – either the man or woman, not both – need have the operation in order to protect against pregnancy.

COMPARING THE VARIOUS METHODS

A 'perfect' method of contraception would be one that was:

- very convenient and easy-to-use;
- totally safe and didn't cause any side effects or medical problems;
- 100 per cent effective (or at least highly effective) at preventing pregnancy.

Unfortunately, no method is perfect. Each method has its particular advantages and disadvantages. Some methods are very convenient to use, but aren't as safe or effective as others. Other methods are totally safe, but aren't always as convenient to use or as effective as others. Still other methods are highly effective at preventing pregnancy, but often aren't as safe as some of the others. In the next few pages we'll be comparing the different methods in terms of their convenience, their safety and side-effects, and their effectiveness.

Convenience

Methods like sterilization, the IUD and the injectable contraceptive are very convenient. After sterilization, a person needn't bother about contraception ever again. Once the doctor inserts an IUD, the woman needn't worry about protection against pregnancy again for three to five years (depending on the type of IUD). A single injection of the injectable contraceptive is good for two to three months.

Other methods are less easy to use. Natural Family Planning (NFP), for instance, requires users to keep temperature charts, to track their menstrual cycles on a calendar and to record daily observations of their cervical mucus. Although some people who use NFP say that it's really no trouble once you make it part of your daily routine, this method does require more effort than others.

Of course, how convenient a method is often depends on the user. The pill is considered a very convenient, easy-to-use method by most women because all a woman has to do is swallow a pill and remember to take her pills according to schedule. But for women who have trouble remembering to take medications, the pill may be a very difficult method to use. Methods such as the condom, cap, diaphragm and spermicides are also considered convenient by some people, but highly inconvenient by others. For example, some people find it difficult to insert and remove a cap or diaphragm. Some find spermicides messy. Some find these methods difficult to use because they have trouble remembering to keep the devices handy and to use them each and every time they have sex. Some people find them inconvenient because using these methods interrupts their love-making and they feel that having to stop to use a device takes away from the romance of the moment. Some find it difficult to use these methods because they are too shy or too embarrassed to tell their partners they need 'time out' to put their device in place. However, others incorporate the placing of the device or spermicide into their love-making, don't feel at all shy about using these methods and don't have any problems in using them. So, convenience, like beauty, is often in the eye of the beholder.

Convenience is an important consideration because if a person finds a method inconvenient or difficult to use, the chances of he or she using it improperly or neglecting to use it at all are much greater. And, of course, if a method isn't used properly and consistently, it isn't going to be effective. If convenience were the only consideration, then people would just pick the most convenient method. But, as we shall see, safety, side-effects and effectiveness are also important considerations.

Safety and side-effects

Some methods are safer and have fewer side-effects than others. NFP, for instance, is a 'natural' method because it doesn't involve the use of pills, devices or chemicals; therefore, it doesn't cause any side-effects or pose any health risks to the women who use it. Sterilization doesn't physically affect a person's hormone levels, sex drive, ability to experience orgasm or cause any other side effects. In *rare* cases there will be surgical complications such as infections or excessive bleeding and a few people find themselves emotionally upset by the loss of their ability to reproduce. Because there are no known long-term risks, sterilization is considered a very safe method.

Methods such as the cap, diaphragm, condom and spermicides are also very safe and have few side-effects.

Occasionally, there will be an allergic reaction to the spermicide or the rubber in these devices, which can sometimes be cleared up by switching to another type of device or brand of spermicide. Occasionally, a diaphragm user is troubled by repeated bladder infections (due to the diaphragm's pressure on the bladder), which can sometimes be cleared up by changing the size or type of diaphragm. Though bothersome, these allergic reactions and bladder infections are not considered serious because they aren't major or life-threatening medical problems.

Other methods have a greater number of side-effects and are not as safe to use. The IUD, for instance, may cause side-effects such as period pains, heavier periods and bleeding between periods (breakthrough bleeding). These side-effects may disappear after a few months, but sometimes they are so severe that the device must be removed. The IUD may also cause serious, and even life-threatening, problems. The device can perforate (go through) the muscle wall of the uterus into the pelvic cavity, although this is rare. Having an IUD in the pelvic cavity could lead to serious problems, so an operation is necessary to remove the device. Another serious problem is that women who do get pregnant despite the IUD may have ectopic pregnancies, pregnancies in which the fertilized ovum implants in the Fallopian tube or some other abnormal location instead of in the uterus. Ectopics can burst the tube, creating a medical emergency and requiring an operation to stop the internal bleeding. They can also cause permanent damage to the reproductive organs, causing infertility (difficulty in getting pregnant) or sterility (the inability to become pregnant at all). Fortunately, though, perforations and ectopics are rare.

If a woman already has, or gets, pelvic inflammatory disease (PID) – an infection of the uterus, Fallopian tubes and ovaries – an IUD can make it worse. PID can cause a woman to be hospitalized, damage her reproductive organs so that she's infertile or sterile, lead to chronic pelvic pain and repeated infections, and in some cases it may be necessary to surgically remove the woman's reproductive organs. In rare cases, PID can be fatal. Of course, most IUD users don't ever develop PID. But because of the risk of infertility, this method is not recommended for young women or any woman who may want to have children in the future. Because the chance of getting PID is also greater if a woman has more than one sexual partner or a sexual partner who may have other partners, this method is not recommended for such women, regardless of their future childbearing plans.

The pill also causes side-effects in some women. Pill users sometimes experience weight gain, sore breasts, headaches and nausea, especially at first. There are also a number of other side-effects. Luckily, most women don't have severe side-effects. When they do, switching to another type or brand of pill may help, but some women have to stop using the pill because of the side-effects.

The pill does not have as good a safety record as some of the other methods. For example, the mini-pill sometimes causes ectopic pregnancies in the small number of women who become pregnant while taking it. The combined pill has caused fatal and non-fatal blood clots in the heart or brain in some users. For a healthy, young pill-user who doesn't smoke, the chances of a blood clot are very small. However, the risk for women over the age of 45 and smokers over 35 is much higher, which is why doctors usually don't prescribe combined pills for such women.

The pill has also been associated with other fatal and non-fatal medical problems. In addition, some doctors think that the pill may cause certain kinds of cancer in a small number of the women who use it. Other doctors think that the pill doesn't cause cancer and that it actually protects against certain kinds of cancer. More research is needed before we can say for sure what the long-term effects of the pill are. However, from what we know now, the pill appears to be safe for young, healthy women.

The injectable contraceptive can also cause side-effects, such as longer periods, spotting between periods or no periods at all. Some women experience weight gain, headaches, dizziness, decreased sex drive or allergic reactions, though these are rare. It sometimes takes a number of months for women to begin ovulating, menstruating and being fertile again after they stop using this method. There have been some women who never resumed ovulating and menstruating, but it is not clear if the injectable contraceptive was responsible for the problem in these cases. Some doctors have been concerned that some users of this method might have an increased chance of breast cancer because of laboratory studies done on dogs; other experts don't think there is any risk. Here again, more research is needed. But from what we know, this method is considered a very safe one, safer, in fact, than the pill.

When they hear about the side-effects and safety problems of some methods, the young people in our classes often wonder why women don't just use the safer methods, the ones with fewer side-effects. Some, of course, do choose these methods for just this reason. However, these methods are often less convenient to use and sometimes less effective as well. Besides, the chances of having a serious or life-threatening medical problem are very small with all of the methods we've been discussing. In fact, a woman would be more likely to die from a complication of pregnancy or childbirth than she would from a problem caused by her method of birth control. So, although it's true that there are risks with certain methods, the risks are relatively small for young, healthy women.

Effectiveness

How effective a method is at preventing pregnancy is another important consideration. No method is 100 per cent effective. People sometimes become pregnant even after sterilization, though this is rare.*

Though no method is absolutely foolproof, most methods are highly effective, provided they are used properly and consistently. However, there are some methods – the contraceptive sponge, the rhythm method, spermicidal pessaries, and spermicidal creams and jellies when used alone (without a cap or diaphragm) – that aren't very effective even if a person always uses them exactly according to instructions. For this reason, these methods should not be used by people unless they really wouldn't mind if they became pregnant. These methods are not recommended for people who absolutely don't want to become pregnant.

With the exception of the methods we just mentioned, the other methods listed in the contraception chart are quite effective, provided they are used properly and consistently. How effective these methods are depends on two things: on the method itself and on the user of the method. Most of the time, unplanned pregnancies are a result of the fact that people have failed to use their methods properly or at all. Even when people use their methods absolutely correctly, unplanned pregnancies can still occur because sometimes the method itself simply fails to do its job. For instance: a woman might ovulate despite the fact that she

---

*Pregnancy after a sterilization operation may be due to the fact that the surgeon operated improperly, that the vas deferens or Fallopian tubes have somehow become unsealed, unblocked and have managed to grow together again, or that the man had sex too soon following a vasectomy, before all the sperm previously in his sperm storage area were depleted. Pregnancy occurs after sterilization in about 1 in every 1,000 vasectomies and in about 1 in every 300 female sterilizations.

took her pills on schedule; a diaphragm might become dislodged during intercourse; a condom might break or leak, allowing sperm to get into the vagina; and so on. Effectiveness Chart 1 gives you an idea of how many pregnancies occur because the method has simply failed to do its job (there are no statistics yet for the female condom).

EFFECTIVENESS CHART 1

In a group of 100 women using the method for a year, and using it absolutely correctly, *exactly according to instructions*, we would expect:

- none or, at most, 1 out of 100 injectable contraceptive users to become pregnant;
- 1 or, at most, 2 out of 100 combined-pill users to become pregnant;
- about 2 out of 100 mini-pill users to become pregnant;
- about 2 out of 100 diaphragm or cap users to become pregnant;
- about 2 out of 100 condom users to become pregnant;
- about 2–4 out of 100 IUD users to become pregnant;
- about 3–4 out of 100 contraceptive foam users to become pregnant;
- about 7 out of 100 Natural Family Planner users to become pregnant.

Of course, people make mistakes. Very few people use their methods *absolutely* correctly and properly all the time. So in a typical group of 100 women, there would undoubtedly be more pregnancies than the figures in Chart 1 would indicate. With the IUD and injectable contraceptive, we wouldn't see more pregnancies than indicated in the chart because the IUD is inserted and removed by a doctor and the shots are also given by a doctor. The woman doesn't have to do anything, so there's little chance of her using the method improperly and, therefore, little chance of a pregnancy occurring due to an error on the user's part with these methods.

But with methods like NFP, the condom, cap, diaphragm and spermicides, people can and do make mistakes. For instance, people make mistakes in their NFP charts and have sex during the fertile time; they forget to put enough spermicide in the cap; they insert their diaphragm improperly or remove it too soon; they neglect to use a condom each and every time they have sex; they allow too much time to pass between insertion of the spermicide and intercourse; and so on. Since people can and do make these sorts of mistakes, we could expect a greater number of pregnancies in a typical group of 100 women than indicated in Chart 1.

With the pill, there'd also be a greater number of pregnancies than indicated in Chart 1 because women can and do forget to take all their pills on schedule. However, women who choose the pill as their method are usually the types who are good at remembering to take pills, and they make pill-taking part of their daily routine. Besides, with the pill people needn't interrupt their love-making to deal with contraception and they don't have to refrain from intercourse for a certain number of days each month as NFP users must. Moreover, all a woman has to do with the pill is to swallow it, whereas some of the other methods, especially NFP, are more involved and therefore more open to error. So you can see that pill-users are generally less likely to have unplanned pregnancies due to errors on the user's part than people who use the diaphragm, cap, condom, spermicides or NFP.

Effectiveness Chart 2 on page 200 is similar to Chart 1. It tells you how many pregnancies we'd expect not only because the method failed to do its job, as in Chart 1, but also because the users of the method failed to use the method consistently and properly. The pregnancy rates given in Chart 2 are based on studies of real people who, as you know, sometimes make mistakes. Of course, for any given couple, a method might work better or worse than the figures in Chart 2 indicate, depending on how careful or how careless they are.

EFFECTIVENESS CHART 2

In a typical group of 100 women using the method for a year, there are usually:

- none or only 1 pregnancy out of 100 injectable contraceptive users;
- about 1 to 7 pregnancies out of 100 combined-pill users;
- about 2 to 4 pregnancies out of 100 mini-pill users;
- about 2 to 4 pregnancies out of 100 IUD users;
- from 2 to 15 pregnancies out of 100 condom users;
- from 2 to 15 pregnancies out of 100 diaphragm or cap users;
- from 3 to 16 pregnancies out of 100 contraceptive foam users;
- from 7 to 24 pregnancies out of 100 Natural Family Planning users.

Abortion

Abortion is not a method of contraception – it does not *prevent* pregnancy. It is a means of ending, or terminating, a pregnancy, and is also called a termination. Most abortions are done before the twelfth week of pregnancy. The woman is given an anaesthetic and when she is asleep, the cervical opening is widened enough to allow for insertion of a small suction tube. The contents of the uterus are then gently sucked out through the tube. Abortions may be done up to the twenty-eighth week of pregnancy, but somewhat different procedures are required.

A properly performed abortion is very safe, with few physical side effects. Although some women do experience pain and bleeding during the first two weeks after an abortion, these side effects are usually not severe. Occasionally, they will be severe, will last for more than two weeks or will be accompanied by a fever or rash, in which case the woman should see her doctor, as this may be a sign of infection or some other problem. Some women feel sad after an abortion, even if they are relieved not to be pregnant any more. They may benefit from counselling, but serious depression requiring a doctor's care is rare.

Questions about contraception and abortion

Even after they've heard the information given in the previous pages, the boys and girls in our classes still have many questions about contraception. We've listed some of these questions along with our answers in the next few pages.

Is it legal for teenagers to have birth control? Do you need your parents' permission to get a method of contraception?

Under the terms of the 1969 Family Law Reform Act young people aged 16 and older are able to give their consent to their own surgical, medical and dental treatment without obtaining the consent of their parents, provided that they have been informed about all the issues that may be involved. Family planning clinics (see page 202) will, therefore, provide contraceptive information, devices and advice to all people 16 and older in complete privacy, whether or not they are married or have their parents' consent.

Whether or not people under the age of 16 should be given contraceptive information, devices or advice has been an issue of considerable debate. At present in the United Kingdom people under 16 can receive contraceptive advice and supplies without parental permission and without notification to their parents, though whenever possible doctors will try to persuade young people to confide in their parents.

Where can you get birth control?

As we explained earlier, methods such as the condom, the contraceptive sponge, spermicides and the cap and diaphragm (providing the woman knows her size) can be purchased at the chemist without a doctor's prescription; however, other methods require a doctor's prescription. All methods can be obtained free from any family planning clinic and from most GPs. Many family planning clinics have special youth advisory sessions to help young people learn about and obtain contraception. Young people can also attend one of the many Brook Advisory Centres (found in the major cities of England and Scotland). Contact their central office at 153a East Street, London SE17 2SD (telephone 01-708-1234) for details. The Family Planning Association (FPA) at 27–35 Mortimer Street, London W1N 7RJ (telephone 01-636-7866) gives information and has leaflets on family planning clinics in the United Kingdom, methods of contraception and all aspects of reproductive health care.

How do people decide which method to use?

The method a couple chooses will depend on many factors, including personal preference, the woman's health and her age, the couple's relationship (that is, whether they just want to 'space' pregnancies or absolutely don't want to become pregnant), and feelings about the issues of safety, effectiveness and convenience. Most people use many different methods over the course of their lives.

Many young people begin by using a condom. The condom has the advantage of being easy to obtain and can protect against AIDS and other STDs. Later, they may switch to one of the methods that require a doctor's prescription. Some couples prefer methods such as the IUD or pill because they don't like to interrupt their love-making by having to use the barrier methods or spermicides. Women who don't have intercourse very often may choose a barrier method rather than the pill, which must be taken regularly, or an IUD, which is in place constantly. The female barrier methods also have the added advantage of providing some protection against some sexually transmitted diseases. Women who are concerned about safety and side effects of the pill or IUD may choose the safer barrier methods. Men or women who have completed their families may choose sterilization. Choosing a method involves weighing the relative effectiveness, convenience and safety of each method. It helps to become fully informed about all available methods before making a choice.

What's wrong with not using birth control and just having an abortion if you get pregnant?

Different people would answer this question somewhat differently. For instance, some people feel that abortion is morally wrong, that it is the same as murder and that it should be outlawed. They feel that a pregnant woman should have her baby and either keep the child or put it up for adoption. Since these people feel that abortion is morally wrong, they would, of course, feel that using it as a regular method of contraception (or, indeed, ever) is not OK.

Other people don't feel that abortion is morally wrong nor that it is equivalent to murder. These people feel that abortion is a private matter between a woman and her doctor, that a woman should have the right to decide what goes on inside her body and that she should be able to decide whether or not she wants to have a baby. But even people who feel abortion is morally acceptable often feel that it's not right or ethical for a person to rely on abortion as a regular method of birth control. They feel that abortion should be used only as a 'back-up' measure when the regular method has failed to prevent pregnancy and the woman doesn't want to continue the pregnancy.

Aside from the moral and ethical reasons, there are also good medical reasons why people shouldn't forego using other methods and have abortions whenever they become pregnant. If a woman didn't use contraception, she'd probably find herself getting pregnant at least once a year, if not more often. Having one or two abortions in a lifetime doesn't do any damage to a woman's body or affect her future chances of having a normal pregnancy, but there is some evidence that having more than two abortions, say three or even four, might make it more difficult for a woman to get pregnant or more likely for her to have a miscarriage or a premature birth in the future. Doctors aren't yet sure whether or not three or four abortions will have bad effects. But almost all doctors agree that having more frequent abortions isn't a good idea.

Suppose your method failed or you used the method wrongly or didn't use a method at all: how would a girl know whether or not she was pregnant?

Most females discover that they are pregnant because they fail to have their menstrual period at the expected time. Sore breasts and nausea are also early signs of pregnancy. However, there are many reasons other than pregnancy that could cause a female to miss her menstrual period or to have sore breasts or nausea. But pregnancy is the most common cause of missed periods in sexually active females. Anyone who thinks she might be pregnant should have a pregnancy test.

Standard pregnancy tests are done on a urine sample collected in the early morning. In order for the test to be accurate, at least fourteen days must have elapsed since the time of the expected menstrual period, that is, the girl or woman must be at least fourteen days 'late' in getting her period. These standard pregnancy tests are available from some family doctors, family planning clinics and Brook Advisory Centres. Pregnancy tests that can detect pregnancy earlier, that is, before the girl or woman is fourteen days late in getting her period, are available from one of the pregnancy charities. Two useful places to contact regarding these tests are the Pregnancy Advisory Service (PAS), 11–13 Charlotte Street, London W1P 1HD and the British Pregnancy Advisory Service (BPAS), Austy Manor, Wootton Wawen, Solihull, West Midlands B95 6BX.

In addition, home pregnancy test kits are available from chemists. If a person follows the directions and uses these tests properly, they are quite reliable. However, it is possible to get a false test result. For example, the test may indicate that someone isn't pregnant when, in reality, she is or vice versa. If the home pregnancy test indicates a female isn't pregnant, but she still doesn't get her period or she has other signs of pregnancy (swollen, tender breasts or nausea) or if she feels unsure about the test results, she should have a test done at a doctor's office or clinic.

What if the test shows that you are pregnant?

If pregnancy occurs, there are three choices: continuing the pregnancy and keeping the baby; continuing the pregnancy but giving up the child for adoption; and abortion. If you are not certain which is the best choice for you, your GP or the doctor at the place where you got your pregnancy test can refer you to a counsellor who will help you decide. Regardless of what decision you make, you have the right to sympathetic counselling and to complete information about each of the choices available. Even if you feel certain about your decision, you may find it helpful to discuss your decision with a counsellor.

Is it legal for a teenager to have an abortion?

Yes, but young women under the age of 16 need the permission of a parent or guardian in order to obtain an abortion. In addition, women of all ages must have two doctors agree that the woman or any children she already has will suffer physical or emotional harm if she continues the pregnancy *or* that the baby is likely to be born handicapped *or* that continuing the pregnancy would endanger the woman's life.

How far along can a woman be in her pregnancy before it's too late for her to have an abortion?

Legally, abortions can be done up to the point at which the baby would be capable of staying alive outside the mother's body. This is about 28 weeks. Most abortions are done before the twelfth week. Late abortions occur only in exceptional circumstances, for example, where the baby is discovered late in pregnancy to have a serious abnormality or where the mother is a young teenager who didn't realize she was pregnant until a few months had passed. Late abortions require more elaborate procedures, which entail somewhat more risk, though even late abortion is a very safe procedure. However, doctors agree that the earlier the abortion is done, the better.

Suppose you do choose abortion, what happens then?

Once you've decided and the first doctor (your GP or the one at the place where you had the pregnancy test) has agreed to the request for an abortion, you will be referred to a hospital or clinic doctor who will perform the abortion. This second doctor also has to agree that you have legal grounds for abortion.

Whether or not you are able to get an abortion on the National Health Service will depend on the agreement of your doctor and the provision of abortion services in the area where you live. Family planning clinics may be able to help with the arrangements, and Brook Advisory Centres offer help for people seeking abortion through the NHS. People who cannot obtain an NHS abortion will have to pay, usually at one of the pregnancy charities.

Sexually transmitted diseases

In the next few pages we'll be talking about health problems associated with the sex organs and sexual activity. The boys and girls in our classes have many questions about these subjects. They are especially curious about sexually transmitted diseases (STDs), which are also referred to as venereal diseases (VD).

STDs are diseases that can be passed from one person to another through sexual contact. There are many different types of STD. The chart on pages 207–13 lists the major types and gives important information on each one. You might find it helpful to read through the chart before you read the questions and answers on the following pages.

SEXUALLY TRANSMITTED DISEASES

Gonorrhoea

This is a common STD that can easily be cured with antibiotics, provided it is detected and treated promptly. Males usually have symptoms severe enough to send them to the doctor (discharge from the penis, pain on urination, frequent need to urinate). Females may have an abnormal vaginal discharge and urinary symptoms if the germs spread from the vagina to the urethra, and these symptoms may be severe enough for them to seek medical treatment. However, the big problem with gonorrhoea is that some males and many females don't have symptoms or have only mild ones that go away on their own. Even if there are no

---

gonorrhoea (GON-eh-REE-uh)

symptoms, the germs are still in the infected person's body, and that person can still pass the disease to others. Undetected and untreated gonorrhoea can be especially serious in a female. If she doesn't know she has the disease and is not treated, the germs may spread from the vagina to the uterus, Fallopian tubes, ovaries and other pelvic organs, causing PID, which can be very damaging and can lead to infertility, sterility and other serious medical problems.

Chlamydia

This is another common STD, which can cause symptoms similar to those caused by gonorrhoea. The information on gonorrhoea also applies to chlamydia. Females are even more apt to be asymptomatic (without symptoms) with chlamydia. Like gonorrhoea, untreated chlamydia in females may lead to PID, infertility, and other serious medical problems.

Genital herpes

This STD is caused by a virus known as herpes virus type II, or HV-2. The chief symptom is painful, blister-like sores in, on or around the sex organs. There may also be pain on urination, fever and flu-like symptoms. Genital herpes is incurable – that is, there is no medication that will rid the body of the virus. However, a person doesn't always have the sores; they go away on their own, usually in, at most, a couple of weeks, but the virus remains in the body. It retreats deep into the body and usually comes back to the surface from time to time, causing new outbreaks of sores. A person can pass the disease during an outbreak and also for a period of time before and after an outbreak, so herpes sufferers must take special precautions to avoid passing the disease to others. Genital herpes is serious because there's no cure and because having the disease increases a female's chances of getting pre-cancerous and cancerous conditions of the cervix (the lower portion of the uterus, which protrudes into the top of the vagina). Women who have genital herpes should have a cervical smear test every year to detect any changes in cells. If a woman has an

chlamydia (KLUH-mid-e-uh)   *herpes* (HER-peez)

attack of genital herpes when she is due to give birth, she might have a Caesarean section.

Genital warts

This is another increasingly common STD. The chief symptom is warts in, on or around the sex organs. A person can have warts without knowing it. The warts may go undetected because of their location, their small size or the fact that they can disappear on their own. However, if undetected and untreated, they tend to recur. Untreated genital warts are a serious problem because they may lead to pre-cancer or cancer of the cervix, and women should have a cervical smear test every year to detect any cell changes. Treatment is by means of a special solution that is painted on the warts, causing them to fall off. In stubborn cases cryosurgery (freezing) or electrocautery (destroying by means of an electric current) may be necessary.

Syphilis

This is a rare disease in Britain nowadays. The symptoms appear in stages, beginning with a painless sore at the exact place where the germs entered the body. The person may not notice the sore, which will eventually disappear, but the germs remain in the body and eventually produce second stage symptoms such as a red rash, mouth sores and an ill-all-over feeling. Most cases are treated by this stage, but if untreated, the disease may progress to a third stage, which can cause serious and permanent damage to the brain, spinal cord and other organs. Treatment is by means of antibiotics, usually given by injection.

Candidiasis

This infection is more commonly known as thrush or yeast or fungus infections. In females this infection causes a white and cheese-like vaginal discharge and itching, redness and tenderness of the vulva. The yeast organisms don't survive well on the penis, so males don't often get the infection. When they do, they are frequently asymptomatic. Male partners of women who are

syphilis (SIF-eh-liss)   *candidiasis* (CAN-di-DIE-uh-siss)

infected are often given treatment even when they don't have symptoms.

The yeast organisms may be introduced into the vagina by sexual contact, but a female may also develop the infection in other ways. Improper wiping after a bowel movement may bring yeasts living in the rectum into the vagina. Yeast organisms are apparently normal inhabitants of some females' vaginas, but the acidity of the vagina keeps them in check so they don't multiply and cause symptoms. Taking antibiotics, being pregnant and having diabetes changes the normal acidity of the vagina in some women, causing the yeast organisms to multiply and producing symptoms. Treatment is usually with special creams placed in the vagina. Though bothersome, yeast infections don't usually lead to major medical problems and therefore aren't considered as serious as some of the other STDs.

Gardnerella

Also known as haemophilus. In females this infection causes an abnormal, foul-smelling, greyish vaginal discharge and sometimes redness or itching of the vulva. Males may harbour the germs that cause this infection in their bodies, but they are usually asymptomatic. If untreated, gardnerella may cause infertility problems. But these problems usually clear up once the infection is treated, so gardnerella is generally considered less serious than some of the other STDs. Treatment is by means of oral medications.

Trichomoniasis

Also called trich and TV, the chief symptom in females is an abnormal, foul-smelling, greenish-yellow discharge, which tends to be frothy and may cause redness or itching of the vulva. Males may harbour the germs in their bodies, but they are usually asymptomatic. Treatment is by means of oral medication. Though bothersome, trich doesn't lead to major medical problems and therefore isn't considered as serious as some other STDs.

gardnerella (GARD-ner-ELL-a)   *trichomoniasis* (TRICK-o-moan-nye-a-siss)
haemophilus (HEM-ah-fill-us)

Non-specific vaginitis

'Vaginitis' means 'vaginal infection' and 'non-specific' means that the doctor can't find a specific organism that is causing the infection. The chief symptoms are an abnormal, foul-smelling discharge and redness or itching of the vulva. Treatment is usually by means of oral medication. Here again, though these infections may be bothersome, they don't pose any major medical problems and therefore aren't considered as serious as some of the other STDs.

Non-specific urethritis (NSU)

Urethritis is an infection of the urethra, the tube through which urine passes as it leaves the body. The chief symptoms are an abnormal discharge from the tip of the penis in males and from the urinary opening in females, pain in the genital area, itching, pain on urination and urinary frequency. The diagnosis of NSU is more common in men than in women. Urethritis may be caused by a number of different organisms, including chlamydia and gonorrhoea, but when a specific organism can't be identified, the diagnosis is non-specific urethritis. Treatment is by oral medication.

Pelvic inflammatory disease (PID)

PID is an infection of the uterus, Fallopian tubes, ovaries and/or other female pelvic organs. The disease is usually caused when gonorrhoea or chlamydia organisms or other sexually transmitted organisms make their way from the vagina up into the uterus. From there the infection may spread to the other pelvic organs. PID may be more severe in women who use the IUD. PID may cause any or all of the following symptoms: period pains; heavier periods, bleeding between periods and other menstrual irregularities; abnormal vaginal discharge; urinary pain or frequency; pain in the lower abdomen or legs; and fever, chills, vomiting or flu-like symptoms. Females may also be asymptomatic, but even these 'silent' infections can cause serious damage to the reproductive organs. Treatment involves complete bed-rest and antibiotics, and may require hospitalization and intravenous antibiotics.

vaginitis (VAJ-e-NI-tiss)   *urethritis* (YOUR-ee-THREYE-tiss)

If the antibiotics don't work, it may be necessary to operate and surgically remove the reproductive organs. Females who've had PID have a greater chance of having ectopic pregnancies. Some females who've had PID are troubled with chronic pelvic pain and repeated attacks of the symptoms. In rare cases PID may be so severe that it is fatal. PID is on the rise and is one of the leading causes of infertility.

Acquired Immune Deficiency Syndrome (AIDS)

This is a very serious, incurable STD that attacks the immune system so the person's body is unable to fight off diseases. It is caused by the human immuno-deficiency virus (HIV). Someone who is infected with HIV may go on to develop AIDS. HIV infection may begin with symptoms such as swollen glands, extreme tiredness, sudden weight loss, night sweats, fever and skin blotches. These symptoms are also common to many other, less serious illnesses. HIV infection can be diagnosed by having blood tests known as HIV antibody tests. AIDS may lead to certain types of cancer, pneumonia and other fatal diseases. People with AIDS usually die. No one has ever recovered.

HIV is passed only through direct blood-to-blood or sexual contact with the blood or body fluids, such as semen or vaginal fluids, of an infected person. It may be spread through vaginal sex, anal sex and possibly oral sex, but is not passed through touching or kissing an infected person, through the air (like colds) or through insect bites (like malaria). In the United Kingdom HIV infection and AIDS are most common among males who have had sex with other males, people who have shared injecting drug equipment, the sexual partners of these people and children born to infected parents. In the past people who were given contaminated blood or blood products also became infected. Now all blood for transfusions and other blood products are carefully screened and treated to prevent them carrying HIV. Although at present it is rare for people outside these groups to become infected, there is evidence that HIV infection is spreading and anyone who is having sex is at risk of contracting HIV.

Pubic lice

Pubic lice are also called 'crabs'. This STD is caused by tiny, blood-sucking lice that can live in pubic hair or sometimes in the eyelashes. The lice may be passed through sexual contact or through contact with infected clothing, towels and bed linen. The bite of the lice causes intense itching, and if you look closely you can see the lice or the shiny, sticky eggs they attach to the hair shafts. Lice are treated by repeated shampooing of the infected area with special lotions (available from a chemist without prescription). Bed linen, towels and clothing must be boiled, dry-cleaned or isolated for two weeks to avoid reinfection. Though bothersome, crabs are not a serious health problem.

Questions about STDs

When they've read through this chart, the boys and girls in our classes usually have a long list of questions about STDs. You'll find some of these questions and their answers on the following pages.

Why are these diseases called sexually transmitted diseases? Can you get them any way other than by having sex?

These diseases are called sexually transmitted diseases because they are capable of being passed from one person to another by some form of close sexual contact. Another thing they have in common is that most are caused by germs that can survive only in the fluids or moist, mucous membranes of the human body – that is, in places like the penis, vulva, vagina, rectum (bowels) or, in some cases, the mouth or throat. Otherwise, these germs die quite quickly. So it is usually only when the infected person's body fluids or mucous membranes come in contact with another person's body fluids or mucous membranes that the disease can be passed along. This kind of contact usually happens only during some form of sexual activity, such as vaginal sex, oral-genital sex or anal (penis in rectum) sex. However, any type of membrane-to-membrane contact can spread the disease, and it isn't necessary for a man to ejaculate in order to infect his partner.

Even though these diseases are *usually* transmitted sexually, in some cases it is possible for a person to get certain STDs in non-sexual ways. For example, pregnant women who have AIDS or syphilis can pass these infections to their unborn babies through their bloodstreams. Also, if a pregnant woman has infections such as genital herpes, gonorrhoea, chlamydia or candidiasis (yeast infection) in her vagina at the time of delivery, the baby may become infected as it passes through the vagina during childbirth.*

In addition, there are other non-sexual ways in which a person could develop certain STDs. For instance, a person could get pubic lice through contact with infected clothes or bedding. AIDS can be passed through transfusions of infected blood or by injecting drug users who share needles or other drug equipment. (But, it is important to note that AIDS cannot be transmitted through touching or through the air like cold germs.)

As we noted on the Sexually Transmitted Diseases chart, the yeast organisms that cause candidiasis in the vagina often live in the rectum, so improper wiping after a bowel movement could bring these organisms into the vagina. A female should always wipe herself from the front to the back, never from the rectum towards the vagina. PID is usually caused by sexually transmitted germs getting into the vagina and then moving up into the sterile uterus, Fallopian tubes and ovaries. Operations, abortions, child-

---

*Babies who get STDs from their mothers may suffer serious medical problems and may even die. This is one reason why it's important for pregnant women to have regular medical check-ups. Please note, however, that candidiasis in newborn infants is not as serious as gonorrhoea, AIDS or syphilis would be.

birth and other non-sexual causes can also lead to PID. Non-specific vaginitis, non-specific urethritis, gardnerella and trichomoniasis can also be contracted in non-sexual ways.

However, even though some STDs *can* be passed in non-sexual ways, they *usually* are transmitted sexually. For this reason, they are considered sexually transmitted or sexually transmissible diseases.

Can you get an STD from kissing?

As a general rule, you can't get STDs from kissing; however, herpes and syphilis can cause sores on the genitals. If you had oral-genital sex with someone who had a herpes or syphilis sore on the genitals, then you could get a sore on your lips. Or if you kissed a person who had such a sore on his or her lips, you could get the infection.

You can't get AIDS from 'dry' kissing, and 'wet', or French, kissing is probably safe too. Although small amounts of HIV may be present in saliva, experts doubt that such small amounts could cause infection. But it's best to be careful who you French kiss.

Can you get an STD from a toilet seat, a drinking glass, a flannel, a towel or from touching some other object?

Again, generally speaking, the answer to this question is no, because the germs that cause most STDs usually die almost instantly when they leave the mucous membranes of the human body and come in contact with the air.

However, there have been some cases of people developing certain STDs from objects. For example, if you used an object, such as a drinking glass, a flannel or a towel, soon after it had come in contact with a mouth sore of a person who had syphilis or herpes, you could pick up the disease. Or if you used a flannel or towel soon after it was used by someone who had pubic lice or an STD discharge from their penis or vagina, you might pick up the infection. Or if you somehow managed to put the mucous membrane of your sex organs in contact with a toilet seat that had just been used by a person with an STD discharge or sore and that person's sore or discharge had come in contact with the toilet seat, it is conceivable that you could get an STD in this way. But such a series of events is highly unlikely. So, practically speaking, it is highly unlikely for a person to get an STD from a toilet seat.

We should also mention that you can't get an STD from a swimming pool, by sitting on someone's lap with your clothes on, from the air, from masturbating yourself or in any ways other than the ones we've mentioned so far.

How can a person tell if he or she has an STD?

There are special medical tests that can be done to determine whether or not a person has an STD, and if so, what kind. One way in which people find out that they have an STD is that they develop symptoms like the ones described in the chart on pages 207–13. The symptoms may lead the person to see a doctor who tests him or her for STDs.

However, one of the big problems with STDs is that people sometimes have the disease without knowing it. For example, it usually takes many years for a person infected with HIV to develop any obvious signs or symptoms of AIDS. Women with chlamydia and gonorrhoea frequently don't have any symptoms, or the symptoms are so mild or so temporary that the woman doesn't see a doctor. However, the germs are still in the body, can be passed on to others and may lead to serious medical problems such as PID. A person may have genital warts without knowing it, which can be a serious problem for women because untreated genital warts may lead to cervical cancer. (Cervical smear tests can detect the presence of an infection as well as any changes in the cells.)

Because a person can have these and other STDs without knowing it and because untreated STDs can lead to serious health problems, it is *vitally important* that anyone who has an STD or thinks he or she might have one should seek medical attention *immediately*. Anyone diagnosed as having an STD should inform *all* his or her sexual partners, so these people can be tested and, if necessary, treated. Even if the sexual partners don't have any symptoms, they must, none the less, be tested and treated.

Can STDs be cured?

As a general rule, the answer to this question is 'yes'. In fact, provided they are detected and treated promptly, most STDs can be cleared in only one or two visits to the doctor.

However, there are two forms of STDs, herpes and AIDS, that cannot be cured. Though medical scientists are searching for an AIDS cure, they haven't found one yet, and people who get AIDS usually die. Herpes, too, is incurable in the sense that we don't as yet have a medication that will rid the body of the virus that causes the disease. However, people with herpes don't die from the disease, nor do they always have the herpes sores. The sores go away by themselves, usually within a couple of weeks. Even though the sores may go away, the virus is still in the body, hiding away, and may return to the surface to cause new outbreaks of sores from time to time.

With the exception of AIDS and herpes, all other types of STDs are curable. But certain STDs can cause lasting damage to the body if they are not detected and treated immediately. For example, untreated gonorrhoea and chlamydia may cause PID. Although PID can usually be cured, there may be so much damage to the reproductive organs and so much scar tissue around the Fallopian tubes and ovaries that the woman becomes infertile or sterile. Syphilis can also cause lasting damage to the body if it is not treated promptly.

Because these and other STDs can result in permanent damage to the body, it is important that anyone who has STD symptoms or has had sex with someone who has an STD is tested and treated immediately.

What should you do if you think you might have an STD?

Anyone, of any age, who thinks he or she may have an STD should go straight to a special clinic for free advice, testing and treatment. It is not necessary to be referred by your GP. The names and addresses of special clinics can be found on posters and notices displayed in doctors' surgeries, health centres, post offices, and Citizens' Advice Bureaux. The special clinics are sometimes called the Departments of Genito-urinary Medicine, STD clinics or Special Treatment Centres. You can also ring a Brook Advisory Centre for advice on how to get treatment (see page 202 for information on how to contact the advisory centre nearest you).

Testing and treatment is entirely confidential. You don't need your parents' permission. The people at the clinic will not inform your parents (or anyone else for that matter) that you have been tested and/or treated for an STD. The people who work at the special clinics are used to dealing with young people who have STDs. You needn't feel embarrassed or ashamed to go to a clinic.

Even if you don't have symptoms, but think you may have had contact with an infected person, it's important that you be tested. Even if your symptoms have disappeared, the germs may still be in your body causing damage, and you can still pass the infection to others. So it's important to be tested even if your symptoms have subsided.

You should go to a clinic immediately so you can be tested and treated as soon as possible. If you do have an STD, it's important that you notify all your recent sexual partners so they, too, can be tested and treated.

How can I protect myself against AIDS and other STDs?

There are a number of things you can do to protect yourself or at least cut down on your chances of getting these diseases.

1. Don't use injecting drugs, not even once. In fact, it's best to stay away from all illegal drugs and alcohol, too, because they weaken the immune system, making you more susceptible to AIDS. They can also affect your judgement, so that you don't follow STD prevention guidelines and, in some cases, using other illegal drugs leads to the use of injecting drugs.

2. Wait until you're married or older to have sex. Experts agree that abstaining from (not having) sex is the best protection for young people.

3. If you do have sex, use a latex condom and spermicide. HIV may be able to pass through natural lambskin condoms, so always use a condom made of latex rubber. In addition, also use a spermicide (foam, jelly, cream, C-film or pessary), as the chemical it contains helps to kill the AIDS virus. It's important to remember that condoms and spermicides are not 100 per cent effective in preventing AIDS and other STDs, so you must also follow the other guidelines.

4. Limit the number of sex partners that you have. The fewer partners you have, the lower your risk of getting AIDS or other STDs.

5. Look for STD symptoms. Although some STDs don't produce noticeable symptoms, many do. So, check for STD symptoms (sores, rashes or redness on the sex organs, an unusual discharge from the penis or vagina) before you

have sex. You don't have to take out a magnifying glass and examine the person, but do make it a point to look.

6. Get to know a person well and discuss possible exposure to HIV before having sex. It usually takes six or more years for AIDS symptoms to show up. Most people currently infected with HIV aren't yet aware of the fact that they're infected. But they are contagious! So, you must ask about a person's past sex life and whether the person or his/her past lovers may have been exposed to the virus either sexually or by sharing needles. If the person belongs to one of the groups among which HIV infection is most common (see page 212), then you should insist on an HIV antibody test *before* you have sex. For more information on testing contact your Brook Advisory Centre (see page 202).

7. Be aware of the fact that personal hygiene is very important. Wash your genitals every day and wear clean, cotton underwear. Avoid using deodorants, perfumes and strong or scented soaps on your genitals, as they can irritate and dry the skin, making it more susceptible to infection. Avoid synthetic underwear, tight jeans and other tight clothing, as they can cut down on air flow and keep the genital area damp, making it more susceptible to infection. Women should always wipe from front to back, away from the vagina, when going to the toilet, to avoid transferring germs from the rectum to the vagina.

Cervical cancer, pre-cancerous conditions of the cervix and smear tests

If you haven't yet started having sexual intercourse, you don't really need to worry about cervical cancer, pre-cancerous conditions of the cervix or smear tests yet. But when you do begin having sex, you will need to know about these diseases and to have regular smear tests.

The girls in our classes usually have a lot of questions

about these subjects. Most of them have never even heard of these things before. This isn't too surprising; there are many adult women who don't know about them either. But it's vitally important for women to know about these health issues, so we'd like you to read this section carefully. You might even ask your mother (or any adult woman you care about) to read this section too, in case she doesn't know about these things.

What are cervical cancer and pre-cancerous conditions of the cervix?

Cancer, as you may know, is a disease in which cells become so abnormal that they start to reproduce wildly, invade the surrounding tissue, spread to other parts of the body and interfere with the body's normal, healthy functioning. Cervical cancer is a type of cancer that affects the cervix, the entrance to the uterus (see Illustration 22 on page 100).

Pre-cancerous conditions of the cervix are abnormalities in the cells of the skin tissue of the cervix that, if left untreated, may eventually turn into cervical cancer. Doctors use a number of different terms when referring to pre-cancerous conditions of the cervix. Depending on how widespread the condition is and on the degree of abnormality in the cells, a doctor may use any of the following terms to describe the pre-cancerous condition: *dysplasia,* cervical *intraepithelial neoplasia* (CIN) or *carcinoma-in-situ.*

What causes cervical cancer and pre-cancerous conditions of the cervix?

Although the exact cause of these diseases is not definitely known, there is a good deal of scientific evidence that

dysplasia (dis-PLAY-shuh)
intraepithelial (IN-trah-ep-eh-THEAL-ee-al)
neoplasia (neo-PLAY-shuh)

carcinoma (car-sih-no-ma)
situ (SIT-you)

suggests that they may be caused by sexually transmitted viruses such as the ones that cause genital warts or herpes. For this reason, many doctors consider pre-cancerous and cancerous conditions of the cervix to be sexually transmitted diseases.

Are some women more likely to get these diseases than other women?

Yes, certain women are at higher risk than others; that is, they are more likely to get the disease than others. For instance, women who have a history of herpes or genital warts are at higher risk. For some unknown reason, women who smoke are also at higher risk. Since these diseases may be transmitted sexually, the greater the number of sexual partners a woman has, or her partner has, the greater her chances of getting these diseases. (However, this doesn't mean that a woman with one of these diseases has necessarily had a large number of partners.) Women who start their sex lives during their teen years are also at higher risk. This may be due to the fact that the tissues of the cervix go through a stage of being very vulnerable to cancer-causing agents during these years. (Here again, this doesn't mean that someone with cervical cancer has necessarily started her sex life during her teens.)

Of course, a woman may have all these risk factors and never get these diseases, and even women who don't have these risk factors can develop these conditions.

How does a woman know if she has one of these diseases?

There usually aren't any symptoms to alert the woman to the fact that she has these diseases. The pre-cancerous conditions usually don't produce much in the way of symptoms. Even with cervical cancer, there may not be any symptoms, at least not at first. Fortunately, though, there is a test, called a smear test, that can detect these diseases.

What is a smear test?

The smear test, which is also called a cervical smear or Pap smear or test, is a simple, painless test that can be done in the office by your GP or the doctor you go to for contraception.

For the smear test, you will be asked to remove all your lower garments and lie down on an examining table. The doctor will gently insert an instrument called a *speculum* into your vagina. This pushes the walls of the vagina apart so the doctor can see your cervix. This doesn't hurt, but it may feel a little uncomfortable. The doctor then collects some cells from the surface of your cervix by gently rotating a small spatula round it. These cells are smeared on a slide and examined under a microscope to make sure they don't show any signs of a cancerous or pre-cancerous condition. Usually, the doctor has to send the slide to a laboratory for the microscope examination and will inform you by post if the test was not normal.

What happens if your test results aren't normal?

This depends on exactly what the test report says. In some cases the doctor will merely ask you to come back in a few months for another smear test. In other cases the doctor may want to do other tests to confirm the results of the smear test.

If it turns out that you do have a pre-cancerous condition, the problem can usually be treated fairly simply and quickly by laser, and other methods that destroy the affected cells. Luckily, pre-cancerous conditions are 100 per cent curable.

If you have an actual cancer, a surgical operation is usually necessary. In its early stages cervical cancer is usually

speculum (SPEK-you-lum)

curable; however, in advanced cases, a cure may not be possible. About 2,000 women each year die of cervical cancer, most of whom could have been saved if they'd had regular smear tests to detect the disease in its earlier, curable stages. This is why it's so important for women to have regular smear tests.

When should I begin having smear tests? How often should a woman have a smear test?

You should have your first smear test within two years of the time when you first have sexual intercourse. After you've had your first smear test, you should continue having one at least once every three to five years. Many doctors feel the test should be done more often, once every two to three years.

If you have any of the risk factors we mentioned earlier (multiple sex partners, beginning your sex life while still in your teens, a history of herpes or genital warts) or if you've had a pre-cancerous condition of the cervix in the past, you may need to have smear tests every year. If you do have any of these risk factors, be sure to discuss them with your doctor so that he or she can tell you how often you need to have a smear test.

Sexual crimes

When we talk about sexual intercourse in class, we often find questions about sexual crimes in the Everything You Ever Wanted to Know question box. So we want to tell you something about this subject in case you too have questions about it.

Parents sometimes worry about bringing up the topic of sexual crimes with their children because they don't want to scare them. Many parents want to protect their children from even hearing about such terrible things. This is understandable, but the fact of the matter is sexual crimes do happen. We feel that the best way to protect children from sexual crimes is to make sure they know about these things and are prepared to handle the situation if they become victims of a sexual crime.

The three types of sexual crimes we'll be talking about here are rape, incest and child molesting.

RAPE

Rape means forcing someone to have sex against his or her will. It can happen to anyone – young children, adults, people of any age. Most rape victims are females and most rapists are males. It's possible for a woman to hold a gun to a man's head and force him to have intercourse with her, or for a woman to force a person (male or female) to have oral-genital sex with her or something like this. And probably somewhere in the world at some time such things have happened. It is also possible for a man to be raped by another man. By and large, though, rape cases involve a male raping a female.

If you are a victim of rape, it's important that you know what to do. The most important thing is to get help right away. Some rape victims are so upset by what's happened that they just want to go home and try to forget the whole thing. But a rape victim needs medical attention as soon as possible. Even if the victim doesn't seem to have any serious injuries, there could be internal injuries that need medical attention. The victim also needs to be tested to make sure that he or she hasn't got a sexually transmitted disease as a result of the rape. (These tests are one reason why a victim shouldn't bath or shower before seeking medical attention.) If the victim is a woman, she needs a test to make sure she isn't pregnant and she may want to take the morning-after pill to prevent pregnancy. And a rape victim should seek help because he or she will need support to recover emotionally as well as physically.

If you are a rape victim, there are a number of ways to go about getting help. You can go to a hospital casualty department or call the police, who will take you to hospital. There are Rape Crisis Centres in most big towns and cities. You can find the number of the centre closest to your home in your telephone directory, or directory inquiries will be able to put you in contact with doctors who are specially trained to help rape victims. Their service is entirely confidential (private), so don't be afraid to ring them.

INCEST AND CHILD MOLESTING

Incest involves one member of a family being sexual with another family member. It may include anything from touching, feeling or kissing the sex organs to actual sexual intercourse. Of course, it isn't incest when a husband and wife do these things with each other. But when it happens between other family members it's called incest.

Most victims of incest are girls who are victimized by their fathers, stepfathers, brothers, uncles, cousins or some other male relative, although it is also possible for a girl to be victimized by a female relative. Boys can also be victims of incest, though this is less common. When incest happens to a boy, it may be either a female or a male relative who victimizes him. Incest can happen to very young children, even to babies, as well as to older children and teenagers.

Brothers and sisters often engage in some form of sex play as they're growing up, which may involve 'playing doctor' or pretending to be 'mummy and daddy'. This kind of sex play between brothers and sisters is very common and isn't always considered incest. It isn't necessarily a harmful thing. But being forced or pressured to have sexual contact with an older brother or sister *is* incest, and it can be very harmful.

Incest isn't always a forced thing, like rape. Because of the older person's position in the family, he (or she) may be able to pressure the child into doing sexual things without actually having to use force. Most incest victims are so bewildered by what's going on that they simply don't know how to stop it or prevent it from happening again.

Child molesting, like incest, may involve anything from touching, feeling or kissing the sex organs to actual sexual intercourse. (The word molest means to bother or to harm.) But child molesting is different from incest because the person doing the molesting isn't a family member. It may be a complete stranger, a friend of the child's parents or some other older person. Boys as well as girls may be victims of a child molester.

If you are a victim of incest or child molesting, the most important thing to do is to *tell someone*. This can be a difficult thing to do, particularly if you are an incest victim.

The logical people to tell are your parents. (Of course, in cases of incest by a parent, you need to tell the other parent.) However, some parents have trouble believing their children at first. If, for whatever reason, your parents won't believe you, you might tell another relative – an aunt or uncle, a grandparent, an older sister or brother – who you feel *will* believe you. Or you could tell another adult – a teacher or counsellor at school, a friend's mother or father, your vicar or priest, or any other adult you trust. You can also ring the local rape crisis centre, Incest Crisis Line, Childline, or the National Society for Prevention of Cruelty to Children (NSPCC). (Look in the telephone directory or ring directory inquiries for the numbers.) The people who answer the phones are specially trained and they understand what you're going through. (Some of them have been victims of sexual crimes themselves.) You needn't give your name and what you say is entirely confidential, so don't hesitate to ring.

Victims of incest or child molesting often find it hard to come forward and tell someone. Sometimes the person who committed the crime has made the victim promise to keep it a secret. But there are some promises and some secrets a person needn't keep, and this is definitely one of them. Or the victims may find it hard to tell someone because they think that what happened is somehow their fault or that they're to blame because they didn't stop it from happening. But this just isn't true. These crimes are *always* the fault of the older person. The victim is *never* to blame and is *never* at fault in any way. Some victims don't tell because they fear the person will harm them or get back at them for telling. But the police or other authorities can make sure the victim is *fully protected*.

Incest victims sometimes hesitate to tell because incest is a crime and it's possible that telling could get the person who has committed the crime into trouble with the police. Even though most victims hate what's been done to them, they still may not want to see a relative sent to gaol. But doctors don't have a legal obligation to report a crime, so the doctor can listen to your problem without reporting it to the police, though he or she will undoubtedly try to get you to agree to involve social services and even the police. Although involving the police or social services may seem like a horrifying idea, it will be better for everyone in the end and will protect any brothers or sisters who may also be suffering abuse.

Some incest victims don't tell because they're afraid that the family will break up, their parents will get divorced or things will get worse than they are. But if incest is going on, things are already about as bad as they could be. People who commit incest are mentally or emotionally ill, but they can be cured. The victim and the other family members also need help in dealing with the situation. None of these people can get the help they need unless the victim has the courage to take the first step and tell someone.

Most victims of incest and child molesting feel a mixture of anger, embarrassment and shame. This can also make it hard to come forward and tell someone. But you have a right to protect yourself from being touched in ways that don't feel right to you. So even though you may feel embarrassed, it's important to tell someone. It's really the best thing for everyone.

Other questions

We hope we've answered many of your questions in this chapter. However, you probably have questions about these subjects that we haven't covered. If so, perhaps your mother, your father, the school nurse, your GP, one of your teachers or another adult you trust can help you find the answers. You might also contact your Brook Advisory Centre for information.

Chapter 10

Romantic and Sexual Feelings

If a girl is 13 and she's had her period and all she ever thinks about is boys and sex, is this normal?

This question came out of our Everything You Ever Wanted To Know question box. Questions like this often come up in our classes because, as we go through puberty, many of us experience stronger romantic and/or sexual feelings than ever before in our lives. For some of us this means spending time imagining a passionate romance with a special someone or having sexual fantasies. For some it means having the urge to masturbate more often. For some it means getting interested in the opposite sex, having crushes or going out with boy-friends or girl-friends.

These romantic and sexual feelings can be very intense and distracting. It may even seem as if romance and sex are all you can think about. Some young people get so preoccupied that it's a bit frightening for them. If, like the girl who asked the above question, you've been worried about your strong romantic or sexual feelings, it helps to know that these feelings are perfectly normal and natural and that a lot of people your age are going through the same thing.

In addition to questions like the one above, we also get questions like this one:

My friends are always talking about girls and sex and everything. But I'm just not interested in girls in a romantic way yet. Do you think there's something wrong with me?

When boys and girls ask questions like this, we explain that although puberty is a time of strong sexual or romantic feelings for many young people, not everyone experiences these feelings. Some boys and girls are more involved in sports, school, music, a job or some other aspect of their lives, and romance and sex just aren't major interests for them. Just as we all have our own personal timetables of development for the body changes of puberty, so we all have our own personal timetables when it comes to romance and sexual interests. Some boys and girls begin to experience strong romantic or sexual feelings while they're still young. Others don't have these feelings until they're older. If you've worried that there's something wrong with you because your friends all seem to be having strong romantic or sexual attractions and you're not interested yet, you can stop worrying. There's nothing wrong with you. Your personal timetable is just different from theirs. So you can relax, knowing that sooner or later these things will start happening to you.

The boys and girls in our classes are curious about anything and everything having to do with sexuality and they're especially curious about the kinds of romantic and sexual feelings that young people have when they're growing up. Therefore, they ask questions like the ones we've just mentioned and also questions about things like sex play, crushes, falling in love, kissing, necking, petting and having intercourse (to mention just a few). You may be curious about these things too, so in this chapter we're going to talk about them. We can't promise that we'll answer all your questions in just this one chapter. But we would like to say a bit about these issues and we hope we'll answer at least some of your questions.

Some of the sections in this chapter deal with topics that come up mostly in our classes for younger boys and girls. Other sections deal with topics that usually come up only in our classes for older boys and girls. So, depending on your age, you may find that you're more interested in certain sections than in others. For instance, if you've just started to go through puberty, you may not be particularly interested in the section that deals with making decisions about how to handle your romantic and sexual feelings. This issue may simply not be very important in your life yet. If you aren't particularly interested in some sections, you may want to skip them for the present. Of course, it's perfectly all right for you to read these sections – it never hurts to think about these issues ahead of time. Whether or not you read these sections now, we hope you will come back to them later, when you're older and these things are issues in your life.

Romantic and sexual feelings before puberty

People used to think that children didn't have strong romantic feelings or much interest in anything sexual before the age of puberty. We now know that even young children may have strong romantic and sexual feelings and that they often are curious about sex at a very young age. Of course, not all young children have strong feelings of this nature and not all are curious about sex. As we've said, each of us has his or her own personal timetable. But many children do have a curiosity about sex and strong feelings during childhood. It's important for you to know that it's normal if you do have strong romantic and sexual feelings during childhood and it's also normal if you don't.

When we talk about childhood sexual feelings and curiosities, one topic that always comes up is sex play. Many youngsters engage in some form of sex play during their childhood. For instance, many children 'play doctor' or invent other games that involve taking off their clothes and looking at or touching each other's sex organs. Because this kind of sex play is so common, we often find questions like the following ones in our question box.

Is it wrong to play doctor? Is it bad for two little children to play around with each other?

Many, if not most, boys and girls engage in some form of sex play during childhood. Psychologists and sex experts agree that this is a perfectly normal and natural part of growing up and learning about sex. It doesn't mean that there's anything 'wrong' or 'nasty' about you if you've done these things.

However, bullying someone else or being bullied into doing something sexual by another child can be harmful. If you are bullied into doing something sexual by another child – or, for that matter, by anyone – it's important that you talk this problem over with your parent or another grown-up you trust.

If it's natural and normal, why do parents make you stop if they catch you playing doctor?

When parents discover their children playing doctor or other sex games, they usually make the children stop. Some parents even become angry or upset with their children if they find them playing sex games.

There may be any number of reasons why parents make children stop and/or get upset. For instance, some parents have religious values that lead them to feel that sex play in children is morally wrong or sinful. Some parents were caught doing the same thing when they were children and their parents stopped them or became angry with them. So they react in the same way their parents did. Moreover, some parents don't realize that sex play is natural and normal, so they become upset by what they think is unnatural or abnormal behaviour.

Even parents who don't have religious objections and

who realize sex play is a natural part of growing up usually put a stop to it when they find children engaging in sex play. Part of the job of being a parent is to teach your children what kind of behaviour is considered proper, polite and socially acceptable. For instance, if someone didn't tell them not to, many little children wouldn't think twice about taking off their clothes and walking down the street naked. In our society it's not considered proper or socially acceptable for people to go out in public nude, so parents usually teach their children to keep their clothes on. The same is true of sex play. In our society it is not considered proper or socially acceptable for children to take off their clothes and look at other people's sex organs or to play doctor. So even though they don't necessarily think playing sex games is sinful or nasty, parents usually stop this kind of thing because it isn't considered socially acceptable or proper behaviour.

Homosexual feelings

This is another topic that always comes up when we talk in class about sexual and romantic feelings people have during their growing-up years. 'Homo' means 'same' and, of course, 'sexual' refers to sex. Having homosexual feelings means having romantic or sexual thoughts, fantasies, dreams, attractions, crushes or experiences that involve someone who is the same sex as we are. Many boys and girls have homosexual thoughts or feelings or sexual experiences with someone of the same sex while they're growing up.

If you have homosexual feelings or experiences as you're growing up, you may realize that this is perfectly natural and normal, and you may not be at all worried about it. Or

homosexual (hoe-mow-SEX-you-ul)

you may feel somewhat confused or upset or even frightened about having these kinds of feelings or experiences. Perhaps you've heard people making jokes or using insulting slang terms when talking about homosexuality. If so, this may have caused you to wonder if your homosexual feelings or experiences are really OK. Perhaps you have heard someone say that homosexuality is morally wrong, sinful, unnatural, abnormal or a sign of mental illness. If so, this, too, may have made you wonder or worry about your own feelings. If you've heard any of these things (or even if you haven't), we think it will be helpful for you to know the basic facts about homosexuality.

Although almost everyone has homosexual feelings or experiences at some time or another in their lives, we usually consider people to be homosexuals only if as adults their strongest romantic and sexual attractions are towards someone of the same sex or most of their actual sexual experiences involve someone of the same sex.

Both males and females may be homosexuals. Female homosexuals are also called *lesbians*. *Gay* is a non-insulting slang term for both male and female homosexuals. There have been homosexuals throughout history, and homosexuals come from all walks of life. People from any social class, ethnic background, religious affiliation or economic level may be homosexuals. Doctors, lawyers, lorry drivers, policemen, artists, business people, ministers, rabbis, priests, politicians, soccer players, married people, single people, parents – you name it – all sorts of people are homosexuals.

The majority of adults in our society are *heterosexuals* (people whose strongest romantic and sexual attractions are towards the opposite sex and whose actual sexual

lesbians (LEZ-be-anz)
heterosexuals (HET-er-oh-SEX-you-uls)

experiences mostly involve the opposite sex). However, about one in every ten adults is a homosexual. Although an adult is usually considered either a homosexual or a heterosexual, this doesn't mean that he or she doesn't sometimes have feelings or experiences in the other direction. Very few people are *strictly* homosexual or *strictly* heterosexual. Most of us have a mixture of feelings. For instance, most heterosexuals have at least some homosexual thoughts, feelings, fantasies, dreams, attractions, crushes or sexual experiences at some time in their lives. In fact, over one-third of the males in this country will have a sexual experience with another male to the point of orgasm during their lives. Although the numbers are somewhat lower for females, many females also have this sort of sexual activity with another female some time during their lives.

Now that you know a bit about homosexuality, you might want to read some questions that the boys and girls in our classes have asked and our answers.

Is homosexuality morally wrong? Is it unnatural, abnormal or a sign of a mental illness?

In the past many people felt that homosexuality was sinful or abnormal, and there are still some who think it's morally wrong or the sign of a mental illness that needs to be 'cured' by a psychiatrist. However, nowadays most people no longer feel that homosexuality is either wrong or an illness. They feel that it's a personal matter, that some people just happen to be homosexuals and that being homosexual is a perfectly healthy, normal and acceptable way to be.

What's a bisexual?

A bisexual is a person who is equally attracted to males and females and whose sexual activities may involve either sex.

If a person has a lot of homosexual feelings while growing up, will this person be a homosexual as an adult?

Having homosexual feelings and experiences while you're growing up has *nothing at all* to do with whether or not you'll be a homosexual as an adult. Some young people who have homosexual feelings and experiences while they're growing up turn out to be homosexuals and some turn out to be heterosexuals. Some adult homosexuals had homosexual feelings while they were growing up; others had heterosexual feelings; still others didn't have strong feelings one way or the other while they were growing up.

Can a person know for sure that they're gay even though they're still young?

Yes. At least, some gay adults say that they knew they were homosexuals right from the time they were teenagers or even from when they were little children.

If you think you might be a homosexual and would like to talk to someone about your feelings, you can ring the Gay Switchboard on 01-837-7324.

Crushes

Crushes is yet another topic that always comes up when we talk about the kind of sexual and romantic feelings young people may have during their growing-up years. Having a crush means having sexual or romantic feelings towards a certain, special someone. Many young people develop crushes. Having a crush can be very exciting. Just thinking about or catching a glimpse of the person you have a crush on can brighten your whole day and you may spend delightful hours imagining a romance with that person.

Sometimes young people develop crushes on someone who isn't very likely to return their affections – a film star, a rock singer, a teacher, another adult or a friend of an older brother or sister. This sort of crush can be a safe and healthy way of experimenting with romantic and sexual attractions. These crushes are 'safe' because, no matter how much we may pretend otherwise, deep down we know that this unattainable person won't really return our affections. So we don't have to worry about real life problems like what to say or how to act. And because we're making it all up, we're free to imagine things turning out the way we want them to, without worrying about whether that person will like us back. In a way having a crush on someone unattainable is a way of rehearsing for the time in our lives when we will have a real romance.

But having a crush on someone unattainable can also cause a lot of suffering. One year some of the girls in our class developed crushes on a certain rock star. They plastered their bedroom walls with posters, wore badges with his face printed on them, pored over fan magazines and generally had a great time sharing their feelings about him with one another. When the rock star got married, they were, naturally, somewhat disappointed, but one girl was more than disappointed. She was really upset. She had become too involved in her crush and the rock star's marriage was devastating for her. If you find yourself developing a serious crush on someone unattainable, it helps to remind yourself from time to time that your crush isn't very realistic and that this person isn't very likely to return your affections.

Not all crushes are unrealistic. You may develop a crush on someone near your own age who you actually know through school, church, temple or some other group. If that person is interested in you, the crush can be especially exciting. But yearning after a person who doesn't return your affections can be painful. If you find that your crushes are causing you problems, it helps to find someone – a friend, a parent, a teacher, another adult or a counsellor – with whom you can discuss your feelings.

When we talk about crushes and being romantically or sexually interested in a certain, special someone you've actually met or know, we're often asked questions like these:

How do you find out if someone likes you? How do you let someone know you like them?

There are basically two answers to these questions: you can do it on your own or you can have a friend do it for you.

If you decide to have a friend do it, be sure to pick someone you can really trust or the next thing you know it will be all over school! It's often easier to let someone else do the talking for you. But keep in mind that if you do this, you don't have very much control over what's being said. Suppose, for example, you want your friend only to bring up your name in a roundabout way to see how this other person reacts. Your friend may not do it exactly the way you'd like; instead, your friend might tell this other person that you're madly in love with him or her!

For these reasons many people prefer doing it on their own. You can let someone know you like him or her by being friendly, starting conversations, going out of your way to be round that person, asking the person to go out with you, showing the person how you feel by the general way you act or simply telling the person how you feel. You can find out if a person likes you by watching to see if that person does any of these sorts of things to you.

Regardless of whether you tell the person yourself or have a friend do it for you, make sure it's done in private and not in front of the other kids. Otherwise the person may be so embarrassed that he or she may say they don't like you even if they really do. The other person may even stop liking you if you embarrass him or her in this way, so it's best to do it in private.

Going out

As they move through puberty and into their teen years, many young people begin going out. This can be fun and exciting, but it can also create problems. For instance, you may want to go out before yourr parents think you're old enough. Or you may not be ready to go out, and your parents or friends may be pushing you into it. You may have trouble deciding whether you want to go steady with one person or go out with lots of different people. If you've been going out with one person regularly and decide you want to go out with others, you may have problems in ending your steady dating relationship. Or if your steady boy-friend or girl-friend decides to change the relationship, you may have a hard time coping with this. On the other hand, if you want to go out and no one is interested in going out with you, you may feel rather depressed.

Here again, if you're having problems that relate to going out, it might be helpful for you to talk them over with someone you respect and trust. One of your parents, another adult you trust, a friend or an older brother or sister might be someone you could talk to. It might also be helpful for you to hear some of the questions about this subject that come up in our classes.

What if you feel left out because all your friends have boy-friends or girl-friends and you don't? Should you get involved with someone you don't really like just so you, too, will be going out?

Not going out when most of your friends are can make you feel awfully 'out of it'. Sometimes young people get to feeling that they should pair up with anyone who seems willing just so they won't feel left out. If you feel this way, you need to think carefully about getting involved with 'just anybody'. Is it really worth being paired up with someone you don't truly care about just so you won't feel left out? Do you really need to be going out in order to feel good about yourself? Is it really fair to the other person to get involved when you aren't really interested in him or her?

Instead of going out with someone you don't really care about, you might decide to make friends with a crowd of young people who haven't started going out yet. Or you could decide to go along when your friends are paired up to do things like going to parties, dances or the cinema, even though you don't have a date. Or perhaps you could ask someone you're 'just friends' with to be your partner in these sorts of situation. Most importantly, remember that it's not going out with someone that makes you a special person; it's being who you are. With or without a boy-friend or girl-friend, you're still the same, special person.

Suppose that you'd like to go out, but you never have and you're beginning to wonder if you ever will?

If the other people you know have already started going out and you haven't, you may begin to feel that these things won't ever happen to you. If so, it helps to remember that, sooner or later, you will find someone special. People always do! It also helps to remember that just as we all have our own special timetables of development when it comes to the physical body changes of puberty, so we all have our own timetables when it comes to romantic matters. It can be awfully hard on us if our personal timetable is moving along more slowly than other people's. But the fact that we're getting a slow start doesn't mean that we won't ever start doing these things. It may take a while, but eventually these things will happen for you. We guarantee it!

Remember too, that you have a lot of years ahead of you.

In the long run it doesn't really matter if you start going out when you're only 12 years old or not until you're 20. What's important in the long run is that you feel good about yourself. So don't let the fact that romance isn't yet a part of your life get you down or make you feel bad about yourself.

Is it all right for a girl to ask a boy out?

Back in your parents' day this was a definite no-no. Of course, even back then there were some brave girls who went ahead and asked the boys out. And most girls did everything they could, short of actually asking, in order to get the boys they liked to ask them out. But the 'rules' that most people went by said that boys did the asking and girls were supposed to wait to be asked.

Nowadays things have changed. Although there are still some people who think it's not 'right' or 'proper' for girls to do the asking, most people don't see anything at all wrong with a girl taking the initiative. In fact, many people think it's a great idea. Almost every boy we've asked has said he wished more girls would do it. Girls are often in favour of this idea too. However, many girls have admitted to being so worried about what others might think or so afraid that the boy might say no, that they can't really bring themselves to ask a boy out.

Our opinion is: go for it! We encourage girls to go ahead and do the asking. After all, the worst that could happen is that the boy will say no, and that wouldn't really be the end of the world. No one's ever died from being turned down for a date. Besides, if a girl waits to be asked, she may never be asked. As one girl put it, 'My boy-friend is so shy. We'd never have got together if I hadn't got the ball rolling by asking him out. I'm glad I did!'

What if you and your best friend like the same person?

If one of you is already dating or going with this person, then we'd say that this person is 'off limits'. But if the person isn't 'taken', then the two of you need to think about how you're going to keep your feelings for this person from getting in the way of, or maybe even ruining, your friendship. Here are some possible solutions. You could decide that you're both going to 'go for' the person, but you agree ahead of time not to let it affect your friendship. You could toss a coin. You could decide to let the one with the strongest feelings have the first chance. Of course, the person you like may already be interested in one of you, so he or she may do the deciding. Or the person may not be interested in either of you, so it may not be a problem at all.

Whatever happens, try to keep a sense of humour about it. And remember, at your age romances come and go, but the friendships you make now may last a lifetime. So don't lose your friendship over a romance.

What if every time you ask someone out, the answer is no?

If you've asked a certain person out a number of times and that person keeps saying no, then perhaps you just have to face the fact that this person doesn't want to go out with you. It can be difficult to know exactly how many times you should ask before giving up altogether. In part it will depend on what the person says when turning you down. If the person tells you that he or she is already dating someone else or simply isn't interested in you, then that's a pretty clear sign that you should stop asking. But if the person says, 'I'm sorry, but I'm busy', or doesn't give a clear reason for saying no, you might want to try again. Perhaps the person really is busy, but would like to go out with you another time. But if you've tried a few times and have had this kind of reply, you might want to say something like, 'Is there a time when we could get together?' The answer to this question will usually give a clear idea of whether it's worth continuing to ask this person out.

If you've asked a number of different people out and all of them have said no, you may start to feel discouraged. You may even start to feel that there's something so wrong or so horrible about you that no one will ever say yes. But before you allow yourself to feel down and discouraged, you might think for a moment about just who it is you're asking out. Maybe you're asking the wrong people. Are you asking only the best-looking or most popular people? If so, this may be part of your problem. For one thing, the best-looking and most popular people may already have lots of people asking them out, so your chances aren't as good as they would be if you asked someone less popular or not totally gorgeous. The fact that someone is popular or good-looking doesn't necessarily mean you're going to have a great time with that person. What's more important is whether the person is nice, whether the two of you could be comfortable with each other, whether you could have fun together. The person's inner qualities are more important than being popular or good-looking.

You might also ask yourself how well you know the people you're asking out. If you're asking people you hardly know, this may be a big part of the reason you keep getting turned down. If you take the time to get to know someone and to let them get to know you first, you'll have a better chance of having the person say yes when you ask for a date.

It might also be helpful for you to have a mutual friend check things out before you ask for a date. Your friend can give you an idea of how the person might respond. If the person isn't interested, you'll save yourself the discouragement of being turned down again. In addition, you might ask some of your friends who they think you should ask for a date. People love to play matchmaker and your friends may come up with someone you wouldn't have thought of by yourself. They may even know someone who's been dying to go out with you! So don't hesitate to enlist your friends' help.

Above all, don't give up. Somewhere out there is someone who'd just love to go out with you. We guarantee it!

Suppose you want to go out, but your parents say no?

Young people usually choose to handle this problem in one of three ways: sneak round behind their parents' backs; go along with their parents' rules and wait until their parents say they're old enough; try to change their parents' minds. Let's look at each of these choices.

Sneaking round behind your parents' backs just isn't a good choice. Sooner or later young people who do this almost always get caught. If you do get caught, you may get into a lot of trouble and may do serious damage to your relationship with your parents. In fact, your parents may find it hard to trust you in the future. Even if you don't get caught, you'll probably feel guilty about lying and sneaking. Going out should be a fun and pleasurable part of your life. Having to sneak round just complicates your life. Who needs the added complication of having to go behind your parents' backs? In short, sneaking round behind your parents' backs just isn't worth the price you may have to pay.

On the other hand, it can be awfully hard to go along with your parents' rules and wait until you're older, especially if there's a special someone you'd like to go out with. But parents who make these sorts of rules aren't usually trying to be mean or unfair. They're trying to protect you from 'getting in over your head' by starting your romantic life when you are too young. After all, you have a lot of years ahead of you. So if your parents want you to wait, think honestly about it. Maybe they're right. If your parents say no, ask yourself these questions: are the other kids my age allowed to go out? would I really lose anything by waiting until I'm older?

If your honest answer to these questions is no, then perhaps waiting is the best choice for you. If, however, you feel that your parents are being too strict or too old-fashioned, you might want to consider the third choice, changing their minds.

Changing your parents' minds probably wouldn't be an easy job, but it's worth a try. For starters, find out exactly why they've made these rules. What are they worried about? Once you understand their feelings, you may be able to come up with a compromise. If, for instance, your parents think you're too young to go out, maybe they'd allow you to go on group dates. Or if they won't allow dates for the cinema, perhaps they'll allow you to go to a boy-girl party or invite someone to your house.

How can you split up with someone without hurting his or her feelings?

It's best to tell the person yourself rather than having a friend do it or having the person hear it through the grapevine. If the person hears it from someone else, he or she is going to feel even worse. The person may feel like you've made a fool of him or her, or that you didn't even care enough to bother being honest. The person may feel even more hurt or angry if he or she has to hear the bad news from someone else.

It's usually very difficult for us to be honest and to tell someone that our feelings have changed. Even though it's perfectly normal and natural for a person's feelings to change, we may none the less feel guilty about it. We may feel that we're some terrible, disloyal, bad sort of person.

Sometimes we may feel so guilty, so disloyal and so afraid of the other person's angry, hurt feelings that we may pick a fight so we'll have an 'excuse' for splitting up. Rather than honestly admitting the real reason we want to end the relationship, we may try to shift the 'blame' to the other person. We may try to pretend that it's the other person's fault, that it's something he or she has done or that it's something about him or her as a person that's causing the split. But if you think about it, is it really right or really fair to shift the 'blame'?

Our advice is be honest, but be kind. You might say something like 'I really want to be your friend, but I don't want to be tied down to just one person' or 'You're really terrific and I really care about you, but I just feel I'm too young to settle down and date only one person.'

How do you know if it's really love?

When they begin going out, many young people fall in love, or at least what they think might be love, so they ask questions like this one.

Emotions can't be weighed or measured and different people have different ideas of what it means to be in love. So we can't give you a definite answer to this question. But we can share with you some of our thoughts on the subject.

We think it's important to recognize the differences between infatuation and true love. Infatuation is an intense, exciting (and sometimes confusing or frightening) fireworks kind of feeling. We may be so wrapped up in our infatuation that it's hard to think about anything else or even to eat. People sometimes mistake infatuation for love. But infatuation doesn't usually last very long; true love does. You may start out being infatuated and have it grow into true love. Or the infatuation may pass and you may discover that you weren't really 'right' for each other after all. In addition, you don't have to know someone very well in order to be infatuated. But in order to truly love someone, you have to know that person (both their good points and bad points) very well. In addition, infatuation can happen all of a sudden; true love takes more time.

Regardless of whether your relationship starts with an infatuation, or develops more slowly and gradually, sooner or later love relationships go through a questioning stage, where one or both of you begin to question whether the relationship is really a good one. During this questioning stage one or the other of you may decide to end the relationship. In our opinion it's only after you go through this questioning stage and decide to stay together that you're really on the road to true love.

If you're uncertain about whether or not it's true love, you might want to ask yourself the following questions.

Am I tired or unhappy most of the time? Does the relationship seem like more of a problem than a joy?

Do I keep hoping that 'maybe things will get better'?

Do either of us frequently ask, 'Do you really love me?'

Do we find it impossible to spend a day together without having a fight?

Do I often have to be careful about expressing certain opinions for fear that he or she might get mad at me?

If you answer yes to one or more of these questions, then chances are that you're not really in love after all and that it's time to make a change in your relationship.

Making decisions about how to handle your romantic and sexual feelings

When young people begin going out or when they fall in love (or what they think might be love), they often find themselves faced with questions about how to handle the strong romantic and sexual feelings they may be having. When two people are attracted to each other, they quite naturally want to be physically close. Being physically close may mean something as simple as holding hands or kissing goodnight after a date. Or it may mean more than this. Physical closeness may even include something as intimate as sexual intercourse.

Some young people don't have much trouble in deciding what kind of physical closeness is right for them or in making decisions about 'how far' they want to go in terms of physical intimacy. For instance, some young people have very strong religious or moral beliefs or other values that guide them in making these sorts of decision. But other young people aren't as certain. For example, some young people aren't sure what's right or wrong when it comes to deciding how far to go. And even those who are sure sometimes have a difficult time sticking to their beliefs when they're actually in a situation in which they have to make these decisions. So we usually spend a good deal of time, especially in our classes for older boys and girls, discussing the topic of making decisions about how to handle romantic and sexual feelings. We don't have enough space to cover everything we discuss in class, but in the following pages we'll answer some of the most commonly asked questions.

Some of the questions you'll find here are questions about what's OK or not OK or what's morally right or wrong when it comes to young people acting on their romantic or sexual feelings. If there were one set of answers with which everyone agreed, it would be easy to answer these sorts of question and our job as sex education teachers/writers would be much easier. We could just give the agreed-upon answers and that's all there'd be to it. But it's not that simple. The fact is that different people have different ideas on these issues and there isn't one agreed-upon set of answers. Therefore, when we're discussing these sorts of question in our classes and in our books, we don't give one answer. Instead, we try to present the many different opinions that people have and to explain why people feel the way they do about these issues, without taking sides. We do it this way because we think it's important for young people to hear all sides of a question and come up with their own answers rather than just going along with someone else's opinion. Far too many young people don't think these questions through on their own, and this can lead to trouble. For example, some young people answer questions about how to handle their sexual and romantic feelings based on what they think everyone else is doing. Not only are they often wrong about what 'everyone else' is doing, but the fact is that just because everyone else does it *does not* mean it's right for you.

Or, to take another example, some young people don't think through these issues on their own and just go along with what their parents or their religions say is right or wrong. Now, please don't misunderstand what we're saying here. We're not saying that you shouldn't follow your parents' or your religion's teachings or rules. In fact, we think parents and religions usually have excellent advice that's well worth following. But we've found that young people who just accept what they've been taught without thinking things through for themselves frequently run into problems when they're actually in situations in which they have to make decisions about how far to go. Often these young people find that they don't stick by the rules they've been taught. The rules sort of 'crumble', 'fall apart' or 'cave in' in the face of the tremendous pressure to experiment sexually that's often put on young people. We think this happens because the rules weren't really their own in the first place. The rules were someone else's rules. We believe that it's not until you consider all the different viewpoints and decide for yourself what rules to follow that the rules become truly your own. And it's not until the rules are truly your own that they become rules you can really live by. So you'll find many viewpoints in the answers to the questions about what's right/wrong or OK/not OK in the following pages. We hope this will help you find your own answers.

I'd like to have a girl-friend, but is someone my age (11) old enough to have sex?

I'm 12 and there's a certain boy in my class that I like, and he likes me too. I'm scared of having sex though. What should I do?

We kissed goodnight after our first date. I want to go out with him again, but what if I get pregnant?

It's usually younger boys and girls who ask these sorts of question. When we first heard questions like these, we have to admit that we were a bit shocked that boys and girls who were so young seemed to be asking questions about whether they were ready for sex. However, when we talked further with the very young boys and girls who asked these sorts of question, we realized that the reason they were asking them was often because they had very mistaken ideas about physical intimacy. Some of them seemed to think that kissing or being physically close in other ways happens almost as soon as you get involved with someone, or at least very quickly – perhaps even before you've had a chance to get to know each other. Some seem to think that going on a date means you have to, at the very least, kiss the person goodnight or perhaps go further. Some even seem to think that having a boy-friend or girl-friend automatically means that you're going to have sexual intercourse with that person.

These things just aren't true, but it's easy to see how a young person could get these mistaken ideas. In the books we read it often seems as if two people no sooner meet than we turn the page and find them madly kissing each other. In the films it sometimes seems as if two perfect strangers no sooner look at each other than the next thing we know they're having sex. Or on television programmes two people will be going out on their first date in one scene and are in bed together in the next!

In real life things don't usually happen quite like this. In real life a romantic relationship usually goes through several steps or stages of physical closeness before things get to the point of having sexual intercourse, if indeed the relationship ever goes that far. In real life it usually takes at least some time before a relationship ever gets to the point where two people are having intercourse. Moreover, in real life many romantic relationships, especially the ones we have when we're young, never do get to the point of having sex. In fact, many relationships never go beyond the holding hands or goodnight kiss stage, if they go even that far.

So please don't be confused by what you read in books or see on TV or in films. Going out or having boy-friends or girl-friends doesn't mean that you have to have sex, kiss or even hold hands. Above all, remember that when it comes to romance and sex, you're in charge and you don't have to do anything that doesn't feel right for you.

What is French-kissing? What's the right way to French-kiss?

French-kissing, which some people call tongue-kissing, means that one or both people put their tongues in the other person's mouth while kissing. Some people like French-kissing; others don't and choose not to try it. There is no right or wrong way to French-kiss. Some people put just the tip of their tongue into the other person's mouth. Others put more of their tongue in; still others manage to get their tongues in each other's mouth at the same time. There aren't any specific rules about this.

What is necking? What is petting?

Necking – or 'snogging' as some people call it – means having prolonged kissing sessions. Different people define petting differently. Some people use the phrase 'petting above the waist' or 'light petting' to describe a situation in which a male feels or fondles a female's breasts. 'Petting below the waist' or 'heavy petting' means touching or rubbing the other person's genital organs. Some people further divide petting into petting outside or over your clothes and petting inside or under your clothes.

What is mutual masturbation?
What do people mean when they say 'doing everything but'?
What does 'going all the way' mean?

Mutual masturbation means masturbating with another person or masturbating each other. 'Doing everything but' means that although two people stop short of having sexual intercourse, they engage in other forms of physical closeness such as heavy petting; getting naked or partially naked and hugging, rubbing or touching each other's bodies; mutual masturbation; oral-genital sex or other intimate sexual contact. 'Going all the way' means having sexual intercourse, that is, the male putting his penis in the female's vagina.

Is it all right to kiss on your first date?
Is necking wrong? How about petting?
How far is 'too far' to go? Where should you draw the line? Is it OK to 'do everything but' as long as you don't 'go all the way' and have sex?

As we explained earlier, if everyone agreed upon these issues, these would be easy questions to answer. But different people have different answers to these sorts of questions. For instance, some people think it's 'too soon' or just 'not right' to kiss on a first date, while others think it's perfectly acceptable to do so. Some people think necking is OK; others don't. Some people have moral objections or think it's 'sinful' to go beyond necking or perhaps light petting. Some don't think this is morally wrong or sinful, but are afraid that young people who get involved in necking or petting might get too 'carried away' or 'turned on' and wind up having sex or doing something else they might regret later. Some feel light petting is OK, but draw a line at heavy petting. Some feel it's all right to 'do everything but' as long as you don't 'go all the way' and actually have sexual intercourse. Other people have still other opinions on these issues; and some people just aren't certain exactly how to answer these sorts of questions.

Young people's answers to the sorts of questions listed above are strongly influenced by their personal situations — by their parents' values, their friends' opinions, their religion's teachings, their own moral beliefs and/or their emotional feelings. These influences may be different in each case and may affect each of us differently, and as we've said, there isn't one agreed-upon set of answers to these questions. But even though there isn't one set of rules that everyone follows, we think there are some basic guidelines that are helpful to anyone facing these questions, regardless of their personal situations, morals or values.

1. Whether it's French-kissing, petting or going further, don't let yourself be rushed into anything. Do only what you're really sure you want to do (or at least as sure as you can be). If you're not sure, don't do it. Wait until you are sure. After all, you have many years ahead of you; you can afford to wait until you are sure.

2. Ask yourself how you feel about this other person. Is this someone you trust? Will this person start rumours or

gossip about you? Are you doing these things because you really care about this person or simply because you're curious to try these things? Young people are naturally curious about how it feels to neck, pet or do some of these other things, but remember that it may not be as pleasurable if you're only doing it out of curiosity.

3. Ask yourself why you want to do this. Your real reasons for kissing, necking, petting or experimenting sexually in other ways may not have much to do with your feelings about the other person or even with your curiosity about or eagerness to try these things. Some real reasons might be: hoping to prove you're grown-up, trying to become more popular or being afraid you'll 'lose' him or her if you don't. But agreeing to kiss, neck, pet or go further for these reasons just doesn't work. It won't solve your problems; in fact, it may create new ones.

4. Don't pressure someone into doing something he or she doesn't want to do. This pressure may take the form of a boy persuading a girl to go further than she really wants to or of a girl acting like a boy isn't 'manly' if he doesn't want to kiss or doesn't try to get her to go further. Or it may take some other form. In any event it's just not fair to put this sort of pressure on another person.

5. Don't let someone pressure you into doing something you don't want to do and don't do something because 'everyone else is doing it'. Make up your own mind.

6. Don't allow yourself to fall for a 'line' like:
'If you liked me, you'd neck with me.'
'If you truly cared about me, you wouldn't say no.'
'If you don't, I'll find someone else who will.'
'Everybody else is doing it.'
   If someone hands you one of these lines, turn it back on them: 'If you truly cared about me, you wouldn't pressure me.'

'Prove you love me by not pushing me.'
'Go ahead and find someone else.'
'If everybody else is doing it, you shouldn't have much trouble finding someone to do it with you.'

7. Don't assume you know what the other person is thinking; ask. Many boys and girls get involved in necking, petting or other sexual activities even though they don't really want to just because they think the other person wants or expects to do these things. But this isn't always the case. Sometimes neither really wants to, so talk things over first.

8. Don't be afraid to say no. Sometimes young people get involved in doing something because they're afraid they'll hurt someone's feelings by saying no. We're all taught not to be selfish or hurt another's feelings. But sexuality is one area of life in which it's right to be selfish and to think of yourself first, so if you don't want to do something, it's OK to say no. Sometimes young people go along with something because they don't quite know how to stop it from happening. But remember, if you don't want to, all you have to say is one simple word: no.

9. Don't be surprised if you don't always know the answers to questions about what's right or wrong for you. If you don't know, remember that you can always choose to wait and to take some time to think through these issues, and to talk them over with others before making a decision.

10. Don't be too hard on yourself if you make a mistake and afterwards find that you've done something you wish you hadn't. Learning to make decisions about how to handle your romantic and sexual feelings is just like learning anything else: you're bound to make mistakes. Remember, too, that if you have done something you regret, you can always decide to behave differently in the future.

How old should you be before you start having sex?
Should you wait until you're married? Is it OK to have sex if
you're really in love, even though you're not married?
Are teenagers mature enough to handle sex?
Why do people make such a big fuss about sex? I mean, if two
people want to have sex, why shouldn't they just go ahead and
do it?

Even though each of these questions is phrased a bit differently, they are all about the same thing – when is it all right for a person to have sex and when isn't it all right? Here again, there isn't one set of agreed-upon rules; different people have different ideas on this subject.

Some people feel it's acceptable for two people to have sex with each other as long as they're both adults or have reached a certain age. Some of these people consider a person to be an adult once he or she has reached a specific age, such as 18 or 21. Others think you're an adult once you're out on your own, that is, once you're no longer living with your parents and/or you're earning your own living and supporting yourself. Still others have what we call the legal point of view. These people feel it's all right for people to have sex as long as they're over 16 because the law says it is *illegal* for a male to have sex with a girl under the age of 16 even if she has given her consent (agreed) to have sex with him. There is no legal age of consent for boys, except for homosexual relationships, and then the age is 21. This law was designed to protect young girls from being seduced – that is, being led or talked into sex, by older men. But technically, it is illegal for a male *of any age* to have sex with a girl under the age of 16. (Apparently the lawmakers didn't feel it was necessary to protect young boys from older women, perhaps because it's much less common for an older woman to seduce a young boy, though this does happen.) This law was designed for protection purposes.

The people who made this law didn't intend to suggest that being over 16 automatically means you're old enough to have sex.

Very few of the people who have definite ideas about when it's all right for a person to have sex are actually concerned about the law. In fact, for most people it's not *how old* you are that's important. For instance, many people feel that you shouldn't have sex until you're married, regardless of your age.

People may have the 'wait until you're married' point of view for a variety of reasons. For some, it's a religious principle. They feel that the Bible tells us very clearly that people should not have sex unless they're married to each other. For others, it has more to do with pregnancy. These people are concerned about what will happen if an unmarried couple has sex and a pregnancy results. Such people are often morally opposed to abortion. They feel that a decision to have sex isn't just a decision between two people but a choice that involves the responsibility for a third person, the baby that might be conceived. For this reason they feel that you shouldn't have sex until you're married and are able to take on the responsibility of raising a child.

There are also other reasons why people have the 'wait until you're married' point of view. One man we interviewed, who we'll call Charlie, explained his reasons particularly well. Charlie was not a religious person but, as he explains, he decided not to have sex until he was married:

My wife and I waited until we were married to have sex, which was a different decision than many people make nowadays. But I think it was a good one. Maybe if we'd had sex with other people or with each other before we were married, we'd have been more experienced or knowledgeable. But learning about sex together, with each other, made it that much more special. Also, we didn't have to worry if either of us was as good as the other lovers either of us might have had before. So we didn't have the jealous, uncertain feelings some couples have.

By being willing to wait until we were married, I felt I was showing her that it wasn't just sex that I wanted from her but real, true love and lifelong commitment with her. And she was showing me the same thing, that we really mattered to each other as people, beyond just a physical, sexual wanting or desire. We really trusted each other and that made us feel safe enough for us to really let go. We didn't have to worry that if we did it wrong or it wasn't great the first time that it would be all over. And, really, it wasn't so great the first time. It was kind of awkward and embarrassing. But I knew and she knew that we'd both be around tomorrow. So we were able to be free and open and to make mistakes and to learn how to make love. If we hadn't been married and hadn't already promised to be there through thick and thin with each other, I think it would have been harder to learn to have good sex. We might have had hurt feelings or uncertainties or shynesses that we couldn't have got beyond. But by the fact of marrying, we had already promised ourselves to 'work things out, come what may'. This trusting and promising made us able to grow to be better lovers than we might have been otherwise.

While some people emphasize waiting until you're married or until you've reached a certain age, others put more emphasis on being mature enough or on the nature of the relationship. For instance, some people feel it's all right to have sex if you're really in love. Some say it's all right even if you're not in love as long as you're really committed to a serious, long-term relationship. Some say it's all right as long as you're both mature enough to handle it. Of course, it's not always easy to know for sure if it's really love, just how serious or long-lasting the relationship will be or whether you're really mature enough to handle it. People who have these kinds of guidelines are concerned about the emotional feelings involved in sex. Having sexual intercourse involves very intense emotional feelings and it's very easy for people to be hurt. When parents don't want teenagers to have sex, many times they're concerned not only about morality or the possibility of pregnancy, but also about the possibility of the emotional pain that can result when two people have sex and the relationship then ends. Also, as Charlie pointed out, sex is something that takes some time to work out. If two people aren't in love or in a long-term relationship that guarantees that the other person will be around to work things out with, one or both people may suffer emotionally.

One young woman we interviewed had something especially interesting to say about why she thought it was important to wait to have sex until you were involved in a serious relationship:

I have girl-friends who think if you get into heavy petting with a boy, it's stupid or artificial or something not to go all the way and have sex with him. They say sex isn't such a big deal . . . Maybe I'm too romantic or too idealistic, but I think sex *is* a big deal – or should be. I want it to be very deep and very emotional . . . I know you can go round having sex all the time and it *won't* be a big deal for you. If you do that too much, though, I think you get . . . well, hard and cold and kind of callous. It's like you deaden yourself. You keep having sex without it touching your deep emotional places and you start thinking that's how it is. You're no longer even capable of having it be deep or emotional. That's what I mean by saying you deaden yourself. The part of you, inside yourself, that can have it be deep and emotional dies or starves to death or gets all lost.

The emotional aspects and the nature of the relationship (that's being in love or at least in a serious relationship) influences many people's answers to questions about when you should or shouldn't have sex. There are also some people who don't place much importance on being in love or in a serious relationship. These people feel that if two people are attracted to each other and want to have sex, then it's perfectly acceptable for them to do so. Such people often feel that society is 'too uptight' or 'too hung up' about sex. They often think moral rules about sex are silly or old fashioned. They argue that sex is normal and natural and that people should be free to enjoy it whenever they want to, provided, of course, that both people consent to do so.

Some people who have these more casual attitudes about sex even say that it's all right for two people to have sex even if they've just met or hardly know each other. Some feel that 'one-night stands' (that is, having sex with someone you don't necessarily expect to see again after the one night you spend together) are perfectly OK. However, not everyone who approves of casual sex is quite this casual about it. Most people who favour casual sex don't think it's OK to have sex with 'just anybody', or to have sex on a one-night stand basis. Still, they are willing to have sex without waiting to find out if they're really in love or if they're at least going to have a serious relationship with the other person.

But the fact of the matter is that nowadays casual sex is far too dangerous, for it increases the risk of AIDS. And, to put it bluntly, AIDS kills. Having casual sex also increases your chances of getting other STDs, which can have serious consequences. For instance, a girl or a woman who has even one gonorrhoea infection has a 15 to 40 per cent chance of becoming infertile. People with genital herpes can't be cured and may suffer repeated outbreaks of the disease. Because of the risk of AIDS, herpes, gonorrhoea and other STDs, many people think that having casual sex is simply not a wise idea.

So far we've talked about people who have one viewpoint or another, but there are also people who simply aren't sure how they feel about the question of when it's all right for people to have sex. If you're one of these people (or even if you're sure how you feel), you might find it useful to talk this over with other people. In the end only you can answer these questions and make your own decisions about how to handle your sexuality. You can get some help by talking it over with other people. You might start by talking with older people who've had some sexual experience. What do they think? Don't (as many young people do) automatically rule out your parents as people to talk to. You may be surprised to find that your parents struggled with these same questions when they were your age. Young people often don't talk about sexual decision-making with their parents because they already know that their parents' attitudes are more conservative or stricter than their own. But even if this is so, your parents may have good reasons for feeling the way they do. And even if you don't totally agree with them, they might have things to say that could prove useful to your life. You might also talk with other people, an aunt or uncle, a sister or brother or an older friend. What about chatting to a teacher you feel close to or your school nurse or school counsellor? You might even decide to go along to a youth advisory centre or Brook Advisory Centre (see page 202) for advice and information.

Chapter 11

A Few Final Words

As you know, there are a number of physical changes that take place in our bodies during puberty. For most of us these physical changes are accompanied by certain emotional changes. For instance, we may feel very proud and excited about the fact that we're growing up and becoming adults. But along with these positive feelings most of us also experience less-than-totally-wonderful feelings from time to time as we're going through puberty. It's not uncommon for young people to have the 'blues', times when we feel depressed or down in the dumps, sometimes for no apparent reason. Part of the reason we have these feelings may be the new hormones our bodies are making. Hormones are powerful substances and they can affect our emotions. It takes our bodies and emotions some time to adjust to these hormones and some doctors feel that the emotional ups and downs many young people experience are a result, at least in part, of hormonal changes. But it's undoubtedly more than that. It's not just our bodies that are changing, it's our whole lives. At times all this changing can seem a bit overwhelming and we may feel uncertain, frightened, anxious or depressed.

One girl wrote to us expressing feelings that a lot of young people share. She said:

I'm going through puberty now and I'm very frightened about it. Everyone says it's normal to feel this way, but every time I'm feeling good and everything, I suddenly get this depressed feeling and I don't want to grow up any more. I just never want to get older and face things like possible rapes, diseases, deaths, etc.

Also, I'm going into my first year of secondary school and I'm really frightened. I'm not sure I'm ready to face all the changes.

It is quite normal to have these kinds of feelings. Knowing that other people your age have the same feelings won't magically make you feel better, but it can help you to know that at least you're not alone.

Sometimes, young people are upset because they feel pressured to grow up all at once. As one boy put it:

Everyone I know is trying to grow up as fast as possible. What's the rush? I'm just not in a great big rush. I want to take my time. I'm tired of everyone trying to act all big and grown-up all the time.

And sometimes, the idea of being more grown-up and independent can be rather frightening. As one boy said:

OK, so now all of a sudden I'm supposed to be all grown-up and have all these adult responsibilities. But I'm not ready to have these responsibilities and make all these decisions. In a few years, I'm going to go to university or maybe get a job and live on my own, and I don't know even what I want to do or if I can really do everything on my own. Sometimes I just want to stay a little kid.

However, there may be times when we feel that people around us, especially our parents, are keeping us from growing up as fast as we'd like to. One teenage girl expressed this point of view:

Sometimes I really hate my parents. They treat me like a little child. They want to tell me what to wear or how I should wear my hair and where I can go and who I can go with and when I have to be home and blah, blah, blah. They're always on at me. It's as though they want me to stay 'their little girl' forever and they won't let me grow up.

Going through puberty and becoming a teenager doesn't necessarily mean that you and your parents will have problems getting along with each other, but most teenagers do run into at least some conflicts with their parents. Indeed, at times it can seem like out-and-out war. These conflicts between young people and parents have to do with the change that takes place in the relationship between the parent and child during these years. When we're little babies, we can't even feed ourselves, change our clothes or go to the lavatory by ourselves. Our parents have to feed us, dress us and change our nappies; we are *dependent* on them for everything. It's our parents' job to teach us how to take care of ourselves so that, eventually, we'll be able to live on our own. And they have to take care of us and protect us until we're old enough to do that for ourselves. Children need their parents, but they also want to grow up, to be more independent, to take care of themselves and to make their own decisions. At the beginning of your teens you are still very dependent, but in a few years you'll be off to university or out earning your own living. So during your teens you and your parents are ending a relationship in which you're very dependent and trying to establish a new relationship in which you are totally independent.

It's not easy to let go of old, familiar ways of relating and to establish new ones. Parents are used to being in charge, to making decisions. They may continue to tell you how to dress, how to wear your hair, what to do and when to do it even after you feel that you're old enough to make these decisions for yourself. This change in the relationship from dependent to independent doesn't usually progress without problems, and much of the stress, anger and other negative feelings that you may experience during your teens have to do with a working out of the change in the relationship with your parents.

Our relationships with our friends also change during these years and these changes, too, can cause uncertain, confused, depressed or otherwise difficult emotional feelings. Chances are you'll be going to a new school, making new friends, perhaps seeing less of old friends. Breaking old ties and making new ones isn't always easy to do. During these years being part of a certain gang or group usually becomes a very important part of your life. It can make things easier and more fun. But groups can present problems, too. You may find that you aren't accepted into a certain 'in' group even though you'd very much like to be part of it. Feelings of being 'out of it' or being excluded from the group can make life seem very lonely.

Even if you are accepted by the group, you may find that there are still some problems. Being part of a group can have a lot of rewards – it helps us feel more accepted, more a part of things, less lonely and uncertain. But sometimes being part of the group 'costs' us. We may have to act in certain ways or do things we don't feel good about doing in order to stay part of the group. Here's what some kids had to say about this:

I really want to be 'in' with this group at school, but they do some things I don't like. Like they're always laughing at people who aren't in the group, making jokes or comments when one of them gets up in front of the class or something. I really want to be accepted, and it's like I have to do what they do to be accepted. But if I do, I don't feel good about myself.

Margie, age 14

I hate school 'cause I either have to act a certain way or be some outcast. Like in class, if you have an idea about something that is different from everyone else's, you can't say it or you'll be out of it and everyone will put you down. You have to do and say the same thing as everyone else or you're not OK.

Tim, age 13

Friends can talk me into doing things I don't really want to do. I'm in with the really 'in' crowd, but they drink and smoke dope 'cause that's cool. My parents would kill me if they knew what I do, and really I'm not so into these things, but I do them to be part of the group.

Sharon, age 15

This business of being part of the group isn't a problem for all teenagers, but it is for many. Another change that many young people find difficult and that can cause emotional problems is the change in the relationships between boys and girls that usually takes place during these years. Sometimes it seems that all the rules have suddenly changed. The 10- to 12-year-olds in our classes usually have a lot to say about this. Here's what one boy said:

I'm going to Jennifer's Hallowe'en party on Saturday, and my sister keeps teasing me, 'Oh, you like Jennifer, you're in love with Jennifer.' Well, I do like Jennifer, but not like that. It's now, all of a sudden, you can't just be friends with a girl. It's got to be boy-friend and girl-friend, like you're all romantic with each other.

Tom, age 12

Another boy and girl, we'll call them Donny and Hilary, who've been friends since they were very young, had this to say:

I went over to Hilary's house to spend the night and we were swimming in the pool. These girls who live next door came over and they were saying things like, 'Oh, you're playing with a girl. Oh, you're staying overnight at a girl's house. Oh, that's peculiar. You must be gay.'

Donny, age 11

Yeah, then they realized they'd seen Donny on TV in that film he was in. Then they started acting all different – 'Ohh, you're sooo cute', and trying to act all sexy. Then they made it like he was my boy-friend and it was all different than when he was just going to stay overnight at my house.

Hilary, age 11

As we explained in the last chapter, we may find that our feelings about the opposite sex are changing. Although having crushes and going out on dates can be fun, they can also complicate our lives.

Growing up is indeed a mixed bag of experiences. On the one hand, there are a lot of exciting things to look forward to; on the other hand, there are a lot of changes – physical changes, life changes, changes in our relationships with our parents, our friends and with the opposite sex. Probably at some time there must have been someone, somewhere, who went through puberty and the teen years without a single problem, but we wouldn't bet a lot of money on it. If you're like most young people, you'll run into some problems as you go through the physical and emotional changes of puberty. We hope that this book will help you in dealing with these problems.

Index

READ MORE IN PENGUIN

In every corner of the world, on every subject under the sun, Penguin represents quality and variety – the very best in publishing today.

For complete information about books available from Penguin – including Puffins, Penguin Classics and Arkana – and how to order them, write to us at the appropriate address below. Please note that for copyright reasons the selection of books varies from country to country.

In the United Kingdom: Please write to *Dept. JC, Penguin Books Ltd, FREEPOST, West Drayton, Middlesex UB7 OBR.*

If you have any difficulty in obtaining a title, please send your order with the correct money, plus ten per cent for postage and packaging, to *PO Box No. 11, West Drayton, Middlesex UB7 OBR*

In the United States: Please write to *Consumer Sales, Penguin USA, P.O. Box 999, Dept. 17109, Bergenfield, New Jersey 07621-0120.* VISA and MasterCard holders call 1-800-253-6476 to order all Penguin titles

In Canada: Please write to *Penguin Books Canada Ltd, 10 Alcorn Avenue, Suite 300, Toronto, Ontario M4V 3B2*

In Australia: Please write to *Penguin Books Australia Ltd, P.O. Box 257, Ringwood, Victoria 3134*

In New Zealand: Please write to *Penguin Books (NZ) Ltd, Private Bag 102902, North Shore Mail Centre, Auckland 10*

In India: Please write to *Penguin Books India Pvt Ltd, 706 Eros Apartments, 56 Nehru Place, New Delhi 110 019*

In the Netherlands: Please write to *Penguin Books Netherlands bv, Postbus 3507, NL-1001 AH Amsterdam*

In Germany: Please write to *Penguin Books Deutschland GmbH, Metzlerstrasse 26, 60594 Frankfurt am Main*

In Spain: Please write to *Penguin Books S. A., Bravo Murillo 19, 1° B, 28015 Madrid*

In Italy: Please write to *Penguin Italia s.r.l., Via Felice Casati 20, I-20124 Milano*

In France: Please write to *Penguin France S. A., 17 rue Lejeune, F-31000 Toulouse*

In Japan: Please write to *Penguin Books Japan, Ishikiribashi Building, 2-5-4, Suido, Bunkyo-ku, Tokyo 112*

In Greece: Please write to *Penguin Hellas Ltd, Dimocritou 3, GR-106 71 Athens*

In South Africa: Please write to *Longman Penguin Southern Africa (Pty) Ltd, Private Bag X08, Bertsham 2013*